UNFORGIVABLE

BOOKS BY NATALIE BARELLI

Unfaithful

The Housekeeper
The Accident
The Loyal Wife
Missing Molly
After He Killed Me
Until I Met Her

UNFORGIVABLE
NATALIE BARELLI

bookouture

Published by Bookouture in 2022

An imprint of Storyfire Ltd.
Carmelite House
50 Victoria Embankment
London EC4Y 0DZ

www.bookouture.com

ISBN: 978-1-80019-153-2
eBook ISBN: 978-1-80019-152-5

ONE

Our suburb is perched on a hill, and what makes it exceptional is its stairs. There are over a hundred of them, zigzagging everywhere, connecting streets from top to bottom and back again so that from above our suburb looks like a giant board of snakes and ladders but without the snakes.

There's a set of old concrete stairs just thirty feet from our house. Once upon a time, they would have connected tramlines to each other, but now they link one end of a cul-de-sac—where we live—to another dead end below. They are divided into three sections by two landings with a sharp turn at each and overshadowed by a large canopy of trees. Hardly anyone uses them because they're steep, crumbling along the edges, and they lead nowhere useful.

The police think this is why she wasn't found sooner. It had rained all night, there was no moon, and for almost fourteen hours, she lay on the first landing with her head at an odd angle, tree leaves slowly falling over her. If you'd stood at the top and craned your neck, you might have seen a leg or a foot, but you wouldn't have been sure. But anyway, nobody stood there and nobody looked.

. . .

But we're not there yet. For now, I'm in the back, unwrapping packages that the courier brought, sent to us for the new exhibition, the one that opens in two weeks. An exhibition that I'm hoping is going to cement my career as a curator. This is what I do, I'm an exhibitions director, a grand title considering there's just me and my assistant Gavin, although Gavin is about to leave and I haven't found a replacement for him yet. I didn't choose what to call myself. My boss, Bruno did. This is his space. A long time ago, I was a painter doing mostly portraits and I had some modest success. I topped up my income by teaching art in elementary schools until I woke up one day and realized I'd been teaching for so long and done so little painting in that time that I probably could no longer call myself an artist. I wasn't even really a proper teacher; I was a primary school relief art teacher with no qualifications, an income that barely covered my living costs and no regular hours. I didn't enjoy teaching back then, although I think I would now. But then later, once I had a family, I decided it was time for a real career and a reliable salary, and yes, I wanted Jack to be proud of me.

I was on the wrong side of thirty and had no skills to speak of except a love for art—is that even a skill?—so I decided to become a curator. I studied in my spare time, and I was lucky to find work at the Bruno Mallet Gallery although, to be fair, he didn't hire me for my curatorial abilities, but because I agreed to adjust my salary according to how much money I made for him.

Turns out, I did well. I have an eye, apparently. We now represent some very successful artists and we do okay.

As I slice off the wrapping, I am thinking about Bronwyn. *Bronwyn Bronwyn Bronwyn*, like a broken record, her face filling up my head, taking up all the available space because *Bronwyn is coming*. That's what Jack said this morning as I was leaving for work, like an afterthought. *Oh by the way, before you go, do you know where my blue shirt is? Oh by the way, the electrician called, they can't make it today. Oh by the way, Bronwyn called, she's coming.*

Beautiful, dazzling Bronwyn with long raven hair and porcelain skin, a face like a Renaissance painting. And that was before she got engaged to a plastic surgeon. I wonder what she'll look like now. Like a goddess, probably. I wish I wasn't thinking about Bronwyn, today, of all days. The artworks I am carefully unwrapping are very important to me. They are to be included in a new exhibition I've planned and curated for over a year now. The culmination of my career so far. So yes, I resent Bronwyn for robbing me of this moment, although to be fair I resent Bronwyn all the time but most days, I manage not to think about her at all.

I am so absorbed in my task—and in my thoughts—that when the front door chimes, I don't register it immediately. It's the sound of rubber soles squeaking on the timber floor that makes me realize that someone has come in the gallery and for a crazy moment I think it's her, that she's already here. I put down the Stanley knife, pull off my gloves and walk into the main area, and of course it's not her. It couldn't have been her; she couldn't have arrived here that fast. It's a young woman in high-top sneakers, skinny black jeans and faux fur jacket in black and gold animal print slumped back off her shoulders. I guess she's too warm, because it is too warm for a jacket like that, and underneath she's wearing a black camisole with thin straps that barely cover her shoulders.

"Hi!" She smiles at me, a lovely big smile, lots of teeth, straight blond hair parted in the center.

She looks vaguely familiar, but I don't think she's a buyer. I would have remembered. She points to one of the artworks and shakes her head. "These are awesome."

I come to stand next to her. "Aren't they?"

The show is called *Little Ones,* and it's by a seventy-two-year-old artist called Claire Carter who is small and shriveled up and claims to have shockingly bad eyesight although I'm not sure I believe her; she builds miniature scenes that are so precise, so beautifully crafted you can't take your eyes off them. They're housed inside glass bulbs, snow domes and test tubes, or sometimes nothing at all, just tiny shop fronts or doll houses that live on a piece of board the size of a paperback and sometimes even the size of a playing card. On the surface, they seem exquisite and delicate and charming, but look closer and that tiny figure lying on the couch isn't sleeping, they're bleeding from the head, and is that a shotgun on the floor? And leaning against the tiny piano is a white cane; does that mean the woman playing is blind? And the little boy sitting cross-legged on the rug is holding a tiny goldfish in both hands, watching it squirm. Her pieces are dark and weird and surreal, but the craftsmanship is flawless. I went to her studio once—a small austere building on Washington Street—and it was like walking into a crazy toymaker's workshop; bits of dolls scattered among dead clocks spewing out their entrails; glass eyes staring at you from the counter; springs and tiny beads surrounding jeweler's tools and absurdly small paintbrushes. She offered me a piece of lemon cake that she took out of a little fridge in the corner, and it had a thin film of mold on it, like someone had sprinkled strands of pale silvery cotton and finished it off with a scattering of gray dust. That was the only time I thought maybe there was something wrong with her eyesight, after all. Or maybe she just didn't like visitors. I ate the cake. That goes without saying. Although I scraped the top layer with my spoon and fed it to the cat under the table.

"They're wonderful," my visitor says.

"This is one of my favorites," I say. "It's called *The Inverted Garden.*" It's a take on the hanging gardens of Babylon but even more magical. Small trees and shrubs in all shapes and colors, tiny mushrooms, ivy climbing everywhere, even peacocks wondering around. Every nook and cranny of the crumbling splendor of a white building, more Roman than Babylonian, is covered by this enchanted garden, with stairs linking tiered levels and columns and arches and even fountains. It's also the only work of hers, as far as I know, that doesn't have a dark side. It must have taken years to make, and if it was mine, I'd never part with it. "But it's just been sold, I was about to put a red dot on it, in fact. But if you're interested, this one is available." I point to the piece next to it, tiny swimmers playing with a beach ball in a swimming pool, ignoring the woman drowning just feet away. "Also one of my favorites." She raises an eyebrow at me. I laugh. "Okay, I'll come clean. They're all my favorites."

She laughs too. "Oh, I wish." Her outstretched hand shoots out from the ripples of her jacket. "I'm Summer. You may not remember me, but I'm a photographer. We met once, at the Carrie Saito opening. We talked about me having an exhibition here, but it wasn't the right time."

"Oh yes! I do remember you. How are you?"

"I'm well, thank you. And that was a great show too, by the way."

I nod. "She's brilliant." I do remember her. It was a busy exhibition opening and everything was going wrong that night. Gavin called in sick at the last minute and I had to rope Jack in to tend the bar which he wasn't thrilled about. She'd brought her portfolio and she wanted me to look at it right there and then. I was distracted, I glanced at the work, I could see she had talent, but I didn't find any of her photographs exciting.

"You said I should develop my own style."

"I'm sorry—"

She raises a hand. "Don't be. It was good advice. I'm still learning."

She reaches into her satchel and I'm thinking she's going to pull out her portfolio, the updated, stylish version, but she says,

"I saw there was a job advertised on your website." She pulls out a simple white envelope. "I brought my resume."

"Oh? But it's an administrative position."

"I know. But I have the skills, I promise. I know I could learn so much working with you, and if you'd give me a chance, I promise you won't regret it."

She tells me about her somewhat limited office experience but I'm not listening because behind me my cell is ringing in my bag. I recognize the ringtone I set for Charlie's school. I raise a finger. "I'm sorry, I need to get that. Could you excuse me for just a moment?"

There's a tiny pause. "Of course," she says, twirling her envelope between her fingers.

I thank her, running over to dig out my cell. "Laura, it's Tara Fuller, from Greenhills Elementary?"

"Yes, Tara, is everything all right?"

"We've had an incident, unfortunately."

"Is Charlie okay?"

"Yes. She's fine." She sighs and I brace myself. "She bit one of her classmates."

"She did?" Oh God. I thought we had moved on from the biting. "I can't believe it's happening again," I say. "Who did she hurt?"

"Valerie."

"Valerie? But they're friends."

"Not anymore. Can you come early and pick her up? And we should have a chat."

I glance at my watch. Five past three. I am supposed to be here until five-thirty. Maybe Jack could do it. "Have you tried her father? He was going to pick her up later anyway, he's probably at home—"

"She asked for you, Laura. She wants you."

She wants you. Is it terrible that those three little words send a ripple of joy every time I hear them? Even when it's because she took a chunk out of another child? *She bit someone. She wants you.*

"I'm on my way."

I put my phone away and when I look up, Summer is smiling at me, her arm outstretched with the envelope in her hand.

I take it from her. "Unfortunately, I have to close up. Family emergency. Are you free tomorrow? Would you be able to come back then?"

"Yes, of course. Is everything all right?"

"Yes, everything is fine. Just a minor... hiccup." I slide her envelope in the drawer. "I'll be here from nine am. What's a good time for you?"

She smiles. "Nine am would be just fine."

Minutes later, Summer is gone and I'm fumbling with my bag, fishing for my keys. I've texted Jack to let him know what's going on and I'm about to call Bruno to tell him I have to close early but then I remember Gavin saying he'd be back. I call him, explain the situation. He says he's still at the bank but he's almost done and he should be back in fifteen minutes. I'm doing three things with two hands. I've still got the phone wedged in the crook of my neck and I'm hanging up the "back soon" sign on the door, adjusting the analog clock and movable hands to four o'clock. As I thank Gavin, I accidentally drop the keys on the ground, and then my phone. The phone now has a cracked screen, and Gavin is gone and when I finally look up, I think I catch the edge of Summer's distinctive black and gold jacket disappearing behind the edge of the building and I wonder if she'd been there the whole time.

TWO

Charlie is sitting on a yellow plastic chair inside Tara's office, her eyes red from crying. She springs upright and rushes into my arms to bury her face in my belly.

"Hey, sweetie! You okay?" I feel Tara's disapproving stare as if to say. *Oh, she's fine, it's the other girl you should be worried about.*

"Charlotte?" Tara says, "Can you go outside for a minute?"

"Go on," I say softly. "You wait outside the door where I can see you. I'll be there in a sec."

"It's not just the biting," Tara says once Charlie's left the room. "She's... taking things again."

We don't say stealing here, in this lovely elementary school. I know this because this isn't our first rodeo. We say, "taking things without permission."

"What did she take?"

"A box of pencils from another student. We found them in her bag."

"I'm so sorry."

"Do you know why she's acting up? She's been so good lately, is anything going on at home?"

These time-honored teacher-parent questions are never meant to be answered truthfully, surely everyone knows that. We're hardly going to tell our child's educator that daddy is having it off with his secretary or mommy's gone to rehab. So, I do what everyone else does. I plaster on my genuinely puzzled face, and say, "No, nothing I can think of. But we'll talk to her, tonight, Jack and I. We'll get to the bottom of this."

"Because she was doing so well, she's very popular with her classmates, she's a lovely child."

"Yes, she is. It's a minor setback, Tara, really. I'll take her home and talk to Jack and let you know."

"Have you considered counseling for her?"

"Not since the last time," I say, "I'll talk to Jack about it. I'm sure it's nothing." I press my bag against my chest and stand up. "Thank you. I'll take her home now."

"Oh and, Laura, also..."

"Yes?" I say, my hand on the door handle, my face for all the world looking like I have no idea what's coming.

"The term's fees. You're fifteen hundred dollars in arrears?"

"Am I? Really? Oh my God, I'm sorry. I thought Jack had taken care of it!" I shake my head. "I'll do it as soon as I get home."

———

We live a ten-minute walk from the school. I try to take Charlie's bag but she shrugs me off. She's sullen because I asked her to wait outside, she probably thinks I'm taking Tara's side. She's angry with me, and she's letting me know. It's raining and I pull the hood of her parka over her head, and she takes off toward the park, toward the playground.

"Charlie, no! Come on! We're going home!"

But she's not done yet. She sprints around the corner, toward the concrete stairs that join up to our street even though she knows full well I don't like to use them when it's raining. She stomps her gumboots into puddles of water, and for a second I consider giving in, but only for a second. If I give in now, she'll be a complete nightmare all evening.

"Come on, Charlie!" I call out to her again and, after a bit more stomping, she comes back and runs home, her backpack bouncing between her shoulder blades.

She waits for me at the gate and we walk together into the house.

I love this house. It's by far the largest house I've ever lived in, but that's not why I love it. It's light and open and airy, views everywhere you look, a yard at the front and at the back. To the left of the hallway, an archway opens to the enormous living room with French doors leading onto the deck. The kitchen is further down the house and there's a formal dining room which we hardly ever use. Then stairs go down to the lower level where Jack's office is, a playroom, the laundry, my work studio and a door that opens to the backyard.

Charlie drops her school bag on the floor and runs up the stairs to her bedroom.

"Jack?"

I hang my coat, pick up her school bag and take it upstairs to her room. When I get there, she's lying on her stomach, her head facing the window. I lie down next to her, rest my back against the bed head, kiss the top of her head. Charlie has long brown hair with a tight curl to it, almost crinkly. I love the feel of her hair. Today it smells like play dough.

"What happened with Val, sweetie?"

She shakes her head, buries her face in the pillow.

"I thought she was your friend."

"She called me a reject," she says, her voice muffled.

"Ah. I see." Wait till I get my hands on that little chimp. "And that's why you bit her?"

She nods.

"You know you're not supposed to bite people. What if they have diseases? What if you turned into a toad? You don't know where they've been."

She looks up, sees my face. I want her to smile, but she doesn't. She turns her head away.

"Seriously, Charlie. There are other ways of dealing with this stuff. What does Miss Lee say?"

Charlie loves Miss Lee. *I* love Miss Lee. "What does Miss Lee say?" I repeat.

"Take a breath, hold it for a count of three, think of the nicest thing you know."

"Okay. Try it now."

She makes an exaggerated sigh and turns around fully to face me. Scrunches up her face to hold her breath, closes her eyes. We count, together, silently. She opens her eyes wide and lets out a big, big, big breath.

"What did you think of?"

"An elephant."

"Good choice!"

"I love you, Mama," she says, and buries her face in my neck.

Mama. That's me. Mommy, on the other hand, lives in Italy with her fiancé, the famous plastic surgeon, in a villa on Lake Como, three doors down from George Clooney. I bet Mommy waves at George from the pontoon of her villa. I bet she thinks George would ditch Amal in a heartbeat if he thought he stood a chance with Mommy. I bet he would, too.

There's a photograph of Mommy on Charlie's bedside table. It's me who put it there. After she left, Charlie, who was five at the time, couldn't even say *Mommy* without having an asthma attack. I absolutely believe they were panic attacks and said so, but I got told off, so now everyone pretends Charlie used to have really bad asthma, then made a full recovery. She also used to bite people and everyone pretended that was completely normal too, and she used to steal—sorry, take things without permission—and that too got swept under the rug along with everything else, so that by then the rug had started to look like the Sierra Nevada.

I spent the best part of two years nursing this sweet child back to happiness, with the help of her lovely teacher Jenny Lee. It was me who had the photo printed, because as I often said to Charlie, *Mommy loves you,* which isn't remotely true. Mommy doesn't love anyone except Mommy, but I believe the illusion of *Mommy loves you* is better than *Mommy couldn't care less, sweetie.* Charlie and I chose the photo frame together —bleached wood with starfish and seashells—and the picture is of the two of them on a beach. Mommy sitting on the sand with the dunes behind her. She's in a polka dot bikini and a wide brim hat and enormous sunglasses. She looks surprisingly happy. Charlie is sitting in front of her, also facing the camera with Mommy's arms wrapped around her waist. She's wearing a matching one-piece polka dot swimsuit and cute sunglasses and she's laughing too. She's missing a front tooth and her hair is bleached by the sun and so frizzy it looks like wild cotton candy. My favorite part of the picture is that she's pushing against Mommy's forearms and clearly trying to get away. Sure, she's obviously having a ton of fun and wants to play in the sand and run into the sea. But still.

I put another two photos of Mommy on the pin board above her desk. The pin board is a jumble, mostly pictures of animals. Charlie is *obsessed* with animals. She wants to be a vet when she grows up, or run an animal sanctuary. Her walls are covered with animal posters—dolphins, cats, chimpanzees, giraffes, dogs, meerkats, and an enormous one of a young Jane Goodall sitting with a chimp eating a banana while she checks for parasites in its fur. On the board there are also pictures of Charlie and her best friends at a birthday party; pictures of her with Jack and I camping at Curly Creek Canyon; a picture of me carrying Charlie, aged six, on my shoulders on a vacation in Yellowstone valley. We even share a pin, Mommy and I. One corner each bonded by a single tack.

In the two years I have been with Charlie's father, I have spent many a night consoling a sobbing Charlie who still doesn't understand what she did wrong, why her mother moved to the other side of the world for a new man with a red Ferrari and didn't take her along.

But we learned to cope, together. Charlie doesn't have asthma attacks anymore. She doesn't bite, or so I thought, and honestly, if biting is all she does, it's not so bad. She used to ram her head against the wall—and people—literally dropping her head down like a goat and running into things, brick walls, whatever. We don't do that anymore. We don't ram anything, thank God.

Mommy FaceTimes once every couple of months. When Jack and I first got together, it was once a week, then slowly the calls became further apart and now they happen whenever Mommy gets around to it.

And that is what's eating at Charlie right now; it's her birthday in just over two weeks, and she wants her mother to be here and celebrate with her, the way she has in the past. Last year she and Leon flew over, first class, stayed at the Four Seasons, took Charlie out shopping at Barney's in Pine Street and out to lunch at Shiro's for sea urchin, and then they flew back. I didn't see Bronwyn on that trip. Jack thought it was best and I agreed wholeheartedly. When Charlie came home, I got her out of her frilly dress and into her favorite jeans and tee, and we went out with Daddy for hot chocolate and marshmallows at the Cat Café in Capitol Hill, which is Charlie's favorite place in the world.

But this time, Mommy has been vague about her plans. She hasn't FaceTimed either, and every day Charlie asks if we've heard anything, and every day we say, *No, sorry sweetie, not yet.*

Until this morning.

"I have an idea," I say, caressing her hair.

"What?" she asks, her sad brown eyes looking up at me.

"I think it's time for the freezer."

"What does that mean?"

"It's an old trick my mother taught me. Tried and true. Works every time." While the story is kind of true, I embellish it a little and turn it into a full ritual. I tell her that for it to work she must write down Valerie's name on a small piece of paper, fold it once then once more, blow on it and put it deep in the freezer.

"Then when you see her again, no matter what she says or does, it won't affect you. In fact, you'll barely notice she's there. All you'll think is, *do I know you? Oh, wait, that's right. You're in the freezer. You can't touch me.*"

Charlie opens her eyes wide. "Really?"

I shrug. "If they're in the freezer, they don't matter anymore. They're frozen out. If she talks to you, you raise your hand, like this." I dislodge myself from our embrace and raise her hand, palm out facing me. "And you say, don't talk to me. You're in the freezer."

She pulls her hand away, rolls her eyes. "It's not true!"

"Yes! It is! Whatever she says to you does not matter. It does not count as long as she's in the freezer. You don't have to actually tell her if you don't want to. Just raise your hand. Or do it in your head. Trust me, if they're in the freezer? They may as well be on Mars."

She pouts and shakes her head. I throw in a hot chocolate and in the end, she gives in and we walk downstairs to the kitchen. She writes down Valerie's name on a square of paper, scrunches it up, blows hard on it, then pushes it to the corner of the freezer between the fillets of bass and a packet of frozen peas. She looks up at me and smiles. She's so content after that, so pleased with herself, it makes me think maybe *I* should put *Mommy* in the freezer. After I dismember her. So she'll fit.

Once that's done and we've flicked the door of the freezer closed and bumped fists, I decide it's time to bring up the elephant she loves so much in the room.

"So... guess what," I say, twirling my spoon in the hot chocolate I've just made us.

"What?"

"Daddy told me something this morning. I was going to wait until he was here, but I don't know where he is so he'll just have to miss out."

"What?" she cries.

I wait a beat. "Mommy's coming."

Charlie's reaction at the prospect of her mother's visit makes it all absolutely, hands down, worthwhile. Her whole face opens up with joy and I laugh as she jumps off her stool and onto my lap, wraps her arms around my neck and plants kisses all over my face, as if Mommy coming was my doing, as if I'd made it all happen.

THREE

Jack's home. He comes in the way he always does: fast, with a whoosh and a slam of the door. I'm always struck by how good-looking he is, in a boyish, forgive-him-anything kind of way. He looks after himself, puts product in his hair, checks himself out in the mirror sometimes when he thinks I'm not looking, flexing his biceps. He dresses well: chinos, trainers, T-shirt under a blazer, super skinny jeans on weekends rolled up at the ankles with no socks. Sometimes I wonder how we ended up together. I'm more the jeans and tee type—the "I-really-don't-care" look— although since we got together I've considerably improved my wardrobe whereas he has downgraded his, so maybe one day we'll meet in the middle.

"Hey! Where were you? I was getting worried."

"Why?"

Ah. He's in a mood. I am acutely tuned to Jack's moods. He doesn't look at me. He walks into the living room while pulling off his tracksuit jacket.

"Did you get my message?"

"Yes. How is she?"

"She's fine. Minor hiccup at school, that's all." Jack doesn't pay attention to what goes on at school. That is well and truly my department. "She's thrilled to bits that Bronwyn is coming. You want to go and say hi?"

"Christ's sake, Laura! I just got home, can you cut me some slack please?" He makes a beeline for the liquor cabinet and pulls out the bottle of Scotch.

I tilt my head at him. "You okay?"

"Why wouldn't I be? I just went for a run." He's about to throw his jacket on the back of a chair but I extend my hand for it. He hands it to me. The sleeves are inside out and I pull them back the right way.

"Did something happen?" I ask.

"Did something happen." He chuckles. "Yes, Laura. Something happened. I didn't get the job."

I make a sound at the back of my throat. "The Boeing job? But I thought it was yours if you wanted it?" That's what he'd said. It was a great job that an old colleague had lined up for him. Jack was the perfect candidate. The job description could have been written for him. The old colleague had assured him the interview was only a formality. Jack had returned from the interview oozing confidence.

"You should have heard the questions that one guy on the panel was asking. It was painful. Obviously knew nothing about quality assurance. I literally had to rephrase every question for him. These management guys, they all think they know more than they do. But I got a good vibe from the team. And I got a tour of the place. Impressive."

"I bet they don't do that for every candidate," I'd said, sounding like something out of *Good Housekeeping* circa 1955: *How To Boost Your Husband And Help Him Get Ahead!*

"No, I'd say they don't," he'd agreed solemnly as I handed him his Scotch just the way he likes it. (Dry, two ice cubes.)

He's poured his own this time. He narrows his eyes at me over the rim of the glass before taking a big swig. "Yes, Laura."

He wipes his mouth with the back of his hand. "That's right. The Boeing job. I didn't get it."

And all I can think is, Oh God. This is so bad.

Jack used to run his own very successful engineering consultancy, but then things happened and the work dried up and a year ago he wound it up and decided to go work for one of the big firms.

It wasn't so bad, at first. We had savings, it wouldn't take that long to find a job. He was highly qualified, well respected in the industry. All he had to do was shake the job tree. Lots of low hanging fruit, he'd said. The very next day he was on the phone talking to old contacts and sounding them out for a position. He'd tell me about these conversations while rubbing his hands together and exclaiming that this was the best thing that had ever happened to him, that life was about to get so much easier from now on, that he'd have more time with his family.

Except there are no jobs; those old contacts are either getting retrenched themselves or they're hanging on for dear life. Lately, there are days when Jack doesn't get out of bed until eleven, and he'll start drinking at four in the afternoon. I will come home and he'll stare at me from under slanted eyelids. *Don't blame me, Laura. I'm trying, it's not my fault. It's the recession. Those jobs have gone offshore. It's not my fault.*

But then there are other days where he'll be the old Jack again, or a more manic version anyway. He'll spend hours at the gym training, he'll lock himself in his office and produce spreadsheets and flowcharts and then announce over dinner that he is going to start another engineering design company, that it was a stupid idea to look for employment. He wasn't that kind of guy, he needed to be in charge. He'd had a chance to reflect on what went wrong last time and he knew what he had to do differently. Charlie and I will squeal with delight because we both know instinctively that's what he needs from us, and he will rope Charlie in to come up with ideas for a new company name, a fresh start, and what about a logo? Would she do that? She could be in charge of public relations, she's so bright, so talented, this could be a father–daughter company, Blackman & Daughter, how's that for a name? Would she like that? And he'll borderline harass her, for more ideas! More enthusiasm! Come on Charlie! Whatchagotforme! Let's hear it! Until Charlie's little face starts to fall because she thinks she's not doing it right, but she doesn't understand what's expected—fair enough, nobody does—and I'll gently tug at Jack's sleeve and point out that Charlie is seven years old and it's time for bed.

Forty-eight hours, that's how long that usually lasts, which is how long it takes for the bank to say *no, we won't give you a loan* and I'm secretly ecstatic because God knows we're in enough debt already, and then we are back to dejected, pacing, sullen, angry Jack, *don't blame me,* and round and round we go.

A few months ago he went off at Charlie. She'd been doing handstands in her bedroom and knocked over a floor lamp cracking the lampshade. It had cost fifteen dollars at the Walmart Supercenter. But Jack was drunk. He kept berating her over and over and it got to the point where I snapped at him to cool it and bundled a sobbing Charlie into the car so I could take her for a drive and calm her down, explain to her that Daddy is going through a very difficult time and he doesn't know what he's saying and he sure doesn't mean it because he loves her more than anything in the world. When we came back an hour later, Jack was beside himself. He was absolutely and genuinely remorseful. He apologized to Charlie, talked to her for half an hour, explained that the stress of everything some-times sent him off and it was very wrong what he'd said but it had nothing to do with her, she was the best thing that had ever happened to him, the light of his life, and he was very sorry. In our bedroom that night I stood in front of him with a finger in his face and told him that he needed to get his shit together. Get some counseling, stop drinking. Be responsible.

"Marry me," he said.

I wasn't sure if I'd heard him right, or if he even meant it.

"I love how fiercely you love Charlie. You are a lioness when it comes to that kid. I know in my bones that she and I will always be safe with you. We need you, Laura. Will you marry us?"

I don't know when I'd ever felt so happy as in that moment. I wrapped my arms around his neck and yelled that yes, yes, yes! I'll marry you! And I cried and he laughed and we danced and finally I said, "Wait. Don't you have to get a divorce first?"

And he said yes, what a very good idea. But it was a joke, obviously. The divorce was well under way, the lawyers were trashing out the last parts.

We set a date. We gave ourselves nine months. That was six months ago. For reasons no one has managed to explain to me, Bronwyn has been dragging her feet.

"I'm sorry about the job," I say now. "What went wrong, do you know?"

He slaps his hands on his thighs and pushes himself up. "I'll go say hi to Charlie."

We're not talking about the job. Got it.

He disappears up the stairs and minutes later I follow him to take his jacket to our closet. I peer inside Charlie's bedroom. He's teaching her a boxing move. "No, like this, Watch. Upper-cut." He demonstrates, then takes her little fist and brings it up, like she's a marionette. "You have to make contact with her chin, here." He points to his own. Between the freezer and the boxing moves I'm beginning to feel sorry for Valerie.

Back downstairs I check myself in the hall mirror. I pat my hair, tuck it behind my ears, straighten my blouse. I'm about to ask Jack for money. Another nod to the 1950s. *Take fifteen minutes to make sure you look your best. Put a ribbon in your hair. A slick of lipstick. He's working hard all day and coming home to a happy pretty wife shows him you care.*

"We're late on the school fees, I don't know if you remember?" I say when he returns. He pours himself another drink. "Jack? You listening? Tara brought it up today."

"Who's Tara?"

"The school principal. Apparently we still owe fifteen hundred dollars in fees." I say *apparently* to soften the blow, make it sound like it's news to me, which it's not. It's not news to him either, or it shouldn't be, and yet he turns around, face shocked.

"Are you serious? Fifteen hundred dollars? What the hell, Laura! She's only ten years old! What are they teaching them in there? Keyhole surgery?"

"She's seven, but okay, I get your point. However—"

"It's time to move her to a state school. That's what we pay taxes for."

"Don't say that. She needs to stay at Greenhills for now."

"Why?"

"Because she still has problems and it's the best school for her right now. All her friends are there."

"She doesn't have problems."

"She was sent home because she bit a classmate."

"So what? They're just playing! I don't know why you worry so much, Laura. Biting's nothing! I used to do it all the time."

"That's nice, honey, but this is not about you." At least he's back to himself now. The old Jack, news about the job forgotten, Charlie's fine, what's the problem? I'll give this to Jack: he loves Charlie, I know that, but he doesn't understand her. When Charlie started biting other kids—and I mean biting hard, leaving purple bruised crescents behind—parents weren't happy. Understandably. They were paying upwards of five thousand dollars a year and getting their kids back looking like they'd just had a run-in with a vampire. But Jack kept saying it was nothing. *She's just a kid! That's what they do! In my day...*

"She needs to stay there until high school, Jack. Jenny Lee is the best teacher for her. She's done brilliantly there. And this is such a great school, they've got that great introductory math program, remember? That's one of the reasons we enrolled her there! It will be a waste to move her now, the state school won't introduce math until next year." What I really want to say is that she'll regress, and we do not want that. I want to grab him by the metaphorical lapels and shake him. *We don't want her to regress, Jack! She'll hurt other kids! Remember what it was like? We've made such progress!*

Jack can't handle the idea that Charlie has emotional problems. But he was very excited to find a school that introduced advanced math so early, and as far as he's concerned, that's why Charlie goes to Greenhills.

"Well, babe, if you can find fifteen hundred bucks, knock yourself out." He knocks back his drink.

I swallow a sigh. "Okay, fine. I'll sort it out. I'll go get dinner ready."

———

Later, when Charlie is asleep and it's just Jack and I sipping red wine over the remnants of a beef bourguignon, I bring up Bronwyn's visit.

"So, when are they coming?"

"Tuesday next week. But it's just Bron. Leon can't make it. He's got too much work."

"Just Bronwyn? This coming Tuesday?"

He mops his plate with a piece of bread. "She wants to stay with us."

"With us?" I blurt. "You mean, here? In our house?"

"Yes."

"You're joking, right?" I snort. "We're not exactly the Four Seasons. Will we have to deliver her eggs Benedict and Dom Perignon in bed every morning?" I laugh, I don't know why, it's probably exactly what will happen. "So, what did you tell her?" I say more quietly.

He gives me a pained look, like I'm exasperating him. "I said sure, you can stay in the spare bedroom. What else did you want me to say?"

Oh, I don't know. How about, I told her I'd talk to you first, make sure it's okay with you.

"Nothing," I say. "So how long is she staying for?"

"Not sure, a couple of weeks."

I smile because it's a joke, obviously. I wait for him to say it, but he doesn't. "Sorry. How long?"

"Two or three weeks, something like that."

"Are you serious?"

"Yes, why?"

And I'm thinking, *oh my God. No, please.* "You know what she's like, Jack. You don't think that's awkward?"

He closes his eyes. "I'm trying, Laura, okay? She wants to visit Charlie. She's her mother."

I let out an involuntary snort. "Sorry. Keep going."

"Don't be like that."

"No, of course not. Like what?"

"Like now. Do *you* think it's awkward?"

"Well, yes, I just brought it up, didn't I?"

"Okay, Laura, you may not have noticed but I'm under a lot of stress right now."

"Right."

"So if Bron wants to come and stay and visit Charlie, I'm not going to say no."

"That's not what I meant. But why can't she stay in a hotel?"

"I don't know."

Okay. That's okay. I'll make it work. I make everything work. Think of the positive, she can help around the house. Haha. Just kidding. But what would happen if I said, *No, she can't stay here?* I'm so tempted, I roll the words on my tongue, just to try them out.

But then Jack says, "There is a silver lining."

"There is? You sure it's not an anvil about to fall on your head?"

"We're going to the lawyers and she will sign the divorce papers." He grins at me.

"Oh my God! Really??"

"She's the one who suggested it." And his face relaxes into a smile, like he was saving this best news for last. I punch his shoulder and he slaps his hand on where I hit him, laughing.

"That hurt!"

"I can't believe you didn't tell me!"

"Sorry." He takes my face in his hands, kisses me full on the mouth. "I love you. Let's go to bed, Mrs. Blackman-to-be."

FOUR

Fall came fast this year. One moment we were spending weekends by the beach and the next I had to pull out the heaviest clothes from storage. There's a biting wind this morning that makes me wish I'd worn a scarf. I was lulled into complacency by a small patch of blue sky which, by the time I get off the bus is well and truly gone, replaced by gray clouds.

I am on a mission. I'm going to ask Bruno for an advance against my salary. I've never done that before, and I'm not completely sure he'll say yes, but I think he will. Bruno likes me. Not *likes* me, but we get on well. I am a valued employee. I sell a lot of works for him. You could say I've turned his business around. That has to count for something.

I walk briskly, past the firefighter memorial where a crow that was calmly perched on a bronze shoulder takes off with a cry, past the plane trees that stand behind the memorial, with their stark, black branches against the sky.

I am rehearsing the conversation in my head. If I may, Bruno, could I get an advance on my pay? Fifteen hundred dollars, is that all right with you? No. Too deferential. What about, Bruno, by the way, I'm going to need an advance on my pay, fifteen hundred dollars. Could you transfer it today? No. Too entitled. Not at all my style.

I turn the corner and I'm at the door of the gallery, my keys in my hand hovering before the lock, but the door is already open. Only by an inch or so, which isn't necessarily unusual—it could be that Gavin or Bruno left it open when they came in—except the bolt has jutted out so the door can't close again. You have to put the key in the lock and draw the bolt back, and this is something that happens some-times with this door. You have to pull it quite hard for the latch to engage, otherwise it gets wedged against the plate and a gust of wind can push the door open, at which point the bolt will spring out, which is exactly what happened here. I was supposed to have the whole lock replaced, as it's old and not the most secure system in the world, but I had other things on my mind. I put it off, and then I put it off again.

The other thing I notice is that the sign I put up before I left yesterday is still there. *Back at 4.* My stomach does a little twist. Just a small one. I'm not panicking yet. I walk in. The light through the passage at the back that leads to the second gallery is on and I can hear footsteps.

"Oh thank God!" I say out loud. I turn to the alarm panel but of course it's already off, as is the CCTV control panel. I take off my coat and drop it on the desk with my bag. "Is that you, Gav? I think I just had a heart attack, for a moment I thought—"

"Hi, Laura!" It's her, the young woman from yesterday. Summer, that's it. She's standing in the open doorway that leads to the second gallery, beaming her big smile at me and holding a black folder against her chest.

I check my watch. "Oh, hi! Of course, nine am, and I'm two minutes late. I'm sorry."

"That's all right. I was early."

I unbutton my coat, glance over her shoulder. "Is Gavin out the back?"

"Sorry, I don't know who Gavin is, but there's no one here. Just me!"

"Just you?" I tilt my head. "So how did you get in?"

"The door was open."

"Oh." And then, from the corner of my eye, something odd.

"Everything okay?" she asks.

I turn my head slowly. On the wall to my right should be six of Claire Carter's works on display. Now there are five, plus a blank space. I walk over, put my hand where the work is missing. "*The Inverted Garden*," I say. I turn to look at her and for a moment, I don't know what to say. "It should be there. Do you know what happened to it?"

"No, should I?"

I'm going to be sick. I turn back to the wall. "When did you say you got here?"

"About ten minutes ago."

"Did you see anyone?"

"No, there was no one here. Like I said, the door was open and I just walked in. The light was on down there, so I called out and walked through to the other gallery, but there was no one there either."

I walk out the back and check the storeroom. It's locked. I rummage through my bag and get out my phone, call Gavin.

"Hi Laura, I'm on my way. What's up?"

I'm biting on a fingernail. "What time did you leave the gallery yesterday?"

"Oh, yeah, I didn't make it back. Things took too long at the bank and by the time I left, it was after five anyway. Why?"

The realization comes to me with a lurch of horror. If Gavin didn't return, then it means that it's me who left the light on last night in the second gallery. It's me who left the front door open.

"I think we've been robbed," I mutter, then hang up. I flick on the lights in the main gallery. Seeing the empty space on the wall like that physically hurts. It's like someone flashing you a beautiful smile with one front tooth missing.

I fold myself onto the front step to call the police with my forehead in my hand.

They ask a million questions, but my head is still spinning and I'm confused. Was anything else taken? I don't think so, I say, but I haven't looked. Any sign of forced entry? I press the heel of my hand between my eyes. "I don't know, I think so." I tell them about Summer, how she said the door was already open. Did I leave it open when I left yesterday? Did I do this? I left in a hurry immediately after Tara Fuller's call. I called Gavin. I can see myself with the phone against my ear and the keys in my hand. Then I dropped the phone, that's it. And the keys. Did I lock the door before or after I dropped the keys? Did I lock it at all? I didn't check even though it happens all the time, that the bolt doesn't engage fully, and I should have checked but I didn't and now it's my fault.

But I'm not saying that to the police. Any sign of forced entry? I don't know, I say. I haven't checked.

"Don't touch anything until we get there. Is there another room where you can wait? Somewhere where they haven't been?"

"Y-yes," I say. "There's a storeroom at the back. It's still locked so they haven't been in there."

"Good. Wait for us there, please. We won't be long."

"I'll come back some other time," Summer says behind me after I've ended the call. I spin around.

"Would you mind staying?" I ask. "The police will want to ask you some questions... I mean, I'm sure they could call you if you prefer, but—"

She hesitates, then gives a little shrug. "No, that's cool, I can stay if you want."

"Thank you so much. You can sit back there, you'll be

comfortable." I unlock the storeroom. There's a big table, with chairs, we use it as a meeting room if we need to. I get her settled in, offer her water from the cooler.

"I'm good," she says. "You go, do what you have to. I'm fine here."

"Okay, thank you, Summer. I really appreciate it."

And now it's just me, standing in the gallery, wringing my hands together, my stomach twisting within an inch of its life. In the silence I can hear my heart pound behind my ears. I should call Bruno, tell him what happened, but instead I stare at the front door with its bolt sticking out, at the empty white wall, and then at the middle distance while I add up the costs. That work was sold for fourteen thousand dollars, and now it's gone. Will the insurance even pay if they find out I left the door wide open all night? Would Bruno pay the client back? He's done nothing wrong. He's not the one who left the door wide open with a sign at the front that said: *Back at 4!* It may as well have read: *Help yourself!*

I try to imagine asking Bruno for an advance on my salary while at the same time explaining that I left the door open last night. If I get fired, Jack and I will both be out of work. Brilliant timing, really. I'm thinking school fees, mortgage, birthday parties, incidentals like food and shelter, and of course I'm thinking, *wedding*, and I'm especially thinking, *Bronwyn*. Bronwyn who is coming to stay with us in a few days, and what will she find? Jack and I broke and at each other's throats. Charlie thrown out of school because we couldn't pay the fees. A mortgage that we will be mere weeks away from defaulting on.

What if Bronwyn decides Charlie is not in good hands with us? That we are not capable of looking after her because we are not capable of looking after ourselves?

I'm not even thinking anymore. It just happens. As if I am watching myself from above in slow motion. My mind is blank, as blank as that empty square on the west wall. I am fast. I am a bullet. I am not thinking. I am an automaton. I am a robot running at warp speed. Before I know it, I have walked over to the desk, opened my bag and fished around for my keys. I catch sight of my metal nail file at the bottom of the bag. Perfect. I grab it, along with my phone.

There's a door in the passageway that is completely flush with the wall. It's a cupboard where we keep the basics: white paint, tools, red dots, hanging wire. It's locked, and I open it gently, twisting the key and pressing on the door at the same time so it doesn't audibly click. I gently lift out the claw hammer before pushing the door closed. In a few quick strides I'm back at the front door and position myself so that if Gavin arrives, he won't see what I'm doing. My fingers are shaking and it takes a few tries to slip the key in the lock and with one quick flick of the wrist the bolt is gone, disappeared back inside the door where it belongs.

I study the lock, the plate, the door. I just want to smash something. I want to make it look like robbers had a really hard time getting in and they had to tear the place down, but I can't because Summer is back there. I consider hacking at the plate, levering it off with the claw of the hammer, but that's not the way to do it. I search on my phone, *How can you tell a lock has been tampered with?* My search takes me to a YouTube video that I watch at three times the speed as it describes something called a bump key. It's used to break into any lock just like ours, and frankly they make it look so easy it makes you wonder there aren't more robberies in this city.

I have the door open about a foot and I stand in that narrow space, hunched over, and make a few nicks with my nail file close to the keyhole. Clear evidence that someone used a bump key, I think. Although, is that what it should look like? Is that enough? I have that YouTube video on a loop on my phone and now I'm on a roll, holding the nail file like it's a dagger and frantically scratching crisscrossing marks all over the metal. My heart is hammering and I'm biting down on my own teeth. My jaw hurts, but I can't stop.

I don't know how long I do that for, but suddenly it feels like I've woken from a really bad dream. I'm breathing hard, panting like I've been running. I look at my work and my heart sinks. That looks bad. Really bad. I look down at my shaking hands, one of which still holds the hammer. My hair has fallen over half my face and I blow it away, swipe it with the back of one hand and when I finally look up, I find that on the other side of the glass door, watching me with detached interest, is Summer.

FIVE

It's Saturday. I woke up with a renewed sense of purpose, the overwhelming relief that I'd *gotten away with it* still bouncing inside me, lifting me up, making me feel *lucky* I managed to drag Jack off the couch, off his iPad, so we could spend the day out as a family. We used to do that all the time on weekends: special outings for the three of us. I try to remember the last time we did that and all I can think is the time we took Charlie to the Ferry Wheel. The flowers were in bloom. Spring, then. Ages ago.

Today, we had lunch at Cafe Nordstrom, then spent a couple hours wandering around Pike Place market, and now we're settled at Bottega Italiana because Charlie *loves* ice cream.

"It was horrible," I say. "Walking in and seeing that blank space..."

Jack and I are sitting at the table and Charlie is in the children's nook, cross-legged on the floor with a book on her lap and a bowl of ice cream in her hands. I'm telling Jack the story all over again even though we went through it last night. *You'll never believe what happened. Her best work too, gone.* But he doesn't seem to mind. He's got his head down, scrolling through his phone and I can't think of what else to talk about, and I have to fill the empty space between us, even if it means repeating myself. He must have realized I've stopped speaking because he makes a sound, a kind of grunt, to show he's listening.

"Then Bruno called this morning while you were in the shower—" this is new information, so I can say it with renewed vigor "—because he saw the CCTV footage, and around midnight a person came and walked right in. That's what it looked like, they just walked right in. They must have hacked the lock before the CCTV came on outside. That's what he said." Oh God. Bruno. He arrived less than ten minutes after I'd finished tampering with that lock, even though he doesn't come to the gallery on Fridays, unless he's got a good reason. The thought that he might have walked in while I was... *No. Don't even go there.*

I wish, with all my heart, that I hadn't done that. The memory of it makes my stomach lurch. When the police told Bruno that the lock had been tampered with, I had this sudden urge to tell the truth. No, it was me, sorry, I panicked. I apologize. But I didn't, then as the day wore on and more questions were asked, and they took our fingerprints "for elimination purposes," I realized with a shock that I wasn't thinking about fingerprints when I attacked that lock, which meant the only fingerprints they were going to find were mine, and I didn't think they'd eliminate me so easily. I wondered if it was too late to go back, back to that fork in the road, and take the path where I told the truth but I thought, no. It's too late for the truth. Also, I couldn't understand why Summer was taking so long to tell them what I'd done, and I thought that's what it must feel like when you stand in the dock waiting to hear the verdict and you know it's going to be bad, but a small part of you still clings to the impossible hope that when they found the body, they didn't notice you were holding the bloody axe.

"You came in first. Tell me what you saw," detective O'Sullivan said to Summer. We were all sitting around the table in the storeroom and we all watched her, Bruno closer than anyone, I noticed. I couldn't bear it and I stared down at my hands, picking at the cuticles around my nails, waiting for her reply with my heart bouncing around my chest.

"I was early for my job interview..."

O'Sullivan nods. We've explained about the assistant position we're hiring for so there was no confusion as to why Summer was here, alone.

"... and the front door was open."

"Was it wide open?"

"No, it was ajar. I pushed it open. The main gallery was dark but there was a light down the corridor at the back. I called out, there was no reply. I went to look for someone but there was no one here. I figured whoever was here had gone out for a moment,"

"Were you surprised they'd left the door open?"

She shrugged. "Not really. I figured they'd gone out for a minute, maybe next door. I didn't give it any thought. I just waited."

"Did you notice anything about the door? The lock?"

This is it, I thought. I bowed my head and waited, feeling my face burn.

"I didn't look closely," she said, and I held my breath.

The detective nodded, took notes. "And what did you do then?"

"I looked at the photographs in the second gallery, the lighting was better there. The front gallery was in darkness." Then she added, sweeping a lock of hair from her face, "I'm an art photographer. I have a special interest in that kind of work."

"What happened then?"

"I heard someone call out from the front and I came back

out and met Laura. That's when I found out there had been a robbery."

"Anything else?"

And then, I caught Laura smashing the front door lock. I was already mentally rehearsing my response which included chuckling with disbelief at the suggestion. Of course not! She must have misunderstood. I was trying to fix it, that's all.

"Laura called you," she said, "then she took me out to the storeroom. I was by myself for a while. I went to the kitchen where I saw a coffee machine. I came back out to see Laura at the front and..."

She glanced my way. And that's when I saw Laura hacking at the lock. She was really manic. She had a hammer.

"And then?" O'Sullivan prompts.

"I asked her to show me how to use the machine," she said simply.

I stared at her. That's exactly what happened. I'd looked up and there she was, staring at me from behind the glass, her face as expressionless as a mannequin in a department store. Then she asked for a coffee.

"I saw you have an espresso machine out the back—" She'd jerked her thumb behind her shoulder. "Could I have one? I don't know how to use it."

I could feel my whole face trembling, heat rising up my neck and into my cheeks. "Coffee?" I said.

"Yes."

"I'll make it," I said after a decade or so.

"You sure? I don't mind doing it."

"No, that's okay, you won't know how to... use the machine." Sweat was prickling on my forehead which I wiped with the back of my hand, and that's when I realized I was still holding the hammer.

She smiled sweetly. It was like nothing going on, nothing strange at all about the hammer, the nail file, the door lock, me shaking like a leaf. So, I closed the front door and she followed me back to the cupboard where I returned the tools, then to the kitchenette where I made her a cup of coffee, black, two sugars.

And that was that.

Then later that morning, the police took our statements, then left, and Bruno asked if I was all right, and I said yes, I'm fine thank you, a bit shocked, that's all, and he said, yes, we all are, very unfortunate, and he went to call the insurance company, and later I asked for an advance because I couldn't wait. I was still a little shaken and he must have taken pity on me because he said, yes, of course, Laura. That's no problem. And I was so relieved I could have cried.

"So yes, just one person," I say now to Jack. "Dressed in black, with a hoodie and a face covering like a ski mask. They walked in, came out with one of our best pieces and seconds later they're out of the camera vision, and that's it. They can't tell who it is from the footage. They can't even tell if it's a man or woman, according to Bruno. And I have to say I felt sorry for Summer, she was the first one in the gallery, and Gav even asked straight up if she was the thief, can you imagine? In front of the police, too. I said to Gavin, 'but you were supposed to come back in fifteen minutes!' And he was furious with me. 'No, Laura!' he was saying. 'I said I *might* be back in fifteen minutes, but I couldn't guarantee it, okay? In fact, if you remember I said I might not get back at all.' And I was like, 'but you said... but I heard you...' and he kept saying, 'No, if you heard that, that's on you, because that's not what I said, okay?' But that's classic Gavin. Honestly, I'm glad he's leaving. Whenever anything goes wrong he always raises his hands and says, 'Not my fault.' He's like a kid in that way. In the end I had to apologize just so we could move on. And then he went back to Summer, and he asked again, 'So, did you steal the artwork, Summer? Yes or no.'" I shudder. "So boorish. She just said no."

After a beat, he asks, still scrolling, "Why would he ask that?"

I get it. Jack is stressed out, especially about the job he didn't get. But still, we went through all that last night. I close my eyes briefly. I won't let it get to me. We're having a family day and nothing is going to get in the way.

"Because she was there first, in the gallery, before anyone else. I walked in and found her there. The door was open, you see?" That must be the third time I've explained that.

He doesn't reply. Scroll, scroll, scroll.

"Credit where it's due, she held her own with the police, and with Gav. Cool as anything. In her shoes I would have been completely paranoid that they'd think I did it." I laugh.

"Who?" he asks.

"Who what?"

"Who did you say was there first?"

I shouldn't complain now that he's finally paying attention to the conversation, but in terms of focus, it's a bit lacking. "Summer. She was there for her job interview."

"What's the job?" he asks.

"Why, you want it?" I laugh. He doesn't. I rearrange my face to serious. "It's for the assistant's job for the touring show I'm curating." I lean forward conspiratorially. "I might even throw in some special perks for the right candidate," I say, trying for coquettish.

He smiles politely.

I sigh. "Anyway, I don't think she's right for the position. She's not..." I'm trying to find the right word. "Office ready."

Office ready?

I did interview her, though. We went back to the storeroom, I brought us a jug of water and two glasses. I pulled out her CV from the drawer where I'd left it the night before. But I didn't want to interview her because I still had that moment seared in my mind, her watching me while I made a complete mess of the lock. I tried to banish it, tried to make myself focus on the present.

"What's the job, exactly?" she asked.

I gave her the basic descriptions. Help organize the openings, go to the post office, make sure catalogues are printed on time. "Our next show is a touring exhibition, so the bulk of the work is contacting venues around the country and confirming the dates and their involvement, getting the freight organized, following up on the marketing assets such as logos and press releases, that sort of thing."

"What's the show?"

"It's called the Museum of Lost and Found. A complete departure for us, we're extending our audience reach and opportunities for exposure." I sounded like the state-funding application I'd sent off to help us pay for such a big event.

She took a sip of water. "That sounds fantastic. I love it! Tell me more!"

"Sure, well, we invite members of the public to send in an object they found with a story as to why it's become significant to them, or if they've lost the object, we will recreate it for the exhibition. Let me give you an example. One person sent an old, framed photograph they'd found in the street trash can. It's a picture of a middle-aged man, a studio portrait, three inches by five inches. She's never met this man, she has no idea who he is, but she'd just lost her mother two weeks earlier and she had no family left. She'd never met her father. Something about the photo, the way he posed, the way he looked, made her feel like he must have been important to someone once, but now he was in the trash. So, she took the framed photograph home and put it on her mantelpiece, and decided she would love this man, because someone had to, she said. Somebody had to love him."

Summer clicked her tongue. "That is just so romantic."

I smiled. "She explains it by saying they were both lost, and they needed each other at that time in her life. She told everyone he was her uncle. Uncle Jeff, she called him. She invented stories about him, how funny he was, how he used to dress as Father Christmas when he came to visit them for the holidays. How he fixed her bike. Then she got married and eventually told her husband the truth about the photo, putting it away in a drawer. She no longer needed to look at him on the mantelpiece, but she didn't want to throw him away either. Then she saw our call for works, so she sent it in with her story." I got up. "Come with me, I'll show you."

I took her through to the back storage area and showed her the works that had been selected so far, including the photograph of Uncle Jeff, and a scarf we had someone knit to match the photo sent in by a woman who'd lost it. "It had belonged to her grandmother who had died, and later this woman lost everything in a house fire when she was out of the house, except for the scarf because she happened to be wearing it. Then a year later, she lost it on a train." I read from the letter. "'It's the one thing I never wanted to lose, my last connection to my grandmother.'" Then I show her the rest. A replica of a violin that was lost on the way to an audition for the Philharmonic. I read from the letter. "'My family was broke, my violin was cheap and battered and hard to tune, and somehow I left it on the bench where I was waiting for the bus to take me to the audition. I was devastated. They let me use another one, a pristine beautiful violin with the most delicious sound I'd ever heard. I got lost in my own playing. I got the gig. I don't think I would have gotten it if I'd played the piece on my old violin, so I'm grateful I lost it.'"

"Incredible," Summer said, shaking her head in wonder. She hoisted her bag over her shoulder. "When will you make a decision?"

"Well, let me think. I have a couple of people still to talk to on Monday. Do you want to go back to the storeroom and we can go over your skillset?"

"I'd love to, but I have to run. But you've got my resume, I'm great on the phone, great with people, great with computers, spreadsheets, I can type fast, all that. I'm a hard worker, Laura. You won't be disappointed."

She took my hands in hers. "It would be an honor to work with you."

"Oh, right, you're sure?" I chuckled. I wanted to tell her that it's not that kind of job, she wasn't going to do any curating or creative work of any kind. That I was in no way honorable, that sometimes I lied and sometimes I broke locks.

But she was already gone.

"You should go with your gut, Laura," Jack says now.

I nod. "Exactly. That's what I'm going to do. Go with my gut."

SIX

I don't really have a gut, not in that way. And if I had one, I left it at the door in the end. I'm too much of a coward.

It's Monday. I feel the way I used to when I was not much older than Charlie: the gentle loveliness of the weekend turning heavy and gray on Sunday afternoon, then the Monday morning rise, the prospect of five whole days to get through before the delicious Friday afternoon release.

Up to the moment when I reached the door of the gallery, I'd successfully fought off my anxiety. We'd had a lovely weekend, then last night Charlie went to bed early, giddy with joy at the prospect of her mother's visit, which made me marvel again at the easy forgiveness of children. Children don't bear grudges. They get upset, and then they forget. Which sure is lucky for Bronwyn, although as I keep telling her in the privacy of my own head, *Just wait till she's a teenager, Bronwyn*.

After Charlie went to bed, Jack cooked us dinner—a rarity these days—of spaghetti carbonara that we washed with a bottle of Chianti as he told me about his plans, which were essentially the same plans as last time. Apply for more jobs, obviously, but how about starting his own consultancy again? "Consultants get paid a mint to write reports. That's where the money is, Laura. With my background I could charge five hundred bucks an hour. Easy."

I held in my sigh as he talked of scouting some office space and I agreed that it was a great idea, while wondering silently where we would find the money to get us through that particular brainwave. At one point there was a lull in the conversation while he opened another bottle of wine, and I plunged into it, grasped the opportunity with both hands and brought up our wedding, I don't know why I did that. Actually, that's not true. We were having a nice time, I was wearing the necklace he bought me when we first got together, fingering the chain, the dangling emerald. "I've trimmed the fat every place I found!" I said. "Our wedding is a lean, mean machine, baby! At this rate we'll get married in the public toilets at Matthews Beach, they're nice enough, right? And our guests will drink straight from the tap at the basins and my train will be made out of those big long rolls of toilet paper. And all courtesy of the City!" I laughed. I sounded like I was braying, I put it down to the wine. He kind of laughed too, although not really, more of a distracted chuckle.

"Joking aside," I said, in case he'd hoped I'd been sincere, "We have a meeting coming up at Sodo Park, remember? So many things to finalize, like the menu, the wines, the band. Of course, we don't need a band. We could get someone to DJ for us, like Mike, would Mike be up for a bit of DJing, do you think? We should ask him! Will you ask him, darling? It's getting so close!" It might be a low-key, small-scale, turn-key wedding where everything comes in the one package and you don't have to hire outside vendors, but there are still decisions to be made. Plated or buffet? Custom cake or off-the-shelf?

I waited, my chin resting on the heel of my hand while he smiled, poured us another glass, but he didn't say anything, just twirled a few strands of spaghetti onto his fork, and I knew I'd nudged us onto shaky ground, so I retreated, changed the subject, looped back to the consulting company idea. It's hard talking about our wedding when we have money problems. Of course, it wasn't supposed to be this way. When we planned our small, intimate, very reasonably priced wedding, we didn't have money problems. Or if we did, we didn't think it would last.

———

Monday afternoon. I interview other two candidates for the position. The first one is not right so he doesn't rate a mention, but the next candidate is perfect. Her name is Janet, and she's a lovely woman in her early thirties who went back to college to become an arts administrator now that her kids were at school. She's tall, thin, with short blond hair. I like her maturity, her approach to getting things done. She loves the arts and wants to work in that world by bringing her best strengths to it: her outstanding organizational skills. We get on instantly and when she leaves, I immediately tell Bruno I've found someone.

"Really? So... not Summer?"

I noticed on Friday the way he looked at Summer, with a serious appreciation, the way he might hold up a fine wine or examine a work of art. And more interestingly, even as I did all I could *not* to look at Summer that day, I caught the way she smiled coyly at him before looking down at her hands.

"I like Janet," I say to Bruno, and I explain why.

"Of course, it's up to you, Laura."

"Yes, thank you. I'm going to go with Janet, then."

And then, Summer calls.

"I wondered whether you'd made a decision," she asks in her sweet voice, and my stomach does a little twist. Only a small one, barely a quarter pretzel. I picture her in my mind's eye coming to the door of the gallery that morning and seeing it open, noticing the bolt sticking out, although she never said whether she did or not. Then I see myself hacking at that lock, a metal nail file in one hand and a hammer in other, and looking up to see Summer standing there, watching me. Was she smiling? I think she was smiling. And every time I think of that moment, the realization that she was there, I want to curl up on my side and die of shame. But she never said a thing about that either, and I think to myself, *Is it possible she didn't see what I was doing? How could she not see? Of course she saw. She just hasn't said anything. Yet.*

And just like that, I tell myself that I'm doing it for Bruno because of what I've put him through, even if he doesn't know it, and because he transferred the money I asked for into my account, and because he'll be pleased when I tell him I chose Summer, after all. *I'll do it to make Bruno happy*, I tell myself.

"I'm so glad you called, Summer. I'm delighted to offer you the position." And she squeals with joy, and says she can't wait to get started and that I won't regret it.

Bruno is surprised, but visibly pleased, when I tell him I've changed my mind.

"Good. She is very decorative," he says in his French accent and I'm not sure if I've heard him right, but I catch Gavin rolling his eyes so I figure I must have.

"She really is the best candidate," I say. "She has all the right qualities."

And already as I return to the main gallery, I feel the weight of regret, like a stone in my stomach, knowing that every time I see her I will be reminded of that moment when I saw her watching me, and I wish I hadn't offered her the job.

SEVEN

This morning, Bruno has decided to have a work meeting before we open. This is the first time we've done this, but it's fair enough, he wants Gavin to do a handover.

I used to call him Mr. Mallet when I first started, "Call me Bruno," he'd said as he showed me around the gallery—a pretty quick tour, obviously—and he put his hand on the small of my back when he said it and I felt a frisson down my spine even though he was sixty with gray hair and skin that was beginning to sag around the jowls. Now as he leads Summer to the storeroom, he's doing the same to her and Summer smiles, delighted, girlish.

"Summer, welcome to the team," Bruno begins. She flashes him a sunny smile.

Gavin checks his watch.

"Are we boring you, Gavin?" Bruno says, and Gavin visibly blushes.

I don't know what it is with those two. Gavin is Bruno's nephew by marriage, he gave him a job because Gavin loves art, but all Gavin does here is run errands for Bruno and serve wine at openings, and Bruno is always putting him down. Which is probably why Gavin decided to leave.

"It's new, that's all, the watch," I say quickly, rushing to help. I know it is because Gavin showed it to me a couple of weeks ago. It's a TAG Heuer, a present from his boyfriend that he wears on his right wrist for some reason. He showed it to me and I admired it and I was happy for him.

Bruno does a kind of harumph and turns back to Summer. "I trust Laura has explained what your duties will be? And Gavin, have you explained to Summer what you used to do around here?"

"Yes," Summer says, smiling at Gavin, then at me. "Very clearly, thank you. I'm very excited to be here, and very excited about the exhibition."

"Good to hear. Now, Laura, tell us what's on the agenda for this week."

"Excuse me, Bruno, but Laura, before we get to that," Summer says. She lays down a large brown leather portfolio on the table. "I was hoping you would consider..." She unzips it. "This entry, for the Museum of Lost and Found. It's a photograph of my partner."

I'm not sure I heard her right. She opens it wide and turns the portfolio around to show us.

The photograph itself is actually not bad. It's an outline in light and shadows, undulating skin, and it takes a moment to realize it's a detail of a man's back lying on a bed. There's no doubt that it's beautifully shot.

She points to the accompanying poem on the other side of the portfolio. "I was very inspired as you can see, Laura. And your concept made me think of when my partner and I broke up for a few months, and I thought I'd lost him, but fortunately he came back and proposed to me." She shows me her diamond ring. A small diamond, but beautifully set in with smaller ones around it. I turn my attention to the poem.

On finding love and losing it and this is not how it ends.
I found my love on a Friday afternoon
I found myself in your arms
Finally, I found you, you said.
That night I found my true north in the moon
I'll never let you go, you said.
You gave me your heart
Keep it forever, you whispered, and I will keep your heart.
For we must never be apart
What did I say? What did I do?
Why did you leave and take my heart with you?
I lost my love on Thursday afternoon.
But I found you again, my love.
And I will never let you go.

I look up because for a moment I'm thinking that this is a prank.

"What do you think?" she says, twirling a strand of hair around her finger.

I'm speechless.

"Very beautiful," Bruno says, nodding. "Your fiancé is a very lucky man. What do you think, Laura?"

I blink a few times, looking for the words. "It's not really in the spirit of the concept—"

"Why not? It seems exactly in the spirit to me," he says.

"Well," I chuckle. "What I have in mind when curating the show is something more... unusual. Something surprising."

"I think the concept of losing love, and finding it, is very original."

"Really?"

"Well, that settles it," Bruno says. "I think it's an excellent idea to include artworks by our staff. Well done, Summer." And Gavin shoots me a look, then rolls his eyes. Meanwhile, Summer blushes prettily. I know it's not her fault. I can understand why she thought I might be willing, she's very young, but I'm angry with Bruno. I've done everything for this project from the concept to the design to the—successful—application for funding. This show is going to put Bruno Mallet on the map like nothing else we've exhibited. It's a big win for him and his reputation, and mine. Sure, the works are not for sale so he doesn't make money that way, but the reputational transaction is priceless and the funding more than covers our combined salaries and everything else we need.

We discuss other things and on the way out of the meeting, Summer slides up to me conspiratorially. "I think I went about this the wrong way."

I give her a tight smile. "What do you mean?"

"With my piece in the show, I should have asked you first. I see that now. I hope you're okay with it?"

I study her face; she seems to mean it. "Let me think about it."

She nods. "Sure, whatever you say, boss."

EIGHT

Bronwyn is here.

She's in my house. *My* house that used to be *her* house. Will she like what I did with the place, I wonder? Because I did plenty. I put up wallpaper in Charlie's room and replaced the metallic silver drapes with blue and gold ones and laid down colorful rugs where there were timber floors. I painted the dark gray walls in light, cheerful colors and transformed that place from an uber modern, clinical showroom to a cozy, warm, soft cocoon. By the time I was done I'd washed that woman right out of my hair.

If only.

I got the text from Jack a few minutes ago.

Flight was late but she's here, heading home now, see you soon x

She's here. I was desperately hoping Leon had come along after all, that they'd be settling in the Four Seasons instead of our house. Even the fact that Jack went to pick her up at the airport almost turned into our first (of many more to come, I'm sure) Bronwyn-induced argument.

"Why?" I wanted to ask. "Can't she hire a limousine? That's what she usually does, isn't it? Doesn't she know how to call an Uber? Walk to the taxi stand?" The actual question I wanted to ask being: *Are we going to be at her beck and call the entire time she's here?* But I didn't. Firstly because there is still so much time to argue about Bronwyn, so why rush? And anyway, who am I kidding? Of course we'll be at her beck and call.

Secondly, and if I was honest with myself I'd say this was the firstly—*We ARE a happy family.* So I'm hardly going to let Bronwyn walk into *our house* and find it filled with an atmosphere so thick with tension you'd smash your face just stepping inside the front door.

I'm thinking about all that as I lean against the railing outside the school, waiting for Charlie who must be bouncing right out of her cat-patterned gumboots by now. I try to think if I've missed anything in preparation for Bronwyn's stay. These days Bronwyn is vegan and, apparently, very particular about what she eats.

I know Seattle has some great health food stores, so it shouldn't be a problem. But I'm on a strict vegan diet, so can you organize a few things before I get there? she emailed Jack.

A few things. Jack forwarded the list to me because while he has a lot more time on his hands, he claims that he wouldn't know what this stuff even looks like, let alone where to find it, and I agreed with that. Because we have to get it right. There is no room for error, otherwise Charlie will be upset. She's been lurching from elation to anxiety and back again all week. She is terrified that if we don't get everything absolutely perfect for Bronwyn's stay, Bronwyn will turn around and walk right out again.

If only, I don't say.

Anyway, as it turned out, I didn't have to run around the

city looking for obscure vegan supplements or cashew milk artisan cheese wheels or wild pine nut butter because, as luck would have it, Summer used to be vegan and she knows exactly where to get this stuff.

She was sitting next to me, eating out of a bag of trail mix while I read the email. I sighed. She offered the bag to me and I took a small handful.

"You're not vegan anymore?" I asked.

"No," she said. "It was too hard. Dexter couldn't deal with it."

But she told me about Vegan Haven and Central Co-op and we made calls and checked stocks online and I took my list and spent two hours trawling the city when I should have been working, but I got every single item on the list which felt like an absolute win. Except for the part where I spent money we don't really have, but I thought of it as an investment. Perfect family, happy family, refrigerator stocked up with fresh fruit and vegetables, pantry bursting with organic lentils and split peas and chia seeds and flaxseeds and hemp seeds and enough seeds to open an aviary.

And then there were the sleeping instructions. Bronwyn is apparently allergic to everything. Like the bubble boy. She wrote in another email that she can only sleep in white sheets, and they have to be crisp, but only a certain amount of crisp, crispness being dependent on the season. So in winter, not too crisp. "One hundred percent cotton, of course," she wrote, "single ply weave only, please. 400 thread count." Allergic to non-white sheets? That's too bad since I don't have white sheets, and I wouldn't have a clue of their thread count or what ply they were.

"She's messing with your head," Katie said when I told her. Katie is my best friend. I've known her since college. She studied museology, I studied painting and drawing. Then she changed direction and became a psychologist. "I hope you're not even contemplating buying new sheets. Let her sleep in flannels like the rest of us."

I sighed. "Except that Charlie is..."

"What?"

"She's... I don't know. She's super excited of course, she's bursting at the seams, but she's also very anxious. She's started to bite her fingernails again, which she hasn't done in ages. She desperately wants everything to be perfect and you know what she asked me the other night?"

"What?"

"She said..." I could still see her vividly, tucked in her bed, her comforter all the way up to her chin. "She said, do you think Mommy will still like me?"

"Oh, Laura."

"Anyway, it's fine, it's only for three weeks."

Katie snorted. "They're going to be the longest three weeks of your miserable life, babe."

"Yes, thank you. I knew that already, but thank you. You've made me feel so much better." And she laughed.

In the end, I bought the white sheets with yet more money I can't really spare and I picked up Charlie from school and we went shopping for more treats to decorate the spare room. We bought a *Jurassic Park* themed banner kit (Charlie's idea, which I supported fully because I liked the juxtaposition of Bronwyn and dinosaurs) that reads *Welcome Mommy!* Charlie wanted *Welcome Home Mommy!* but I said *Welcome Mommy* is better. We made flowers out of tissue paper and hung pretty fairy LED string lights. Then Charlie made a pretty tableau with her felt board of a colorful garden, and we put it up on the wall, and in the end, we stood back, admired our work, and it was perfect.

"Hello, Laura!"

I've spun my head around and I'm staring at Erin who is standing next to me, leaning against the same railing, waiting for her daughter Brielle who is in the same class as Charlie's. I'm so in my head I don't even remember her showing up, and yet there she is, staring at her gloved hands, at her watch.

"Can you believe I'm on time for once?" She laughs, then shakes her head. "I'm always late. We read *Alice in Wonderland* the other night, and Brielle said I was just like the rabbit." She makes a face and I laugh.

"I heard Bronwyn is in town. Lucky you! Charlie told Brielle and Brielle told me. I'd love to see her again. Is she here for long?"

I shake my head quickly, confused. "You know her?"

"Yes! Of course! Mothers' group. You know what it's like around here, we all know each other. She used to call it the circle of love." She laughs. "But after she left, it wasn't the same. She's so lovely, isn't she? Is she staying long? I could organize cocktails at our house, it would be very nice to catch up."

The bell has rung and the children are spilling out, and there's Charlie, half skipping, half running, and at the same time she's saying goodbye to her friends so there's some hugging and shouting going on, and it's all a bit chaotic and I smile. She runs to us with Brielle, her school bag banging against the back of her legs, and comes to a stop in front of me like a gymnast at the end of a routine, with her face turned up, her hair flying out in all directions from under her green beanie and her cheeks flushed—from excitement?—and I want to pick her up and kiss those pink cheeks, and for some strange reason I find myself getting unexpectedly teary.

I put my hand on her head. "Let's take you home." And she hugs me, the way she does, with her arms wrapped around my waist and looks up at me. "Is Mommy at home?"

"Yes, Mommy's at home."

"Can we get flowers for Mommy?"

I groan, internally. "Good idea."

Charlie jumps and squeals and starts skipping ahead, her backpack bouncing around.

"Well, someone's excited!" Erin remarks. Then to me she says, "Let me know about drinks, whatever day works for Bronwyn." She takes Brielle by the hand. "Bye!"

"Bye!" I say, half raising my hand.

Because that's the other thing about Bronwyn. Everybody loves Bronwyn.

Except me.

NINE

Although I did too, once, a long time ago. Bronwyn and I were in school together from the age of twelve. Then my mother died when I was fourteen years old. My friend Katie says that's why I'm so fiercely protective of Charlie. I am making up for what I perceive as my own mother's abandonment. And she should know, she's a psychologist, although as I like to point out to her, you could just say that the reason I am so fiercely protective of Charlie is because I know what it's like not to have a mother. Sometimes, the right explanation is the one staring you in the face.

Bronwyn was already very pretty in those days, her dark hair in two braids that she flicked over her shoulders. Nobody else could sport that look and not look lame, but she looked cool and sexy, in a Lolita kind of way, and I say this in retrospect because at twelve years of age I had no concept of sexy, let alone Lolita.

I loved her, for a while, the way girls do at that age, until I didn't. We had our own circle of love back then and for some reason only Bronwyn got to decide who was in, and who was out.

I was smack in the middle of it, and then I got booted out. Big time.

"Mommy!"

Inside the front door, crouched next to an open travel bag—Yves St. Laurent—is Bronwyn.

"There you are!" she exclaims. "Come here, beautiful girl!" she chirps as she picks up Charlie and kisses her on one cheek, then the other. "Just like they do it in Roma!" She says "Roma" with an Italian accent. Charlie wraps her arms around her mother's neck and rests her head on her shoulder and a small, very small, barely worth mentioning little dart of jealousy nicks at my heart. Jack appears in the doorway and leans against the wall, his arms crossed, smiling, but not really, not all the way up to his eyes.

I smile too, benignly, anything to hide the little twist of anxiety in my chest. This is the first time I've come face to face with Bronwyn since Jack and I got together so yes, I'm nervous. I'm hoping she won't kill me, essentially. Bronwyn may have a very wealthy, very nice, very devoted fiancé, but I bet she'd still like the previous ones to be visibly pining.

I'll just tell her he was on the rebound. An easy catch. Never would have happened, otherwise. I come to stand next to him and he puts his arm around my shoulders.

I forget how well put together Bronwyn is. Or maybe I don't *forget*, exactly. I just try not to remember. Still, it's a shock to see her up close and be confronted by her beauty, those long, tanned legs, the fabulous clothes that drape themselves around her like liquid.

"My God, Charlotte!"

"I know," I say, unbuttoning my coat and wishing I'd done up my face. "She's grown so much since—"

"Your hair is so long!" she exclaims. Charlie has curly hair and likes to weave it into a single braid that she drops over one shoulder.

Bronwyn holds Charlie's braid in the palm of her hand and studies it closely.

"It's the Greta Thunberg look," I say. No idea why.

Bronwyn looks up at me, puzzled, but not unfriendly. "Don't you put conditioner in her hair?"

"I'm sorry?"

"She's got split ends! Look!" She points to a microscopic point on the end of Charlie's braid. Jack and I both lean forward and frown at it, as does Charlie, so that we're all examining the first of my failures as a stepmom, with many more to come, of that I have no doubt.

"I think it's a two-in-one brand," I say.

She smiles, pats Charlie's head. "Well. Never mind. You need a haircut anyway, we'll pick up some treatments at the same time."

"Treatments?" I snort. They're all looking at me and I pretend to cough. "Sure, good idea," I say. What I mean is, good luck with that. Because if there's one thing Charlie hates it's washing her hair. She's old enough to bathe on her own—after I've checked the bath temperature of course—but if I ask her to wash her hair she'll sulk, then drop a perfunctory minute drop of shampoo, scratch at her scalp and barely rinse it, so I still wash her hair for her. It's traumatic enough as it is, so the idea of adding conditioner into the mix, let alone treatments? Let's see how that pans out. I can't wait.

She stands up straight and takes Charlie's hand. "Anyway, come on. Why don't you show me your room?" She gazes around. "I wonder what *that* looks like," she muses. "There's been a few changes around here."

"Okay," Charlie replies happily.

"Did you see what she did there?" I whisper to Jack. I'm dragging him to the kitchen so I can start dinner.

He opens the cupboards and grabs two wine glasses. "What are you talking about?"

I give a small scoff, one side of my mouth raised in mockery. "I mean, seriously? Split ends? She's seven years old. Who cares?"

I expected him to laugh with me, but instead he just shrugs. I pull out vegetables from the crisper drawer of the fridge. "Anyway, I couldn't see any, could you?"

"I have no idea what split ends look like, Laura. But so what? You know what Bron's like."

"Yes, yes. You're right." I pull out the colander, turn on the cold tap. "What *is* she like?"

"You know, she's a perfectionist."

I scoff. "Then she'll be over the moon because Charlie is perfect!"

Jack picks up an already-opened bottle of wine from the bench and studies the label. "You want one?"

"Yes, thanks," I say. "This wasn't about perfection or Charlie's hair, Jack. She was having a dig at me. Christ! She's only been here five minutes and she's already found something to criticize about my mothering skills. God! She can talk. She wouldn't know a mothering skill if it punched her in the face."

"Okay, you know what, Laura? How about we lay off the snarky comments and enjoy this time together, as a family, okay?" He hands me a glass of wine. "It'll be over before you know it."

If only.

———

"And how is Leon?" I ask as I serve dinner: portobello mushroom ragout with polenta, a recipe I found that I believed satisfied Bronwyn's dietary requirements. "I'm sorry he couldn't make this trip."

"He's very well," she says, looking dubiously at the mess on her plate. "He works too hard. I keep telling him that, but it makes no difference." She sighs. "He's the best plastic surgeon in the country, so you can imagine, everybody wants him. Everybody. All the time."

"Mama works very hard too," Charlie says. I catch Jack flinch from the corner of my eye.

"Only because I'm busy with the new exhibition," I say quickly.

Bronwyn looks at Charlie, her lips into a thin smile. "Mama?"

Charlie nods, looks at me.

"But her name is Laura, sweetheart. That's what you should call her."

I laugh. I'm so nervous, I sound like a hyena. "That's what she likes to call me. Don't you, sweetie? I..." I was going to say, *I love it, actually,* but of course Bronwyn knows that. That's the point. "And you're Mommy! Of course you are! I mean, obviously you are!" I laugh again, sort of. I really need to calm down, and I shove my empty glass at Jack so he can fill it up.

Bronwyn raises an eyebrow at me and gives me a quick nod. "Of course. So, tell us about this exhibition you're working on, *Laura.*"

"Well..." And I tell her about the Museum of Lost and Found. Or I try to, but it comes out all wrong, like I've lost the thread of my own exhibition. When I finish, no one says anything. Bronwyn lifts a forkful of polenta which slops between the prongs and right back onto her plate. She frowns at it.

"I don't know what went wrong," I say. "Normally it comes out fine," I lie.

"I don't understand," Bronwyn says. "You want people to send some broken umbrella they found in the back of a taxi?"

I laugh. "Not exactly, it's hard to explain in a few minutes—"

"And these... things sell, do they?" she asks, looking dubious.

"We're not selling those works. We got state funding to develop the exhibition, and to tour it, involving local communities to contribute artworks. It will welcome new objects and new stories when it's on the road." She's still looking at me expectantly, like there should be more, surely. "So yes, it's a departure for us. We got a significant art grant to put the show together, and the touring, and it will bring us new audiences, raise the profile of the gallery significantly." I choose to finish with that. "So, what are your plans, Bronwyn? While you're here?"

"Well, Charlotte and I are going shopping for clothes first thing tomorrow! Aren't we, Charlotte?" Charlie nods, frowns at her food. I'd offered to make her something different—Mac 'n' cheese, usually a no-brainer—but she wanted the same meal as Mommy.

"I think you need new clothes. And a new haircut to go with them. What do you say, Charlotte?"

Charlotte nods enthusiastically.

"What does that mean, she needs new clothes?" I ask, forcing a smile.

She cocks her head at me, smiles. "I know how busy you are, it's hard to find the time to shop for clothes, and it's expensive too. You're not very fashion-conscious, Laura, you never have been, and that's totally fine. That's you. But Charlotte's wardrobe..."

"What's wrong with it?"

"Nothing!" She laughs. "Oh Laura, I'm sorry. I forget how sensitive you are. I didn't mean anything by that." She smooths one eyebrow with the tip of her finger. "How can I put this?" She thinks about it for a second. "I had a look in her closet, and I think, and please don't bite my head off, but I think her clothes are a little on the tomboy side."

"No, they're not. It's a style, and it's what she likes. She's old enough to wear what she likes."

"She's not a tomboy, Laura."

"Right!" I say, but I'm thinking, *You know this how, exactly?* I smile. "She's an adventurer."

Bronwyn tilts her head forward and slightly to the side so that she leads with her ear, eyebrows raised. "I'm sorry? She's what?"

"An adventurer!" God. Kill me now. I have no idea how we got here so fast, but she's managed to make me sound defensive and unhinged. "She's Charlie the Explorer!" I say, digging myself deeper into my own grave. "She adores animals! You know that, right?" There. A little dig at her cleverly disguised as a question. I keep going. "She wants to be a vet and run an animal shelter. Was it an animal shelter, honey? Or an animal sanctuary? Anyway, she wants to be like Jack Hanna or Steve Irwin! She'd wear khaki all the time if you let her!" I laugh. Sort of.

She smiles. "Well, Charlotte is right here. Why don't we ask her?" She turns to Charlie. "Charlotte, sweetie, would you prefer some... boys' clothes? Or some pretty girls' clothes, with lots of pink, like all the other girls your age?"

Charlie looks up at her mother like it's a test. "I want some girls' clothes?" She makes it sound like a question.

I sigh. "She's just saying that to make you happy."

"Are you just saying that to make me happy, Charlotte?" Bronwyn asks.

"For Christ's sake, Bronwyn. Give it a rest," I snap.

"I want girls' clothes," Charlie says.

"This isn't fair on her."

"Laura, please. I just want to spoil my daughter. That's all. That's all right, isn't it?"

I close my eyes briefly, take a quick, discreet breath. "Of course. But she's got school tomorrow."

"So we'll shop after school."

"And apart from shopping, what do you have in mind for Charlie's birthday?" I ask, just to change the subject.

"I thought we could have a birthday party."

"A birthday party? Where?"

"A party?" Charlie squeals.

"Well..." Bronwyn looks around. "What about here?"

"Yes! A party here!" Charlie shrieks.

"But her birthday is on Saturday next week! When do you want to have a party?" I say.

"What about Saturday next week!"

"Yes! Saturday next week!" Charlie shouts.

"But that's... a week and a half away! It's not a lot of notice, all her friends are bound to have other plans. And it's going to take organizing, isn't it? You never said anything about a party! I thought you were going to do something like last time, take her out somewhere, spend the day together..."

I turn to Jack for support but he's staring at his plate.

"But I thought..." Bronwyn hesitates, tucks her hair behind her ear. "I just assumed, being Charlotte's birthday, that you would have organized a party for her."

"And I thought—" Jack kicks my foot. I take a breath. "Okay..." I say. "Look, we can do something here, sure. If that's what you want."

"Well, it's for Charlotte, not for me, but thank you, Laura." She turns to Charlie. "Who would you like to invite?"

Charlie blurts out names, a roll call of her friends. Brielle, Isobel, Nikki, Omar, Jolene, Mohamed, Alex, Ruby, Yolanda, Eric, Val, Shalina—

"Val?" I blurt. "Does that mean you're friends again?"

She nods enthusiastically.

"Yes. I took her out of the freezer."

"Excuse me?" Bronwyn says. "Out of the what?"

"The freezer," Charlie says. "Mama showed me—"

"*Laura* showed you," Bronwyn admonishes gently.

Charlie nods once, frowning. "Laura," she repeats. Like this is a lesson, nothing more, sending a little dart into my heart.

"Good girl," Bronwyn says.

And honestly, she's lucky I can't reach her on the other side of the table because I am nanoseconds away from grabbing her plate and smashing it on her head.

I smile. "Mama's perfectly fine, sweetie."

"—showed me how when you don't like someone anymore, you write their name on a piece of paper and you fold it twice and put them in the freezer," Charlie says.

"Really?" Bronwyn looks at me, so does Jack, who had been so quiet all evening you wouldn't know he was in the room.

I shrug. "It's something my mother used to do when I was a kid."

"Did she?" she asks with a raised eyebrow, and I wish I hadn't brought up my mother. Bronwyn turns to Charlie. "Tell me about the freezer. What does it do?"

"It's like you've sent them to Mars," Charlie says. "And then you cut them off so they can never come back. They're stuck in space. Forever."

I chuckle. "Well, I don't think I put it quite that way!" *Did I?*

Bronwyn makes a tutting sound. "That's not very nice. Please don't do that again, Charlotte."

Charlie flicks her eyes in my direction, and I give a quick nod. Tell her whatever the hell she wants to hear so we can get through this dinner in one piece.

"I won't do that again."

"Good girl," Bronwyn says, tapping her lightly on the head.

TEN

The dogs bark and the caravan rolls on. That's what the last few days feel like, and I'm probably the one doing the barking. I can't stop thinking about Bronwyn, obviously. She is in every single thought, every single moment. She's been taking Charlie to school and picking her up, and taking her out after school for shopping and ice cream or whatever.

"She's regressing." I'm talking to Katie. One long stream of frustration that I pour down her ear, all of it about Bronwyn. Or Jack.

And Jack is so stressed, of course, I tell her. He says he just wants everyone to get on. "And you think I don't?" I said to him. And you know what she bought for Charlie yesterday? An iPad, for goodness' sake. Charlie's not even allowed a phone. We're trying to bring her up without screens, and now all she wants to do is watch YouTube. And of course, I can't say anything. I'd be the bad person if I pointed out we've successfully brought her up without screens for two years and were hoping to get a few more years like that. God, you should see the sunglasses on her. Pink, of course, because according to Princess Bronwyn, there are no other colors in the spectrum, and heart-shaped, with dark purple lenses, can you imagine? She's turning her into some kind of Lolita. She's barely eight years old, for Christ's sake.

"She wet her bed last night."

"Oh shit."

"Yes."

I was asleep and I heard something, so soft it was barely there. I remember opening my eyes and listening to the silence, then I heard it again and I knew. I went to her bedroom. She was biting her lip, holding back sobs as she tried to wrench her sheets off her bed. I didn't say anything. I helped her get the sheets off. I made it look like it was no big deal, not even worth mentioning. Sometimes, you have to know when to speak and when to keep your mouth shut. I took her to the bathroom and helped her clean herself, then I wrapped her in a towel while I got some clean pajamas, put clean sheets on the bed. I spooned her while she fell asleep.

"Don't tell Mommy."

"I won't."

I didn't tell Jack either. He was fast asleep when I got back to bed. I didn't tell him because I knew she wouldn't want me to, so I told him in my head instead.

What does it say that I'm the only one who hears her when she needs one of us? I didn't tell him that after that first night with Bronwyn, I put the mattress protector back on Charlie's bed. *Just in case.* That's what you do when you love someone. You anticipate what could go wrong, what might hurt them and you provide safety nets. And you do that all day.

"Oh and the other thing, she smokes. I mean, normally I wouldn't care but she smokes in the backyard and leaves her cigarette butts on the ground for me to pick up. Sometimes I swear I think she smokes in her room. I can smell it in the house."

"How is your protégée?" Katie asks now. She calls Summer my protégée, probably because I've gushed about how great she is, but so young, only twenty-five, and a talented artist too! But I suspect the only reason Katie is asking about Summer is because she's tired of listening to me rant about Bronwyn, and I don't blame her. She has her own problems. So my tirades are met with occasional *uh huh* and I don't even care. I'm still talking. I just need to get it out.

"She's great. Bruno loves her. I love her. The visitors love her. Plus she's a good photographer. Speeds up the documentation process and gives us all the material we need for the exhibition website."

"So, everybody's happy?"

"Oh yes. I'm deliriously happy. Can't you tell?"

She laughs.

"Oh and you know what Bronwyn did this morning?"

I'm sure I can hear Katie sigh but I don't care. "Tell me what Bronwyn did this morning," she says.

"She made breakfast for Charlie. You know what she made?"

"No?"

"She made pancakes."

"And?"

"With maple syrup, vanilla ice cream and chocolate sauce."

"And?"

"And she had them too, although only a teaspoon's worth, she wouldn't want to upset that waistline. So did Jack, a gallon's worth. I was there, I watched it all. While sipping on my coffee."

"And she didn't make any for you? Is that it?"

"I was going to work, I didn't want any. Don't you get it?"

"No?"

"She's strictly vegan-sugar-free-gluten-free-dairy-free, remember? I asked Jack about it on the way out, and he said apparently her condition cleared up so she can go back to her normal diet now."

I didn't say anything, just watched him with my jaw half on the floor. He shrugged and I made myself let it go. *Let it go,* I told myself, then I told myself again, like a mantra, *Let it go.* "I've been cooking vegan dishes for days, can you believe it?"

"I told you she was messing with you," Katie says.

I sigh. "I know."

"You want to come out for a drink later?"

I hesitate. "It's tempting, but I think I should be home."

"Why? It's Friday night, Bronwyn's there, you may as well make the most of it."

"I just feel like I should be there."

"Suit yourself," she says.

———

If I'd been smart, I would have taken her up on it. Instead, I go home and find that Bronwyn and Charlie have gone out.

"How was Charlie today?" I ask Jack in the kitchen. He's leaning against the counter, drinking a beer from the bottle, scrolling his phone. He shaved this morning, I note, and part of me is glad we're moving on from the beer-drinking, track-suit-wearing, couch-lying look. Part of me is deliriously happy he's looking more like his old self. But another, tiny, barely-worth-mentioning part of me, wonders if this change is for Bronwyn.

"Charlie was perfectly fine."

"Oh, good."

"She was happy."

"Okay. That's good." The kitchen counter is in a mess with crumbs everywhere, and an open jar of Nutella. I grab a sponge and begin to clean up.

"You don't have to do this now, Laura."

I snort. "I think you'll find I do because nobody else will! Where are they anyway?"

He shrugs. "No idea. What's the matter? Why are you so uptight?"

There are so many ways I could answer that question, I wouldn't know where to start. "I'm just tired. I've been running all over town getting things she wanted and she hasn't even said thank you, did you know that? And Charlie and I got her bedroom ready, with all the decorations Charlie made, and she hasn't even commented on it."

"She did, she told Charlie she loves it."

I look up. "She said that?"

"The other night, we were upstairs. You were downstairs."

"Yeah, right. Cooking yet another delicious strictly vegan dinner even though she was only vegan for a minute and a half, but hey, anything for Her Royal Highness."

"I don't know about delicious," he says, pulling me to him. He takes the sponge from my hand and throws it in the sink, then pulls me into a hug

"She could have said something to me," I mumble into his chest. "She must know Charlie didn't decorate her bedroom all by herself." I look up. "What did Charlie say?"

He doesn't reply right away, his eyes darting sideways. "I don't know, she was happy her mom loved it, what do you want me to say?"

"No, nothing. I mean, that's great. I'm glad."

There's a burst of noise, a gust of air. Bronwyn and Charlie are home. I stay right where I am, my face buried in Jack's polo shirt, but he quickly disentangles himself just as Bronwyn appears in the doorway, masses of shopping bags looped over both arms. "Hello there!"

"Mama!" Charlie yells out. "Look!" She has slipped past Bronwyn and runs to me, holding up as many bags as she can carry.

"Laura..." Bronwyn corrects softly.

"Well, look at all those bags!" I blurt. "And look at you! Wow! That's quite a... transformation, sweetie!"

She's wearing a red woolen dress with a weird white frilly trim at the hem, a brand-new purple coat with a large hood down the back, a matching beanie with a large green flower on the side, black leather boots—flats, thank God—and a brand-new haircut, all curls, lots of curls, with shiny new highlights, tumbling out of her beanie. I lift the beanie off and rearrange a lock or two.

"Wow! You look amazing, sweetie!"

"We saw Harold, I asked him to my birthday party and he said yes!" Birthday party, right. I was hoping we'd all forgotten about that.

Bronwyn reaches for Charlotte's head, rearranges the two locks of hair I just touched. "We'll see, Charlotte. He might not want to spend all afternoon with a bunch of screaming eight-year-olds!"

"Harold is lovely," I say. "He's a nice old man, he adores Charlie. He's very lonely, I think. His wife died many years ago. His son lives in Denver with his family, so we like to have him over for Thanksgiving, and Easter Sunday. Don't we, Charlie?"

"Oh! Laura!" Bronwyn laughs.

"What?"

"You're so funny!"

"Why?"

"I know who Harold is! This is my house, remember?"

"*Your* house?"

"You know what I mean."

I turn to Jack who is busy pretending he's not listening, while scratching something off the countertop.

I swallow a sigh. "Sorry," I say. "Of course, you used to live here."

"Anyway, it doesn't matter," she says, "You're the one

throwing Charlie a birthday party. You can invite whoever you like." And with that, she's gone.

I grab the sponge again and start wiping invisible stains with more vigor than ever. "What the hell is wrong with her?" I snap. Jack leans against the counter, arms crossed, eyes raised to the ceiling. "Seriously, she dresses Charlie up like a runner-up in *Little Miss USA Beauty Pageant*. Charlie's not like that. She's not a doll."

"Why do you take it so personally?"

"She knows how to push my buttons, that's all."

"You sure know how to get your buttons pushed, Laura."

"That doesn't even make sense, Jack, but whatever." I sigh. I stop scouring, squeeze the sponge over the sink. "Are we really having a birthday party for Charlie next Saturday? Or was that just a bad dream."

He chuckles. "Come on, it'll be fun. I'll help."

"How about Her Royal Highness lends a hand too, or is that too much to ask?"

"Don't be like that."

"We can't make it a big party, I just don't have the time. Half her friends will probably have other things to do anyway."

"Let's do what we can, okay? Bron is here, and Charlie wants this too. She misses her so much, and Bron misses Charlie—"

I snort. It escapes out before I have time to stop myself. "Sorry," I mumble. He holds me by the shoulders. "Laura, Bron loves Charlie. It's awesome that she wants to spend so much time with her daughter. You should be happy for Charlie."

"You've changed your tune." I pull away and start rearranging things on the table.

"What does that mean?"

"Bronwyn doesn't love Charlie, Jack. Apart from having the maternal instincts of a brick, Bronwyn is too self-obsessed to love anyone but herself. Everything Bronwyn does is about perception. The only purpose of these occasional visits is so that no one can accuse Bronwyn of being a bad mother. Even though she is. She's a bad mother. She's a shit mother."

There's a beat of silence. When I look up at him again, his face is pale and he's gazing at a point over my shoulder. I turn around, my stomach lurching slowly, bringing with it a tidal wave of nausea.

"Well. Why don't you say how you really feel?" she says, one contemptuous eyebrow raised. Everything inside me twists. "I only came down to suggest we get pizza for dinner so you wouldn't have to cook." She turns on her heels and goes back upstairs.

"Great job, Laura," Jack mumbles, walking past me.

"Wait." I reach for his arm but he flicks me off, his whole demeanor stiff with anger.

And I stand there and wonder how the hell I got to this point where both Jack and Bronwyn are angry with me, and it seems so unfair I want to cry.

ELEVEN

I do it all weekend long, the cleaning up after everybody. The cooking, too, and the shopping, and the loading up of washing machines and dishwashers and making beds (although not Bronwyn's, thank God). It's my penance, for being *a real bitch*. That's what Jack hissed at me when he returned from his run on Saturday.

"You can be a real bitch sometimes."

"Sorry," I replied. What I really wanted to say was, *Sorry not sorry. I meant every word.*

"You've got to stop reacting to everything she says, Laura. You've got to think of Charlie."

I think of Charlie all the time, I wanted to say. *She's all I think about.* But of course he's right because the last thing I want is for Charlie to be upset. "I'm sorry," I said, again. Then I said it another fifty times, and eventually I managed to coax him out of his angry shell.

"You'll have to apologize to Bron."

I groaned. "Seriously?"

"Yes, Laura! I don't need this grief right now, okay?"

"Apologize?"

"Yes!"

There was so much I wanted to say, but I didn't. I swallowed my pride and went to find Bronwyn in the living room, where she was relaxing on the sofa, flicking through a magazine.

"I'm sorry," I said, about as convincingly as Henry the Eighth to Anne Boleyn after swinging the axe. Then I added, "About what I said yesterday."

She didn't even look at me. Just kept flicking her magazine. "Why do you hate me so much, Laura?"

"I don't hate you," I scoffed. "That's a ridiculous thing to say!" But beneath the makeup I could see the fourteen-year-old girl who had spread vile rumors about me and made my life miserable and I thought, *okay, maybe a little bit.*

She closed the magazine and put it down beside her. She was wearing a pearl-colored silk shirt and a gray tweed skirt, and she crossed her legs in a way that looked so elegant, so feminine, with her legs parallel, her knees angled to the side and her hands resting together loosely on her right hip. I felt frumpy in my weekend clothes—sweatshirt and jeans and sneakers— whereas Bronwyn looked like she'd just returned from deportment school.

"Tell me, Laura. How long did you wait before fucking my husband?"

Oh God. That didn't take long. "It didn't happen like that."

"Really? You were *my* friend, you came to *my* house, this house, and now you're getting married to him? It's a little fast, wouldn't you say? You can tell me, I don't care anymore, I'm just curious. Were you fucking him when we were still together?"

I bit the inside of my cheek. *Don't get your buttons pushed, Laura.* "It wasn't like that. Never. Jack's not like that. And neither am I. Also, you left, Bronwyn. You can't resent me for falling in love with Jack after you left him." I bit my fingernail. I'm thinking she can absolutely resent me, and probably does.

Bronwyn sets the parameters of resentment, as I know full well. It has nothing to do with logic or her own actions or even the truth.

She shook her head slowly, like I just didn't get it.

"I didn't know you were a couple, you know." She glanced at her magazine again. "I knew, vaguely, that you were around. I assumed you were the babysitter, earning money on the side, until Jack told me you were getting married." She turned to me again. "By the way, is he still screwing other women behind your back? I've often wondered about that. That's what he used to do to me, remember?"

"He's not like that."

She smiled at me and for a moment she looked like she almost felt sorry for me. "How do you know? Oh wait, don't tell me. You're the one who's going to change him, is that it?"

I could feel my stomach drop with every passing minute. I'd come to apologize, and instead we were rehashing history, old and new. I knew I should just shut up, say my piece, walk away, but instead I found myself defending him.

"Maybe he was unfaithful, back then," I said, even though I didn't believe it for one second. "But that's a long time ago. He's been through so much, he cares so deeply for me and Charlie. He's not like that anymore, Bronwyn."

For some reason, I thought she was going to laugh, but instead she just smiled, and in a soft voice she said, "Whatever you say, Laura."

I was turning to leave when she sighed. "He's deeply depressed, you know."

"No, he's not!"

"You must be joking. Have you looked at him lately?"

"He's a bit down, of course, because... anyway, look, he's fine. We're doing fine."

"If you say so."

"I say so. So anyway... I just wanted to apologize. About

yesterday. That's all. I've done that now, so I'm going to..." I waved vaguely in the direction of the door and again turned around to leave.

"He won't stay with you, you know? He's just using you, until someone better comes along."

"I'm not listening to you," I said.

"I'm only trying to help. And I probably should let you know, since you... live here, that I've decided to extend my stay by a few weeks."

"A few weeks?"

"That's right."

"And then what?"

"And then... we'll see. Who knows what the future holds?"

I stood there, my head spinning, my mouth opening and closing like a blow fish dying on a hot beach, and when I felt sure my legs could carry me again, I walked out of the room.

———

Later that night, in bed, I asked Jack if he knew how long she was staying.

"A few days I think."

"Oh, right. I think it might be longer. Did she talk to you about that?"

He frowned. "No."

"Don't you think it's strange that she's here at all?"

"Of course not. She's here for Charlie's birthday, and we have an appointment with our lawyer to sign the divorce papers."

Our lawyer.

"And then she'll leave?"

"Of course."

"She said a few weeks."

"She's just pushing your buttons, Laura."

I studied him, wondered if I should trust him, and decided that I should. For now. "Are you feeling depressed?" I asked.

"No, not really. I mean, things have been better, but I'm okay. Why?"

"Just checking. You'd tell me if you were?"

He shrugged. "Sure!"

"You know what you should do?" I asked, propped on my elbow.

"What should I do, Laura?" he sighed.

"I think you and Charlie should do a project together. At the moment, it's just Bronwyn spending a lot of time with her taking her shopping, all that stuff. I think you should talk to her, and find something she'd like to do, and that you could help her with."

He frowned, and I didn't think he'd pursue it.

The next morning, the two of them are hunched over the dining room table, which is covered with bits of electronic components, wires, a soldering iron.

"What's all this?" I ask.

"We're citizen scientists!" Charlie says excitedly. Jack smiles at me.

"I told Charlie about the community wildlife monitoring project," he says.

"The what?"

"We're looking for coyotes!" Charlie squeals. She's so excited she's jumping in place, her fists in front of her mouth. I laugh, take her head in my hands and kiss her cheeks.

"We're putting up remote sensors around the neighborhood, wherever there might be urban wildlife," Jack says. "Any traces or sightings gets sent back to the project database and mapped."

"I have no idea what you're talking about, but I think it's

great," I say, and I kiss his cheeks too. And when I walk out, he mouths, *thank you*.

I'm so happy that when I greet Bronwyn on the stairs later and she doesn't speak to me, I laugh. I don't care. We're going to be just fine. And if Bronwyn thinks she's going to hang around *a few weeks*, she has another thing coming. Because I don't know what she's doing here exactly, but I don't believe it's just for Charlie's birthday and signing the divorce papers. She's up to something, and I won't rest until she gets on her broomstick and gets the hell out of here.

TWELVE

It's Tuesday afternoon. Countdown time. Three days to the opening of the new show, four days to Charlie's birthday party. There's so much to do, and yet I can barely function. I spent Monday on autopilot, trying to understand what, *We'll see what the future holds...* actually means. I've been telling myself that it means nothing, that's what, that Bronwyn can come and go as she pleases and so what if she wants to spend a few days or weeks back in Seattle? It's not going to make any difference to us, except that Charlie will get to spend time with her mother, so that's good, right? Other than that, it means nothing.

If only.

I haven't looked at Bronwyn's Instagram account for months. Last time I checked, it looked like something out of a Conde Nast travel magazine. Endless shots of Bronwyn and Leon on boats, strolling hand in hand on narrow cobbled streets, eating at some gorgeous restaurants, strolling along the Amalfi coast with its colorful villages and clear blue seas, Bronwyn on a yellow bicycle with the front basket full of flowers. An ideal life that everyone in their right mind would envy. Which is the point, obviously. Unless you're me. There is nothing about

Bronwyn's perfect life that I envy. I got everything I ever wanted right here.

I'm looking at her Instagram now, my stomach twisted within an inch of its life. We've finished hanging most of the works and I'm sitting at the front desk with my forehead resting against the palm of my hand, poring over each new post with a lurch of my heart and a pounding behind my ears, berating myself for not checking sooner.

Her latest posts consist of selfie after selfie after selfie of Bronwyn and Charlie. Bronwyn and Charlie on top of the Space Needle with the view of the city behind them; Bronwyn and Charlie outside the Children's Museum—which personally I think Charlie has outgrown, but whatever. Bronwyn and Charlie in a place I don't recognize; outside the pop culture museum; ice-skating; eating ice creams... and then I see it, and for a moment I wonder if this an old image that has popped up in her timeline. But of course, it can't be. This is a recent photograph, you can see that this is Charlie now, today. I check the timestamp and see that it is from yesterday.

I recognize the setting since it's one of my favorite places in the world. They're standing outside the Chihuly Garden and Glass, near the purple sculptures that Charlie says look like a family of octopuses. From the angle it's clear that it's Bronwyn who is holding the phone. Jack is carrying Charlie on his back, she is beaming with her arms around his neck, Bronwyn is on the other side of Charlie, her hand on Jack's shoulder, her head forward so that their cheeks are almost touching. Actually, now that I take a closer look, I think they *are* touching. The three of them look unbelievably photogenic, natural, the perfect little family, and the sight of them squeezes at my heart.

This was yesterday. I was here, of course, at the gallery, all day. Why didn't Jack tell me that they went? Nobody told me. Not even Charlie. What did we do last night? I went to help Charlie with her homework but she said she'd already done it.

Mommy helped me, she said. Even hearing that sent a little pinprick at my heart. A tiny one. Just a prickle really, a toothpick's worth, and I recognized that I had no right to feel even slightly hurt because it was a good thing. That's what I told myself as I went to make dinner. *It's a good thing that Bronwyn is helping Charlie with her schoolwork.* I took out the Bolognese sauce I'd defrosted from the fridge that morning and cooked pasta for everyone. We acted like everything was great, but I noticed Charlie was a little quiet with me. She interacted more with Bronwyn and gave monosyllabic answers to my questions about her day. Now I wonder, when exactly, did they go to the Chihuly yesterday? Has Charlie not been going to school? Is that even possible? And as I scroll through the rest of the images, I can't tell if that's why I feel so shaken, or if it's because in every image Charlie looks so happy. She is positively beaming from ear to ear, or she's got her arms around her mother's neck, kissing her on the cheek, or she's sitting on her lap, laughing, and that one especially reminds me of the photo I framed and put in her room, except that in this one she's not trying to get away.

"Your step-daughter looks adorable."

I look up with a start. Summer was out the back unpacking the last of the artworks and I was so focused on my phone I didn't hear her come in.

"Thank you. Yes, she is," I say.

"Can I see?" I look at her outstretched hand, bangles jingling on her wrist, and hesitate for a moment, then I hand it over. She scrolls through them. "She looks very sweet, very happy."

She says this with the best of intentions, and yet her words send a tiny sting into my chest, even though I was just thinking the same.

I nod. "Yes, she does."

"And this is Bronwyn?"

I told Summer about Bronwyn. Summer has been with me for a week and Bronwyn has been around all of that time. *Charlie's mother is staying with us for a few days. Yes, it's very nice. It's for Charlie's birthday, you see? Yes, Charlie is thrilled. Bronwyn lives in Italy. With her new fiancé, Leon.*

"Yes, that's her."

She nods thoughtfully, points at the photo taken at the Chihuly Garden. "And this is your husband?"

"That's Jack, yes." I feel an unexpected sharp twist in my stomach. "My partner, we're not married yet."

"Hot. Good for you."

———

Hot. He hasn't been so hot lately. He's been prone to lying in bed until late. Although when I have complained about house chores being left to me—and what if he got up in the morning instead of sleeping till midday? How about trying that for a change?—he snarls at me.

"You don't know that! You're not here, Laura! You don't *know* what I get up to when you're at work. You want to know what I do all day? I look for work, Laura, I call people, I send application after application. That's what I do, all day, okay? So stop being such a bitch, because you don't know, okay?"

Oh, but I do know, I don't say. I *know* the bed is unmade, I *know* from the trash can that you've drunk at least three beers and ordered take-out pizza for lunch. I *know* the dishwasher hasn't been emptied and the kitchen tap is still dripping, and while I don't *know* you've been watching TV all day, your bare feet on the coffee table, I *imagine* it's probably true. I *know* you haven't shaved for days, and I *know* you haven't called anyone to set up job interviews because your cellphone log for the day shows you only made one call, to Rocco's Pizza.

But in this photo, Jack looks different. Dressed well, twinkled-eyed, happy, *hot*. At least she doesn't comment on the obvious, that the three of them look like they're doing a photoshoot for a perfect family ad. That there is no place for me, in this photo. Not even a gap where I'd fit.

I stare at the zoomed in photo of Jack and Bronwyn and Charlie together, their cheeks almost touching, their faces radiant.

"Very modern family. Nice. All power to you, Laura."

"Why do you say that?"

She points to the tags. I'd been so focused on the photographs I completely missed the tags. I snatch the phone from her.

#homesweethome #familyiseverything #familycomesfirst #lovemyfamily.

I stare at the pictures, then at the tags, all the likes she got, all the comments from people I've never heard of. *Beautiful family! You're so lucky! Awwwww! So cute!*

"Does he post them too?" she asks.

"What do you mean?"

"On his Instagram feed."

"He doesn't have one. I mean he does, but he never uses it. I think there's just one photo of Charlie at the beach and that's it. Jack doesn't like social media."

"Really?" Summer's watch beeps. She looks at her wrist. "Five o'clock. Do you want to go for a drink?"

"A drink?"

"It's still happy hour at The Good Bar. What do you say, boss?"

I hesitate, but only for a moment. "Okay, why not, that would be nice."

———

Outside the bar I call Jack. "I'm going for a drink with a friend," I say. I make it vague because I want him to think I'm going for a drink with a *male* friend.

"What time will you be home?"

"Mmm... I don't know. I'll be back for dinner. Maybe you can pull together something."

A beat. "Sure. I'll get pizza. Everything okay?"

I've got tags in bright neon signs zigzagging through my brain. *No, not really, what's #homesweethome #familyisevery-thing #familycomesfirst #lovemyfamily about?* Instead, I blurt, "Has Charlie not been going to school?"

Another beat of silence. "I was going to tell you—"

"You were *going* to tell me what?"

Silence.

"Tell me, Jack."

"Bron insisted. She wants to have time with Charlie, that's all. It was just a couple of days, I swear."

"And why wasn't I told?" My voice has risen an octave and is starting to sound dangerously close to shrieking. I take a breath. "It makes me feel... odd, that I wasn't consulted, or even told."

"I know, you're right. I'm sorry. Honestly, I thought you'd say no, that's all. I wanted to avoid another confrontation."

Another confrontation.

I glance through the door to the bar and spot Summer carrying two glasses of white wine. I shouldn't be doing this now. "Charlie didn't tell me either last night. I think that's odd. Do you think it's odd, Jack?"

Silence.

"Oh, come on! Don't tell me you asked her to lie to me!"

"No! Of course not! Not lie! I just asked her not to mention it—"

"What?"

"—unless you asked! About school. Or about her day."

"Oh my God, Jack! You're kidding me, you can't do that! You can't ask Charlie to keep things from me! That's... that's just so screwed up! And I did ask about school, by the way. Of course I did! And you know what she said? Nothing! She just shrugged. She didn't want to discuss it. What the hell?"

He sighs. "I know. I'm sorry. You're right."

"Was that Bronwyn's idea? For Charlie to lie to me?"

"Not lie—"

"Was it Bronwyn's idea!?"

"Yes."

"Oh my God. That's so bad, that's just so wrong."

"You're right. And I apologize. I should have consulted you."

"Damn right you should have."

"Anyway, you have fun, okay? I'll take care of everything down here."

I can't bear it. I just hang up.

THIRTEEN

Two guys in suits leaning against the bar are checking out Summer. They make a show of it, appraising her with their eyes, winking at each other, puffing out their chests, laughing loudly. I feel like walking up to them and telling them off. *She's much too young for you! For Christ's sake! Hit on someone your own age!*

"Sorry I got caught up. I was talking to Jack."

There's a glass of white wine in front of my chair. She jerks at it with her chin. "I made an executive decision. Sauvignon Blanc."

"Perfect, thank you," I lie. I would have preferred a vodka anything. Or a tequila. I take a sip. The glass is already sweating with condensation and I wipe my fingers on my jeans. I try to remember why I came and I wish I hadn't. I'm tired, I have so much to do. I want to be home with Charlie, I want to sit with her in her room and read books with her, her head against my chest. I miss the smell of her, I miss brushing her hair, I miss the softness of her cheeks. Except that even if I were home, I doubt Bronwyn would let me spend time with Charlie.

"Tell me about your boyfriend," I say, swallowing back a sigh as I sift through my brain for his name. "Lester?"

"Dexter. He's a lawyer."

"That's nice, where does he practice?"

"Downtown. He works with his dad."

"That's nice," I say again, my vocabulary having shrunk down to two words. "Do you have a photo?"

She pulls out her phone from her brown leather bag. The photo she shows me is not what I expected, I suppose because she's so pretty whereas the man in the photo looks kind of... ordinary. He has dark hair, a round face and a nice smile. He's wearing a simple black T-shirt and he's a tad on the heavy side. A big tad.

"He looks nice," I say. And I mean it, he looks like a nice, regular guy. She smiles at the phone when I pass it back.

"He is," she says. She tells me they live in a two-bedroom apartment on 23rd Avenue South.

"Cherry Hill?"

"More like Atlantic. We're getting married soon," she says.

"Yes, I remember. Congratulations."

"Thank you." She leans back in her chair, tilts her head at me. "So, tell me about this Bronwyn. Is she nice? She's not nice, is she? I have a feeling she's not nice." She takes a swig of her wine.

"What do you mean?"

She shrugs. "I'm getting a vibe. I'm being curious. Dexter always tells me my curiosity is going to get me into trouble one day. Hey, speaking of which..." She looks around as if someone might be eavesdropping.

"Did you take it?"

"What?"

"The Inverted Garden!"

"No!" My heart does a somersault as I look around quickly, in case anyone heard her, but no one is listening. Not even the two guys in suits at the bar. They've found two young women with long, tanned bare legs more amenable to their charm.

"I didn't steal anything," I hiss.

"Hey, it's none of my business, Laura. And just so you know, I haven't told anyone about what you did. But I did wonder." She tips her glass in my direction.

I feel a touch of vertigo. "I don't know what you think you saw. I was checking the lock, that's all. Sometimes the bolt sticks out—"

"Oh, okay."

"—so I checked the lock, and I used my key to check the bolt, that it was sliding in and out the way it was supposed to do. That's all."

"You did look like were you hacking at that thing like you were trying to kill it. No offense."

"Cut it out!"

She tilts her head at me. "Honestly, I'm not going to tell on you. I was curious, that's all."

I drop my head. "Listen," I lean forward again. My lips are trembling as I speak. "I didn't take anything, okay? I accidentally left the door open the day before. That's the truth. When I came back the next morning, an artwork was missing. I scratched the lock to make it look like a robbery, I mean a real robbery. Rather than me just... screwing up."

She takes a moment to think about this, one eyebrow raised. My heart is beating in my throat. She nods slowly. "Well, there you go! See? There's always a logical explanation if you look hard enough."

I breathe out. "What are you going to do?"

"Nothing."

"You're not going to tell anyone?"

"Who would I tell? And why would I? It's none of my business."

I drop my face in my hands. "Thank you." I look up. "It was

for the insurance, I swear to God. Please don't tell anyone. Please don't tell Bruno."

"Only if you share the loot with me." She winks.

"But I didn't—"

She laughs. "It's okay, I'm just kidding. Why don't we have another drink and you can tell me about Bronwyn?"

I nod. A lot. I feel dizzy. I keep waiting for her to say something else about it but she's rummaging through her purse, pulls out her wallet.

"No, hang on. I'll get it."

"Okay, thanks!"

I push my chair back, stand up, my stomach clenched. I feel sick and I don't think it's the wine. "Actually Summer, if you don't mind... maybe we should do this another time. I probably should go home."

She pouts. "Come on, Laura. Don't be like that. Let's have another drink."

She makes it sound like we've done this before, like she knows what I'm like, how I get. *Don't be like that.* "Okay," I say. "Sure. One more."

She rolls her eyes. "You don't have to sound so oppressed. I'm not asking you to take a shot of cyanide."

"No. Sorry. No cyanide."

"Can we get cocktails? You choose. And can you get crisps or something? Or one of those." She points at a plate of assorted dips at her nearby table.

"Okay. Cocktails. Got it. I'll be right back." This time I do my best to sound upbeat. I splurge on two drinks called The Ciao with rye whiskey and Dom Benedictine, and throw in a plate of hummus and some olives. It takes two trips to the bar to bring it all back.

"So. Bronwyn," she says, dipping a piece of bread into the hummus.

"What would you like to know?" I ask. Again, upbeat, like

this is fun, this is two girlfriends catching up after work. This is not weird, at all.

"Well, you ran all over town getting her shopping list, you do a lot for her, which is really nice, I guess, lots of women wouldn't. Then you're at work and they're at home enjoying themselves. There's a story there, surely. How long have you known her? Is that okay if I ask? I'm so nosy, I know. Ask Dexter!"

I take a sip of my drink. It burns my throat. "We've known each other since we were twelve years old. We went to school together."

"Wow, long time. Around here?" She picks up an olive.

"About thirty-five miles north of here. Northwest Everett."

"Is it nice?"

She holds the pit of the olive between her teeth and looks around for somewhere to put it. I hand her a paper napkin. She takes it, spits it in the napkin, scrunches it up and puts it on the edge of the table.

"People say so."

"But not you?"

I shrug. "It's just where I grew up. I didn't have anything to compare it with. I wasn't a happy teenager, my mom died, my dad brought me up." I don't tell her that whenever I think of it, I feel like I'm standing on the edge of a precipice so deep with despair just looking down will make you cry.

"I'm so sorry, that must have been tough."

"Yeah, but you know, you get over it."

"Where's your dad now?"

"In a dementia care facility."

"I'm sorry."

"Don't be. We were not close. He has no idea who I am anymore and that's fine with me."

"And Bronwyn? What was she like as a child?"

I shrug. "We were friends, for a while, then we had an argument over a boy called Jimmy. She wanted him, he liked me, she spread rumors about me, told everyone I was a slut, whatever. It wasn't nice."

"How awful. So how did you hook up again?"

"Bronwyn and I lost touch after high school. Then about three years ago, I was in a group portrait exhibition at a gallery in Bellevue."

And just like that, I skip over two decades at least, including the part where Bronwyn and I were briefly in college together, except not together. We didn't hang out. She waved at me once down a corridor, even said my name, and I pretended not to see her and that was that. I made a point not to take any class she was in, and I wouldn't have anyway. She was enrolled in Feminist Studies which made me think that irony isn't dead, while I was more or less permanently drunk in Art & Painting, lurching into self-destruction. I took every risk I possibly could. I snorted every drug I could lay my nostrils on. I cut myself, of course, what self-respecting death-wishing nut job doesn't, I'd wake up on someone's couch not knowing where I was or who I was with. If you'd asked me what the hell I was doing in college, I'd say the only reason I was there in the first place was because I'd had a scholarship to study art, and it meant I could sit at the back of the class with my head on my arms and nurse my hangovers in peace. I failed more or less every exam, often for not showing up, but I did love art, I loved the idea of making art more. And anyway, she was only there for the first year, and then she disappeared.

"She turned up to the exhibition with Jack. She looked stunning, even better than I remembered. There was a moment where our eyes locked and I did feel a twist inside me. It was a long time ago, but somehow Bronwyn and the boy we argued over, Jimmy, and my mother dying and my shame at having been shunned by my schoolfriend and branded a *slut*, they all merged together, jumbled up, so that at the sight of her for a moment I felt like she'd been responsible for my mother's death, because in my mind, my mother dying meant my mother did not like me, even though deep down I knew it made no sense."

I have no idea why I'm telling her all this. It's like someone has turned on the tap and I'm just blurting whatever comes into my head. Maybe Dom Benedictine has untied my tongue. It must have something to do with it because I see now that my glass is empty. I rub my forehead. "If you think that sounds nuts, you should hear my friend Katie," I snort a laugh. "She's a psychologist," I say, as if that explained everything. And maybe it does because Summer nods thoughtfully.

"Anyway, there she was in the gallery, and I wanted to turn away and run, but her face softened and she said, 'Laura! Is that you?' We talked a little, she admired my work. Then later Jack came over and gave me his number scribbled on the back of the room sheet. He said Bronwyn really liked my portraits and he wanted to commission one of her. I wasn't remotely interested in doing it, but a few days later, he called me. He'd tracked me down, he thought I might have lost it. He offered me twenty-five thousand dollars to do the painting."

Summer makes a low whistle. "Wow, okay, now you're talking."

"I said yes. The money was amazing, I started to fantasize about what I could do to her portrait. I would paint a really unflattering, ugly portrait, like a sad Egon Schiele, take the money and run." I laugh.

"She looked shocked when I showed up on her doorstep, but Jack was there, all pleased with himself and his brilliant idea, and she immediately went with it. I wasn't sure if it bothered her, that it was me, considering our history, but she never brought it up. I went to her house two hours a day while she stood by the window in her living room wearing a red and gold kimono, her face in three-quarter profile, her eyes looking directly at me. It took two weeks, and you know what? In the end, the portrait turned out beautiful. She loved it. I don't know what happened, but it's certainly one of my best works."

"Where is it now?" Summer asks.

"It used to hang in the living room, but Jack took it down after she left. Threw it in the attic."

"God, sounds gothic. Is it aging while she stays the same? Have you checked?"

I laugh.

"So why did she leave? Did she meet someone else?"

"Eventually. After she found out that Jack was having an affair."

"Oh wow. How did she find out?"

"She found a cute loving note in his pocket, then lipstick on his shirt. She couldn't handle it. Around that time, she got a commission to design the interior for Leon's house on Mercer Island, and suddenly, they were gone, together, to Italy."

"That's so sad. I guess Jack didn't want Charlie to go overseas with Bronwyn?"

"Bronwyn didn't want to take Charlie."

"Really? Why not?"

"Because she has a peanut where her heart should be."

"Well, that explains it then," she says wryly. "How old was Charlie?"

"Five, almost six. Jack called me, he needed help. He had to go to work. I took time off from whatever teaching I had and helped take care of Charlie. I found a good preschool for her. I asked Jack if I could move in for a while, so that at least she'd have me around. He was grateful. We spent a lot of time together as you can imagine. One thing led to another, as they say in the classics."

She nods. "And you guys are happy?"

Happy? "Yes! Of course! We're very happy. Deliriously happy. I couldn't be happier." I rub my hand on my face. "Maybe, I don't know, not at the moment. Maybe not *deliriously* happy, right this second. Bronwyn is very demanding and Charlie is desperate to keep her happy, so I do my best, but Bronwyn uses that, in a way. She never shops for food, never prepares any meals, never cleans anything, not even to put a plate in the dishwasher. She knows I'll do it."

"Charming." She points to the phone. "But seriously, if I'd hazard a guess, I'd say she's treating you this way to make a point to Jack."

"What point?"

She shrugs. "She's making it clear she's the real woman of the house. So, is it because she wants him? Or because she hates you? Either way, I don't know how you do it, Laura. If that was my fiancé, I'd have killed her by now."

"You always say exactly what you think?" I ask.

"Always. Filters are for losers."

I smile, twirl my drink, clink the ice cubes against the glass. "I think…"

"What?"

"I think maybe she wants to come back for good," I blurt.

"Come back for good?"

And immediately tears prickle at the back of my eyes. I haven't voiced that possibility before, not out loud, not even to myself. And now it seems so obvious. Things didn't work out with Leon. That's why she's back, she wants to test the waters, see if she'd like her old life again. And she's right about one thing. If she told Jack she wanted to come back, he wouldn't hesitate. I mean, I believe Jack loves me, yes, in a distracted kind of way. I think he loves the little family unit that we are. He likes the solidity of it, the sweetness of it. But what he had with Bronwyn was a whole other level. They were the golden couple. They led the most amazing life together. Would he sacrifice what we have for a chance to do it again with Bronwyn?

"Wow, where does that leave you, then?" Summer asks.

I try to laugh. I sound like I'm braying. I rub a hand over my forehead. "She can't stay, she can't get any ideas into her head. But you know, Bronwyn believes in Bronwyn more than anything. The only way she'd change her mind is if she thought Jack was having another affair! Like, right now! Today! She'd be out of there before he'd have time to say, 'I have no idea whose panties these are.'"

She raises an eyebrow at me. "Interesting concept. You're wishing Jack would have an affair while he's with you, so that he wouldn't have an affair with her. Very twisted. Kind of meta. I like it."

She pushes a strand of hair off her face. Her very pretty face. Not beautiful, but youthful kind of pretty.

"Maybe you could do it," I blurt.

She was dipping a piece of flatbread in some kind of dip. She brought it to her mouth, bit the corner of it with her perfect white teeth. "Do what?"

"Have an affair with Jack." I moved forward, my heart racing. "Not literally, obviously, but if you could flirt with him, in front of her, do the whole thing—"

"The whole thing?"

"You know, go all out! A big seduction number! It's just for show. Bronwyn is really insecure. If she thinks Jack's eye is roving, she'll bail. I know she will."

She laughs. "You're so funny, Laura! So, when would I do this grand seduction number? Do I come to your house? Jump out of a cake? Do I get to wear suspenders?"

"They're coming to the opening. Jack, Charlie and Bronwyn. You could give Bronwyn a show!"

"You want me to flirt with Jack at the opening."

"In front of Bronwyn."

"Give her a show."

"Yes, please."

She clicks her tongue. "Are you sure?"

"Yes! Please! Do it! Tell me you'll do it!"

"It's a little weird, I won't lie, but okay, look you gave me the job and I'm super grateful so... why not? If that's what you want, boss..."

I rub my hands over my face. "Thank you. Thank you. No, wait, won't Dexter mind?"

She shrugs. "Dexter won't mind. He's used to me flirting. He says flirting is just non-verbal communication for me. Like morse code. Do you want another round?" She holds up her empty glass. "I'll get this one."

FOURTEEN

"Shit."

I was trying to be quiet, but I've stubbed my toe. I hop on one foot and pull off my shoe. The house is dark except for the light on the porch and a lamp upstairs on the landing. I drop the keys twice before I manage to get the door open. I take my shoes off and lurch up the stairs, holding onto the banister for balance. As I pass the archway I see the remnants of dinner still on the dining room table, and it dawns on me that Bronwyn is doing it on purpose. That she is reclaiming her previous rightful place and putting me firmly in mine. She is the mistress of his house, and I am the spinster friend who hangs around because they've adopted me, and I'm to be grateful for that, and also understand I need to work for it.

You're in the wrong bed.

The words pop into my mind. I don't want them there, but I know why they're there. They are whispering to me what I've always known, deep down. That I am the usurper, and who did I think I was? Bronwyn is back. Thank you for your help. You can go now.

Do you love me like you loved her?

I still remember the first time Jack and I kissed. I was walking out of Charlie's room, having just put her to sleep, and he had been watching me from the doorway. When I reached him, he pulled me away from the door and pressed me against the wall with his body. His mouth tasted of Scotch and salt. I woke up next to him the next morning and I was so happy I was dizzy. And that was it. We were together after that.

The first time we went out together, as couple, was to a barbecue at his friend Mike's house. It was summer, I was wearing a white wrap dress with a pattern of small flowers all over, and white sandals with a thin leather strap that wrapped twice around my ankles. It was a complete change from my usual attire, but it felt great. I felt grown up, with Charlie holding onto the hem of my dress and Jack bringing me a fresh ice-tea whenever he caught my empty glass. This was my family. It was my life now.

I was bringing some empty beer bottles from the backyard into the kitchen when I saw Jack and Mike talking on the porch. Instinctively, I made my movements quiet, put the bottles down from my arm so they wouldn't make a sound.

"You're sure about this?" Mike said.

Jack was smoking a cigarette, one that he'd rolled himself. He'd picked up the habit after Bronwyn left, although he gave it up again after a few months. I watched him pick off a strand of tobacco from the tip of his tongue, pondering his reply, and I waited for it with my heart beating too fast.

"It feels good not to be alone anymore, what can I say? And Charlie loves her."

"Of course Charlie loves her. She's her babysitter. She's nice enough, but she's not Bronwyn, Jack."

I felt my cheeks burn and my eyes prickle, and when I heard voices coming toward the kitchen, I left quickly before anyone caught me eavesdropping. For those few weeks leading up to that barbecue, I'd felt like I was emerging from a chrysalid. I was no longer unwanted and unloved. I'd started to swap my generic baggy clothes I'd pick up from Walmart for next to nothing for more feminine dresses. I started wearing makeup. I wasn't beautiful, but I felt pretty. I belonged, I had a family, I had a purpose: Charlie. Everything I did was for Charlie. I learned to cook, I baked, I stopped ad hoc teaching and turned to curating so I could make more money plus benefits. I had shed my old skin and emerged into the light, and I was happy. Desperately happy. Happier than I'd ever been.

Coming back from the party, I felt like someone had pulled the cloak away and that night I saw myself in the mirror for what I really was. Dull, plain, nice enough. The babysitter. Not Bronwyn. But all it made me do was try harder because I was not going to lose that family. I improved my wardrobe by another notch, with linen suits and elegant dresses. I started coloring my hair to make it shinier. I taught Charlie how to ride a bike, how to tie her shoes, how to read the time. I encouraged her love for nature and took her on long walks in the parks so we could look for birds, learn their names, identify insects, collect leaves and paste them into a book. I watched that child transform before my very eyes and whenever we saw Mike, I thought to myself, damn right I'm *not Bronwyn*. Someone has to be *not Bronwyn* if that child is going to have half a chance at a decent childhood.

When I peer into Charlie's bedroom now, I'm surprised to find her moon-shaped nightlight on. She hasn't turned it on for months. I pad in softly, lean over her bed to take a closer look. She's fast asleep, the covers up to her chin. A strand of hair has fallen over her eye and I gently move it away. My eyes swim, as they so often do at the sight of that perfect child, with her perfect face and her perfect brain and her perfect tastes and her perfect everything. On the way back out, I note how tidy her room is—very un-Charlie like. But I overheard Bronwyn tell her she was messy the other day. And also, that she was slow. *Stop dawdling!* And it made me sick to hear her criticize her child like that. Stop dawdling? How about, stop screwing other men! Stop moving to the other side of the world and leaving your child behind! Stop being such a shit mother! But I didn't say anything. Obviously.

I walk back out silently, then pad my way to my own bedroom and slip into bed next to Jack.

I love you. I whisper it softly, my breath on his cheek. *Do you love me? Like you loved her?* I think about the day Jack told me. "She left me, she's gone," he'd said, sobbing, and it was only later that I wondered about his choice of words. That he hadn't said, *she left us,* but *she left me.*

Now, as I lie there next to Jack, I feel the way I did at that barbecue. *Not Bronwyn. In the wrong bed.* My mind harks back to the way they used to be, the two of them. The perfect couple. Alpha meets alpha. A bit cool, a bit distant, but it suited them. It made them look like they had a secret connection they didn't need to share with anyone. They were the grown-ups in the room. Confident, larger than life. The perfect family.

I know I shouldn't, but I can't help it. I huddle under the blankets with my phone and scroll through her feed again. This time I get back further and find a post that I'd missed earlier; God knows how, considering it's a doozy. It's a selfie of the two of them, Bronwyn and Jack, in our kitchen—their kitchen?— with the wall I had retiled painstakingly with white and blue French-style tiles as background. Jack has his arm around Bronwyn's shoulder, and she's the one holding the phone. *#homesweethome, #homebeautiful*

Home beautiful all right. I painted those tiles myself and laid them too. And now Bronwyn stands in front of them, her head tilted toward Jack, so close their temples almost touch. Thank you for the backdrop.

What does Leon think of all this? I wonder. I scroll back quickly through her posts from before she came back, the last ones when she was still in Italy and I find plenty of them together, mostly sitting in their amazing gardens sipping on drinks in tall glasses, Bronwyn looking happy as ever. Then one of Bronwyn alone on a terrace, a wide brimmed hat on her head, looking out to sea. A caption: *Your value doesn't decrease based on someone's inability to see your worth. #selflove*

I knew it. I just knew it. Her relationship with Leon is over. I read the caption again and I'm thinking, actually, she's wrong about that one. It does. It's called working for minimum wage, which I bet she used to pay everyone that toiled for her and not a cent more. Jesus. How about, *#shutthefuckup*. Before those idiotic platitudes, there were seemingly thousand of snaps of Bronwyn: solo Bronwyn; Bronwyn on a beach; Bronwyn in a garden; Bronwyn baking something—no, Bronwyn *pretending* to bake something. Bronwyn has never baked anything in her life. Bronwyn doesn't *do* anything.

I put the phone on my side table and turn to Jack, propping myself on one elbow. His eyeballs are running behind his fluttering eyelids. I wonder what he's dreaming about. I lean in to kiss him softly on the lips. He smells of soap, a whiff of toothpaste.

And something else. It takes no time at all for me to place it.

Perfume. Bronwyn's perfume.

FIFTEEN

It all went wrong this morning, even before I got to work. I woke up angry, tiny facial muscles flexed between my eyebrows. I read somewhere that it takes eleven muscles to frown and twelve to smile. I must have been using all eleven, for sure, and I must have done it all night because it hurt. I could hear the shower running in the ensuite and I immediately turned to Jack's empty side of the bed and tried to catch it again, the cloying smell of her perfume. I'd woken up in the middle of the night with the horrible thought that they'd slept together in our bed while I was at work, and then I remembered that technically it was *her* bed, and I didn't sleep much after that. Plus my head felt like a construction site and I was trying to remember if I'd said too much last night but I couldn't. And I berated myself for doing something so stupid: get drunk, come home late, sleep badly.

I guess we all woke up angry because after I made breakfast for Charlie, I told her I'd take her to school this morning, and while she was upstairs getting ready, I was rehearsing what I'd say to her. That I knew she'd missed a few days of school lately, that Daddy had told me, that she wasn't in trouble but that it wasn't okay to lie to me, no matter who was asking. But after twenty minutes, she still hadn't come downstairs and I went to get her, and I don't know why I was surprised to find Bronwyn had beat me to it. She was crouched next to Charlie—who had changed into yellow and black striped tights, a yellow skirt and a red sweater so that she looked half bumble bee, half lobster—and was fastening the buckle on her shoe: a shiny black pump with a square heel, small, but definitely a heel, and a strap around the ankle.

I said something about Charlie being able to tie her own shoes, and Bronwyn sighed loudly, like I was being irritating. She tapped Charlie's foot. "There. Shall we go, Charlotte?" She said it like I wasn't even in the room, and to be fair, that's how she'd been treating me the whole time, so I don't know why I was surprised.

"Bronwyn, you've done the school run every day since you've been here. Let me take her for a change. Then she and I can have a chat."

"Laura," she said, in a tone that wouldn't have been out of place during the ice age, "I've taken Charlotte to school every day, that's correct. That's because I rarely get to see my daughter, you understand? So, I'm making the most of it. Is that all right with you? I assume it is since you're always the first to point out I am a bad mother who doesn't even like her own child."

"No!" I hissed under my breath. I prayed I'd spoken low enough that I could reach Bronwyn without Charlie hearing me. But it's clear she did. She was looking from Bronwyn to me with a frown on her face and her mouth wobbling downwards dangerously.

"Mommy likes me," she said.

"Mommy loves you to bits," I said, taking her face in my hands because Bronwyn hadn't and was still focused on me. "It's just an expression, baby."

Bronwyn bristled visibly at the *baby,* but she still didn't speak to reassure Charlie, immersed as she was in her own outrage. "No... what, Laura?"

"Don't. Please don't." Then I extended my hand to Charlie and said, "You're ready, sweetie?"

Bronwyn turned to Charlie. "Charlotte, would you prefer that Laura take you to school? Just like she does every day? Or would you like Mommy to take you?"

"Please don't do that," I whispered.

"Charlotte?"

There's a real art to such passive aggressive behavior, and I have to say, Bronwyn is a virtuoso of the technique. Charlie looked at me with pleading eyes. I nodded and blinked my acquiescence.

"Mommy?" Charlie said, still looking at me.

"Of course. I'll see you later, sweetie." I wasn't sure if she'd done it to keep the peace, or if she really wanted *Mommy* to take her to school, so I decided she'd understood my hint, and that really she wanted *me* to take her to school but it was all too hard, all fraught with danger with grown-ups saying things she didn't understand and I took her head in my hands again and kissed her cheek. "I love you. Have fun at school," I said. Bronwyn rolled her eyes, and I knew I sounded forced, fake, the fake mom with the cliched instructions.

I went to my bedroom and heard Jack come out of the shower, and I went in there looking for... I'm not sure what. Support, I guess. He had a towel wrapped around his waist and he was drying the back of his ears with another, and I opened the drawer of the vanity and rummaged for a lipstick. I didn't need the lipstick, I just wanted something to do.

"What's wrong?" he said.

Are you sleeping with her?

"Bronwyn won't let me take Charlie to school," I blurted. I sounded childish, whiny.

"Please, Laura. Not all that stuff again." He, on the other hand, sounded weary.

"It's just..." I couldn't get the right words. I was still rummaging around the drawer and I pulled out a peach-colored tube which was worn out all the way down so that when I tried to put it on, nothing came out, just the bottom of the tube scraping my lips.

He met my eyes in the mirror. "She's her mother. Surely you understand that, don't you?"

Surely you understand that, don't you? Even you, who is not a mother, must surely understand that?

"Did you ask her?" I blurted.

"Ask who what, Laura?"

"Ask Bronwyn about the divorce? Is it ever going to happen?"

He picked up his electric razor and turned it on. "Yes, we're doing it next week."

"Next week? I thought it was this week?" I closed the tube of lipstick.

"She had to postpone it."

"Yeah, right," I snorted.

"You're going to do this the whole time?" he said, shaving.

I'd run out of self-control by then. My mouth was snapping without me having to do a thing. "Do you *want* her here? Seriously, Jack. Do you *like* having her around? Please tell me, because it's a lot of work for me and I need to know that it's worthwhile. Is it like the old days, maybe? Is that it?" I was shaking. Although to be fair, I was also massively hungover so it could have been that. I also knew I should shut up around about now. I wasn't ready to open Pandora's box, because I was fairly certain I wouldn't be able to shove Pandora back in it. But my mouth had other ideas. "Do you guys like, play happy families when I'm at work? Is that it? Is it fun?" I had found another tube of lipstick in the drawer, a bright red one, not empty. I brought it to my lips but I was shaking so much when I applied it that I made my mouth both enormous and lopsided.

Jack put his hands on my shoulders and squeezed. "Don't be like that."

"Like what?"

"Jealous. I just don't want any trouble from Bron, that's all."

"How can she possibly give you any trouble?" I muttered. "When she gets her own way every single time?"

―――――

I don't notice it right away, the new work hanging on the back wall. Probably because I walk in with my sunglasses on and a pounding headache. I go out the back to put my coat away. I can hear laughter in the storeroom and when I open the door, I find Summer and Bruno chatting.

"Hi Laura!" Summer says brightly.

"Hi, we should probably get working," I say. They exchange a look, and I turn back and walk to the main gallery.

And it's when I reach the passageway that I see it. It's the change in the layout on the wall that draws my attention. The violin we hung yesterday has shifted further to the right and in the newly created space, in all its glory—How could I miss it really? I need my eyes checked—is an enormous print of the photograph she showed me under a sheet of glass. Nicely framed too. And below it, the poem, also under glass.

"What do you think?"

I turn around. Summer stands there, admiring her own work, her arms crossed over her chest.

"But we never discussed it!" I blurt.

She opens her eyes wide. "But we did, Laura!"

"No! I mean we talked, at the meeting the other day and then you said..."

She clasps her hand over her mouth. "Did I do the wrong thing?"

I take a breath. "I said I'd think about it. When we were leaving the meeting. Remember?"

"I'm sorry," she whines. "Bruno said I could, and I thought you said it was okay."

I sigh. "Never mind. It's too late now anyway."

"Are you sure?"

"Positive. We're great."

"Okay! Great. So? Do you like it?"

I gaze at it again. "It's great."

"You're sure? Because I wouldn't want—"

"Nope, it's great. Perfect. Thank you."

"Okay!" She says with renewed energy. "Phew! Thanks, Laura. Let's get to work."

I'm dying inside, and I don't think it's just the hangover. I don't mind the photograph at all—although at three feet by three feet it's making a statement—but the poem grates me. It cheapens the other stories we chose. But maybe I'm overthinking it. Maybe it's not so bad.

I read it again.

I found my love on a Friday afternoon
I found myself in your arms
Finally, I found you, you said.
That night I found my true north in the moon
I'll never let you go, you said.
You gave me your heart
Keep it forever, you whispered, and I will keep your heart
For we must never be apart
What did I say? What did I do?
Why did you leave and take my heart with you?

I lost my love on Thursday afternoon.
But I found you again, my love.
And I will never let you go.

Admittedly, maybe it's the mood I'm in, but there's something vaguely sinister about it. But then, what do I know? They're engaged, they're happy, they're getting married. I should worry about my own situation, I guess. Maybe I could learn something.

SIXTEEN

It's Friday, the opening of the Museum of Lost and Found, and suddenly my big idea, the one I've been working on for a year seems small and clumsy and childish. I feel like I'm about to be found out. I'm a fake, a try-hard, I was just pretending to be somebody who had ideas. I went home in the middle of the afternoon to get changed, and I think a part of me—the big loser part about to be exposed—wanted to surprise them, even maybe walk in on them screwing in our bed—*her* bed, *their* bed. When I found the house empty, I wasn't sure if I was relieved or disappointed. I changed into my silver wrap dress that I wear with a wide leather belt cinched at the waist and black boots, and I did my hair and makeup with great care, and in the end I thought I looked okay.

On the way out, I glance in Charlie's bedroom and find it, again, very un-Charlie-like-tidy, and I'm about to close the door when something catches my eye on her bedside table. The photograph that used to be there—the one I put there of Bronwyn and Charlie on a beach—is gone. In its place is a different photograph, this time of the three of them, another happy family snap. It's similar to the other one of the three of them, the one I saw on Instagram, and clearly taken at the same time, but in this one Bronwyn is facing the camera, with Jack and Charlie on either side of Bronwyn, kissing her cheek, very hard in Charlie's case and Bronwyn is grinning with her eyes screwed shut.

I hold up the photograph in both hands, biting down on my own teeth so hard my jaw hurts, and it's all I can do not to throw it out the window, or spit on it, or snap it in two against my knee. There is so much wrong with this image my brain can't even process it without making my temples throb. What the hell is Jack thinking, for one thing? Taking Charlie out with the two of them and playing happy families? She's been through so much, it has taken so much care and counseling, and caring teachers like Jenny Lee to get Charlie to where she is now: a happy, well-adjusted kid who plays and laughs and is curious about the world and secure that she is loved and she is safe. Does Jack not see how tenuous all that is? How easily she could go back to what she was when I moved in: unmoored, frightened, aggressive, lost. What will happen to her when Bronwyn goes back to Italy?

I sit on the edge of her bed staring at the photo, my stomach knotted onto itself, in full double pretzel mode. *If* Bronwyn goes back to Italy. I'm beginning to think that she's already ensnared him. They're back together again. Hashtag happy family back together again. I mean, random thought here, but shouldn't somebody have mentioned this to me by now? Looped me in? Or are they worried they'll have to wash their own socks, load their own dishes in the dishwasher?

And as I study the photograph, it occurs to me, again, that there's something seriously wrong with Bronwyn. The fact that she placed herself in the middle of the shot when surely it should be Charlie being kissed so fiercely by her parents.

Charlie squinting and grinning and screwing her eyes shut with Jack and Bronwyn's faces pressed almost flat against her cheeks. Was it so necessary to make Bronwyn the focus of their attention? *Hey everybody, look how much they love me, everybody! Hashtag Bronwyn is the best! Hashtag happy Bronwyn!* And then to choose *that* photo to display on Charlie's bedside table.

I put it back, very gently because I am afraid I might accidentally smash it repeatedly against the corner of the bedside table, and it's only when I walk out of the room that I notice the gaps in the corkboard, where all the photos that had included me used to be.

———

At five-thirty, the gallery opens its doors to the public, and by six pm, it is packed. It is, already, by far, one of the most successful openings we've ever had in terms of audience numbers. And now Bronwyn is here, looking impossibly elegant and perfectly made up with her hair up, loose tendrils framing her face.

"Laura!" She opens her arms wide and walks straight over to me, and it's something to behold, the way complete strangers smile at her, get out of her way so she can walk past without brushing against anyone. I'm sure I hear someone whisper, "Is that Angelina Jolie?"

"This is fabulous!" she says, even though she hasn't seen a thing yet. She wraps her arms around me and I stiffen.

"It's fabulous!" she says again. "Congratulations, sweetheart."

Nicely played, I think. Firstly, she'd never show me this much affection without an audience, but the *sweetheart* is smooth. She's saying it like I'm that student who wasn't smart enough for any of the big prizes, so she got the one for showing up.

"Thank you," I say, holding back a sigh. She releases me, picks up a glass of champagne from a passing waiter, looks idly around the room, lightly touching her hair. Then suddenly Bruno is by my side. He takes her hand and brushes his lips on her knuckles. She's wearing a diamond ring the size—and cut— of a pineapple and if only he'd move his lips to the right, quarter of an inch, he could slice his lips on it.

"Bruno Mallet, gallerist," he says. I think I'm going to be sick.

"Bruno Mallet, gallerist." She gives him her best smile. Mysterious, tantalizing, promising. "It's a pleasure to meet you. I'm Bronwyn. Jack's soon-to-be ex-wife."

And then, to my mortification, Bruno—who has no idea who Jack is because while he met him a few times, he wasn't remotely interested—says, "his loss, I'm sure." And Bronwyn can't resist a glance my way as she laughs prettily, her hand at her throat. I have a sudden urge to take that hand and squeeze it, make her tongue stick out and her eyes bulge. *Not so pretty now!* Fortunately, Jack and Charlie walk in—he must have been parking the car—and Charlie runs up to me and just like that, everything is right with the world again. She puts her arms around my waist and I kiss the top of her head, take in the scent of her which is different lately. More white lilies than bubblegum.

"I miss you," I whisper.

"What?"

"Nothing. Hello, pumpkin."

"Hello, Mama."

Her scarf tickles my nose. Except it's not a scarf, it's a feather boa. A pink feather boa. I loosen it and she grimaces, scratching the side of her neck.

"How was school?"

"I didn't go. Mommy and I went shopping." I take a deep

breath in to stop me from saying anything I might regret. "Did you have fun with Mommy?"

"Yes," she nods, a lot, and a volley of darts land in my heart.

Bruno is saying something to Bronwyn, who laughs her pretty pearly laugh, throwing her head back, displaying that perfect swan-like neck. Her fingers lightly finger the pendant at her throat, a gold heart with a big fat diamond in it, before touching his elbow, his shoulder, his wrist, and honestly, the only words that come to mind are *resistance is futile*. It's like having a high-pressure hose spraying you with charm and I almost feel sorry for him as he stands there, all puffed up like a peacock, nodding, listening, smiling, his head tilted down slightly so that they are so very close, so close he must surely smell her perfume, her breath. One of our regular buyers gets his attention by touching his shoulder, and Bruno sighs. "I must attend to my other guests, but it was a pleasure to meet you." And again, he does that kissing of the hand thing, and I'm thinking, *go on, quarter of an inch, if that*.

Bronwyn places her hand on Charlie's shoulder and proceeds to reel off all the fabulous stores they went to, which makes me realize she was listening to us the whole time she was talking to Bruno Mallet, gallerist.

"And then we went to the Bravern, and we found a lovely little handbag in Chanel, didn't we, Charlotte? Show Laura your new handbag." Charlie raises her hand. The handbag is black, with the Chanel logo and a gold chain. About as appropriate for an eight-year-old girl as a pair of nine-inch Louboutins.

Then Charlie's eyes grow wide, and she blurts, "And we saw a beaver!" and I laugh as she rambles on excitedly about the beaver. "This long," she says, making a space between her hands, while Bronwyn insists it was "probably a rat, Charlotte." And I'm laughing inside and out as I look up at Bronwyn, and

I'm thinking, you're not even making a dent in her. Underneath all the glitter, she's still Charlie the Explorer.

"Now Charlotte sweetheart, don't bother Laura," Bronwyn says. "You know she said she doesn't have time for you today."

"No, I didn't!" I blurt, because I'm yet to see a bait I wouldn't rise to in a heartbeat. But Bronwyn has Charlie's hand firmly in hers and is already pulling her away. "Let's take a look at the pretty things on the wall."

"Don't worry about it," Jack says next to me.

"Oh but I am worried about it," I mutter too low so he doesn't hear me. I glance at him sideways, lean slightly toward him to take a sniff of him. He smells like Jack, aftershave, soap, normal. "Looks like you had quite a time at the glass museum the other day." He raises his eyebrows, but I see a patch of crimson on the side of his neck, small, pale at first, then quickly turning darker.

"The show looks great, Laura," he says. The patch fades.

"And you must be Jack," Summer's sweet voice says from behind us. She's wearing a backless black dress so short she's tugging at it with her free hand, with enough décolletage to glimpse the mound of her breasts and a hint of the lacy edge of a black bra. And it's funny, but I completely forgot that I'd asked her to flirt with Jack. For a moment, I consider pulling her aside and asking her not to do it, but then I think, screw it.

"This is Summer, my assistant," I say.

"I think that you, sir, need a personal tour," Summer says lightly. Jack chuckles and looks at me.

"All part of the service," I say, shrugging one shoulder. I am grateful that she remembered, I won't lie. The most important person in my life is Charlie, and I'm never giving her up, and certainly not for Bronwyn—selfish, narcissist Bronwyn who doesn't even know her own daughter's favorite color, can't remember how old she is, has no idea her little girl knows all the planets by heart and used to have a pet caterpillar called Mr.

Fluffles that roamed happily in our backyard. The only person Bronwyn is interested in, is Bronwyn. And right now the only person that can help me get Bronwyn's sticky claws off my family is Summer, and when I turn to Bronwyn, I see that her perfect face is starting to slide down around her mouth, like melting wax.

So that's nice.

SEVENTEEN

I give a speech that is nothing like the one I've prepared and won't remember two hours from now, and declare the show official open. People clap. I'm so proud I'm bursting. I watch people studying every piece, standing back, discussing every work. My friend Sarah is here, lovely Sarah who is an assistant curator at the Art Museum. I take her through my own mini guided tour, my favorite highlights sort of thing, skipping past Summer's photograph, and she loves the show. At one point I catch sight of Bronwyn—I say catch sight as if it was an accident when, in fact, I can't peel my eyes off her—staring at Jack and Summer who by now have meandered down the gallery, Summer with her arm hooked into his in a way that is strangely intimate.

Gavin is back this evening taking photographs for our social media pages—it should have been Summer, she's the better photographer, but Gavin wanted to be here, and he needs the money—he gets Summer to pose with Jack, and if I'd set this up, I couldn't have done a better job. I watch Summer playing it up for the camera, her arm still locked with Jack's and her other hand on her waist. Jack looks uncomfortable, and for a moment

I feel sorry for him but the look on Bronwyn's face? Priceless. It's not even a look. More like a rotting fruit, her whole face falling inward, no longer supported by the liquified flesh beneath that once taut skin. She taps Charlie's shoulder quickly and even though she is too far for me to hear, I can make out the words on her lips: *Let's go.*

I smile to myself. Can this really be mission accomplished? Can I celebrate? Grab a flute of champagne for myself and go all out?

I make excuses to go and say goodbye to Charlie when Adrian Kurilak from the *Seattle Times* walks in. Adrian who I'd invited to review the show, along with other reviewers, but I never expected to turn up. I glance back at Bronwyn and Charlie and see that they are walking to the door. I catch Summer's elbow on my way through the crowd and whisper that Adrian Kurilak is here, very important reviewer, could she go and talk to him? Take him through the show? And please tell him I'll be there in a minute.

"Of course," she says, and puts a hand on Jack's arm. "Thank you for talking with me. I'll see you soon."

Jack nods, smiles like an idiot, blushes, then notices me.

"Bronwyn and Charlie are leaving." I point them out. "I'll just go and say goodbye."

He glances in Summer's direction who is now deep in conversation with Kurilak. "I should go too, then."

"Why?" I ask. "You can stay a while longer, can't you? Stay till the end, we'll go home together."

He makes a show of thinking about it, but then he says no, he should drive them back. I pout, he kisses the side of my head and we walk to where Bronwyn and Charlie are standing.

"You're leaving already?" I say to Bronwyn, bending down to hug Charlie.

"Yes. Charlotte is bored, Jack is obviously busy... I thought I'd take Charlotte to the movies instead."

"Oh? Isn't it a bit late?" I ask.

"Not for *Harry Potter and the Half-Blood Prince*. It's on at seven at the Regal Meridian. In 4D! Whatever that means. We can pick up something to eat on the way, okay Charlotte?"

I don't know what's wrong with me. I should let it go, but I don't. "Okay, I mean, it's her birthday party tomorrow, the movie is two and a half hours, isn't it?" I lean forward. "Don't you think she's a little young for that one? We love reading *Harry Potter* but the later films? They're a little dark and she's so impressionable..."

She tilts her head at me, smiles. "I don't know what's wrong with my hearing, but I could have sworn you were giving me advice about what movies I can take my daughter to."

"I want to see *Harry Potter!*" Charlie whines.

"I know, honey, but..." I lean closer again so I can keep my voice low. "I'm sorry, Bronwyn. I didn't mean to... I just think it's a little scary for her, right now. And it's her birthday party tomorrow and she should get a good night's sleep."

Her face breaks into a wide smile. "You do understand it's only Harry Potter, don't you? You couldn't possibly object to me taking *my* child on a special mother-daughter evening out, surely! That would be... not very nice of you." She's loud enough that a hush has descended around us.

"It's not that," I whisper.

"Oh, good! For a moment, I thought you might be upset that I'm taking my daughter to the movies. Anybody would think you were jealous of our special mother-daughter bond!" She laughs. "Surely not. After all, I've made a big effort to be kind and inclusive and get on with you. Is this about Jack? Because I really don't know what else I could possibly do to make you feel comfortable about my close relationship with Jack. We're just trying to be good co-parents, Laura. That's all." She smiles, puts her hand on my forearm. "Are you all right? You look angry. Have I said the wrong thing?"

I'm dying. By now this is a performance for everyone's benefit and judging from the silence in the room and the glances people are throwing at each other, it's a hit.

"Of course I'm not angry," I say through gritted teeth. "Why would I be angry?"

"You sure?" She frowns, solicitous. "You're turning red."

"Well, I'm not. I'm sure."

"Okay," she says dubiously. "So it's all right for me to take my daughter to the movies?"

I bite a fingernail. *Let it go, Laura, let it go!* "Maybe a different movie?" I say.

She tilts her head at me. "Laura, sweetheart, stop. You're embarrassing yourself, and me. Charlotte and I are going to leave now, and we are going to enjoy our evening together. We'll see you at home."

Jack shoots me an apologetic look over his shoulder as they walk out the door. What a coward, I think as I turn around. He could have stepped in. Then I realize everyone is looking at me, and my cheeks burn as I walk away. Summer joins me, grabbing two glasses of wine from a passing waiter along the way.

"I'd get you something stronger," she says, passing one to me, "but this is better than nothing." She walks me toward the corridor.

Once we're out of sight I lean against the wall and breathe out. "Thank you."

She flaps her hand. "That Bronwyn is something else," she says.

"God. I feel so bad." I risk a glance at the crowd, then quickly look away. "Did everybody hear every word, you think?"

She shrugs. "Don't worry about it. Everybody's got a Bronwyn in their closet. Some ex-wife or ex-boyfriend or whatever that'd pick at everything you do in the middle of your big moment. They just felt sorry for you."

"Yeah, right." I knock back the rest of my drink. "But thanks. I should go and talk to Adrian Kurilak."

"He left."

"Oh! When?"

"Five minutes ago. But I took him around the exhibition, and he was very impressed. He took the catalogue. I'm sure he'll do you a nice write-up."

"Oh, okay. God, I hope so."

I spend the next hour or so walking around with a smile plastered on my face—the kind that pulls my lips away from my teeth—as I thank people for coming and tell them how lovely it is that they could make it, and what do you think about the show? And no one brings up the elephant in the room, which is how I like to think of Bronwyn. As an elephant. Big trunk sweeping and smashing everything in her path. So we all get to pretend there's nothing to see here.

Then it's over, and it's just us left. Bruno opens a bottle of champagne to toast his congratulations.

"I've been getting wonderful feedback all night," Bruno says. "This is a hell of a show, ladies and gent. I suspect it's going to raise our profile to the next level. Congratulations to all of you!" He pours champagne into three flutes that he's holding in the one hand, each glass by the stem between two fingers and tilting the hand as he pours, and I must be a little drunk because I can't stop staring with a mix of awe and envy. I wonder if it's a French thing, if they learn to do it at school, or kindergarten, the way we learn to tie our shoelaces. He hands the first one to Summer, then to me, then to Gavin.

"Congratulations, Laura!" Summer says, tipping her glass to

me, and I'm a bit annoyed that she had to say it, instead of
Bruno.

"And thank *you,* Summer, for all your hard work, really,"
Bruno replies, tipping his glass back to Summer with a little
bow, and I raise my own glass, waiting for my turn, my tipping
of the glass, my expression of gratitude, *And Laura! Wow, what
can I say? I can't believe what you achieved. To think this is all
your hard work, from the very inception of the idea to getting
state government funding to making it all a reality and even
organizing the year-long touring schedule. Incredible. Bravo, and
thank you.* Which I realize is the speech I would give to myself,
and in fact I just did, inside my head. But Bruno just sips his
champagne while throwing glances at Summer, even though
I'm standing right next to her and at this point, I may as well not
be in the room. Anyway, I don't care. Summer and I start to
gather empty bottles and put them in a box. Gavin slides up
to me.

"I'm getting paid for taking photos tonight, right?"

"Yes, of course, that's what Bruno said."

He nods. "Do you have any other work for me?"

I look at him in surprise. "In what way?"

He shrugs. "Sitting the show? Maybe on weekends?"

That's interesting. Gavin is the one who wanted to quit, but
it sounds like he didn't have a job to go to. I think about it for a
moment. I'd like to help him out if I can, and we can afford it,
thanks to the grant money. I turn to Summer. "Do you want the
weekend off? You can work on the other days, instead."

"Sure, sounds great."

"Okay," I say to Gavin. "You can sit the show on weekends.
Starting tomorrow?"

"Thanks," he says.

I walk out the back to give him a spare set of keys. "Oh, and
I asked Bruno to borrow two trestle tables for Charlie's birthday
party tomorrow. I was going to pick them up in the morning

with the van, but if you can deliver them to my house instead, I'll pay you."

"Sure, thanks."

I give Gavin my address and he leaves with Bruno, and Summer and I pick up all the last of the dirty glasses and bring them to the kitchen, stick them into the dishwasher, put away the linen tablecloths and fold up the trestle tables. When we're done, Summer opens another bottle of champagne and pours us both a glass.

"You did good," she says, and I laugh.

It's only when we're outside, about to walk into the icy night that I remember Dexter.

"Your boyfriend," I say. "I didn't meet him, was he there?"

"No," she says breezily. "I told him not to come."

"Why not?"

She shrugs. "It's not his thing. He'd just be in the way."

EIGHTEEN

It's half past nine when I get home. The light is on inside, and I stand at the door for a moment to collect myself. I assume that means they're all home, the whole happy family unit, and I am fervently praying Bronwyn is in bed already, but she is not. She and Jack are standing in the living room, in front of the fireplace, a glass of wine in hand. They're laughing at something, stop abruptly when I walk in.

"How was the movie?"

He shakes his head. "We didn't go to the movies."

"Oh?"

"She was upset," Bronwyn says. "Thanks to you. She was crying. Bawling her eyes out, really. We were not going to go to the movie with her in that state."

"Bawling? Why? Is she okay?"

"No, Laura, she's not! So thanks for ruining our night." She takes a slug of wine.

"I'm sorry. I didn't realize she was so upset. But I did, I do, think that particular movie is a little too much for her. Don't you think, Jack?"

Jack pokes at something on the carpet with his toe.

"Jack?"

"Maybe, a little. Also, it's late."

Bronwyn glares at him.

"Okay. Thank you. Anyway, I'm going to bed. I have to get up early, very early, to get the house ready for the party because as far as I can tell, neither of you has done anything."

"The bike has been delivered," Jack says sheepishly. "It's in the garage."

I sigh loudly. I'd completely forgotten about Charlie's birthday present, the new bike, to replace her old one that got stolen. "Well, that's great, Jack. I'm going to bed."

At the bottom of the stairs, I snatch my bag from the console table. "It would be nice for Charlie if you two could help out. For a change. I'm sure she'd appreciate it."

I quickly disappear upstairs, and pop in to check on Charlie who is asleep. Her occasional shuddering breath tells me she must have been really upset and I feel a wave of guilt.

"I'm sorry," I whisper, kissing her soft cheek. She doesn't stir.

In my own bedroom, I lie on the bed, fully clothed, staring at the ceiling. What is wrong with me? I keep trying to do the right thing, but I make a complete mess of it. I think of what Jack said the other day, *You sure know how to get your buttons pushed, Laura.* The implication being what, exactly? That I poke and prod at Bronwyn until she snaps? That it's all my fault?

Is it all my fault?

I swing my legs out of the bed and grab my phone out of my bag, quickly send a text to Summer.

Wanna come to an 8-year-old's bday party tomorrow? I could use your help again. Like you did before. wink emoji. Two pm.

Then I think about it, gnawing on a fingernail, and add:

Only if you're free.

Seconds later comes the reply:

To do what?

Flirt with Jack, please.

Then I add:

I'll pay. A hundred bucks.

Deal.

Great. I'll tell Jack you've come to help me entertain the children.

Whatever you say, boss.

NINETEEN

Two hours later, I can't get to sleep. I'm thinking of Charlie. I desperately want her to have the most wonderful birthday party ever. So I get up again, wrap my robe around me and pad downstairs to my studio.

It used to be Bronwyn's studio when she started working professionally as an interior designer. She'd lay out her samples on her big drafting table, pin bits of fabric to corkboards on the walls.

When I moved in, Jack said I could have it as a painting studio, but I never got that far. I use it as storage mostly, it's where all my supplies are, and for the next few hours, I sit in there and make things. And it's nice. It reminds me of the hours in the middle of the night I used to spend in my own small apartment making art, making things. I'd paint portraits of women and they always had the same round face, round shoulders and no one would know this, but they all looked a little like my mother. You didn't need to be a brain surgeon to figure out I was trying to conjure her up during those years, so I wouldn't forget what she looked like.

But it's my years as an art teacher that I draw on as I make flowers, lots of flowers, because Charlie loves flowers. I make them out of tissue paper and card stock, and I make them in every shape and size, and I build garlands with them that I hang around the living room. I dress up the porch with fairy lights, make little air balloons with lanterns and strings and card stock which I hang around the house so that they look like they're floating below the ceiling, then I make garlands out of shiny paper, and I blow balloons, lots of them, and use the white ones to make more air balloons, which I hang over the dining room table. Then I make tiaras for the girls out of cardstock and wire and beads, and I make shiny swords with jewels stuck on the handles for the boys. I make pinatas shaped like big fat stars and hang them in the backyard, and I write up HAPPY BIRTHDAY CHARLIE in big letters using confetti that I glue on the living room wall.

Then I make food. I make mini pizzas that I'll bake later and pop on paddle pop sticks, and fairy bread truffle balls, and jelly custard tarts and little blueberry cupcakes, and finally the birthday cake, and that one I made easy for myself. It's basically mashed up ice cream in three flavors stacked up in a bowl which I pop in the freezer.

By the time I fall back into bed, the sun is coming up.

———

It's a glorious day, sunny and crisp and bright blue. Just warm enough for the kids to run around outside if they want to. Not that we have a huge garden, but we're lucky, we have more space than most.

Summer comes early. I laugh at the sight of her. She is dressed in full fairy godmother regalia: in a pink dress with bouffant sleeves that surely must be flammable, white wings on her back, white lacy gloves, a silver crown and a silver wand. I laugh so much I'm bent over in two, but maybe I'm just delirious because I'm so tired. My head had only just hit the pillow when Charlie got up and ran squealing around the house. So I got up again and made pancakes with Nutella for breakfast while Jack and Bronwyn were asleep, and together Charlie and I made more decorations, blew more balloons, cut up more flowers, and it was just like before, before Bronwyn, just Charlie and I together, chatting, making things, her talking at a million words a minute. I felt our bond in my bones, warm and golden like liquid caramel, and then Katie arrived and Gavin arrived with the trestle tables I'd borrowed from work, and the four of us set up the chairs and tables and games outside, and guests arrived, big and small and suddenly it was mayhem.

"Thank you for coming," I whisper to Summer. Then I hug her awkwardly.

"You kidding? I love birthday parties!" I hook my arm into hers and walk around the front yard, pretending to show her around. I launch right into it. "Fabulous job yesterday, but we're not out of the woods yet, so if you could strike a fatal blow, somehow, make Jack do something that Bronwyn would find intolerable, unforgivable, I would be eternally grateful."

She tips at her forehead with her fingers. "Fatal blow. Got it."

"Great, thank you. But maybe entertain the kids also, so it doesn't look strange..."

"I brought supplies." She opens her bag to show me. "Face painting, dress ups, roleplay. These kids won't know what hit them."

"Okay, great, thanks."

I had completely underestimated how difficult it would be to keep twenty or so children happy for the afternoon, so Summer is literally a godsend. She paints their faces, teaches them line-dancing, tells them scary fairy tales that sends them squealing with terror around the yard.

"Who the hell is that?" Katie says.

We're both resting back against the table, surveying the damage in progress in the flower beds. I follow her gaze to where Summer and Jack are talking, drinking beers straight from the bottle, Summer picking a leaf out of his hair.

"Summer, I told you about her."

"Summer... your protégée?"

"Yes. My protégée, if you must. She doesn't need protection, though. Not from me."

She shoots me a look, a very Katie look with one eyebrow raised. "She's very relaxed around Jack."

In her ear, I whisper. "It's not how it looks. She's helping me out."

"Helping you how?"

"It's because of Bronwyn." I tilt my head toward her, and she does the same, so our temples are almost touching. "You know how Bronwyn always says Jack was unfaithful to her?"

"Sort of."

"Okay, well, she did, and lately her and him... they spend so much time together..."

"Who?"

"Bronwyn and Jack."

"Really?"

"Yes."

"Like, *spending* time together?"

"Yes, exactly like that. Anyway, Summer is a new friend of mine, and I thought if Bronwyn sees them together like this, she'll back off. So this is a strategy, you see? It's a pre-emptive strike. Maybe not pre-emptive now that I think of it, but it's a strike. A fatal blow to the possibilities. Because Bronwyn would hate that." I tug at Katie's sleeve and tilt my head toward Bronwyn to make my point, as in *wait till you see her face!* But unlike yesterday, Bronwyn doesn't seem to notice the scene playing out in front of her, or care, or if she does, she hides it well. Maybe she's given up. Maybe she's realized it's a hopeless cause, and she's moved on. She wouldn't be heartbroken about it since obviously she doesn't have one.

"I hope you know what you're doing," Katie says.

"Nope, no idea. Help me with the cake?"

We slip in the kitchen and get out the frozen ice cream cake which I turn over and pop out onto a plate, cover with sprinkles, and I'm about to stick sparkler candles into it when the children erupt into a loud *Happy Birthday!*

I turn to Katie. "What?" We both rush to the window and when I see it, I am not as surprised as I should be. In fact, I wonder why I didn't anticipate it.

In the garden are two waiters pushing a trolley with an enormous, multi-tiered cake, and if it wasn't for the candle in the shape of an eight crowning the whole edifice, you'd think this was a wedding cake for a party of five hundred.

Hip hip hip hooray!

I slide the ice cream cake into the trash and throw the plate into the sink where it breaks into shards.

Outside, one of the waiters—Where did they come from?—is taking photos of Jack and Bronwyn and Charlie, with Bronwyn holding the knife to cut the cake. For once I'm glad I'm not included. I don't think I could resist snatching that knife from her cold fingers and driving it right into her heart. If I could find it.

"Wow. That's a heck of a cake," Katie whispers, her arm around my shoulders.

I sigh. "Well, if we're doing surprises, then we should get her bike." I go straight to Jack. "Can you get the bike?"

Jack tears himself away from the little group and Bronwyn raises one arm toward me. "Laura! Sweetheart, come and get some cake!"

"That's okay, thanks," I mutter.

"Oh but you must! It's fabulous! Come and take a photo with me!"

This is the longest conversation I've had with Bronwyn since she left the gallery yesterday.

"No, thanks!" I say again. And from the corner of my eye, I catch Erin looking at me, head tilted. She's probably thinking I'm not being very friendly, but I don't care. Waiters cut the cake and pass portions around on china plates, real china, not the cheap paper stuff I picked up from Target on University, on sale at six dollars fifty for a pack of twenty. Then Jack comes out with the bicycle—*Happy Birthday, Charlie!*—which to his credit, is perfect. Lime green, big wheels, tassels hanging from the dual handbrakes. Charlie's face lights up with joy and I no longer care about the cake.

Until the van pulls up outside our house literally one minute later

Bronwyn rushes to the front gate like she's been waiting for this, and I close my eyes. When I open them again, all the kids are bouncing on their feet with anticipation, little fists in front of their mouths while their parents are craning their neck to see. Two women get out of the front and open the back of the van. A ramp slides out and connects the back of the van to the ground, then one of the women walks back in and comes out holding a pink glittery lead. She gently tugs at it as she walks down the ramp, small steps—*there there, it's all right, good girl, tug tug*—and we all wait with bated breath for whatever is at the other end of the pretty pink lead.

It's a fucking pony.

TWENTY

"You have got to be kidding me," I mutter.

Charlie screams. With excitement, obviously. She shrieks so loudly I have to put my hands over my ears.

"Happy birthday, Charlotte!" Bronwyn says, pulling the pony behind her, her sharp heels sinking into the lawn.

I walk over to Jack, try to speak through lips so tight they feel like I've got rigor mortis. "What the hell is this?"

For some reason that I don't understand, Jack is laughing. "It's a pony, Laura!"

"Yes, I see it's a pony. Why is it in our yard? Did you know about this?"

"No!" The children are surrounding the pony, patting it. Charlie has wrapped her arms around its neck.

"What do you want to call it?" Bronwyn asks.

Call it?

"Is it mine?" Charlie asks.

"Yes, Charlotte. What would you like to name your pony?"

"David Greybeard!" she shouts. If I wasn't so angry, I would have laughed. David Greybeard was the name Jane Goodall gave to her favorite chimpanzee.

"David? No! That's a boy's name! Look at the pretty pony, she needs a girl's name!"

"Greta Thunberg!"

"No! That's a silly name, it's too long!" says Bronwyn, who has no idea who Greta Thunberg is. "Let's call her... Tallulah."

"Tallulah!" Charlie shouts, wrapping her arms around the pony's neck again, *Ohmygodohmygod it's my pony is it really Ohmygod Tallulah I love you Tallulah.*

I, on the other hand, am shaking with rage. Not just because Jack and I have been outsmarted—outspent, outplayed—but because we discussed presents, and I asked her to contribute to the bike, (total: $380) and she said, no, that's okay, she'd give Charlie a fifty-dollar voucher for Magic Mouse Toys, which I actually didn't think was a bad idea.

I watch the children pat the pony, try to guide it down the path, which has steps. Needless to say, it's dangerous, but nobody else seems to care. I'm trying to figure out how to deal with this but I'm so angry it's making my head pound.

Bronwyn catches my eye and beams. "Come and meet the new addition to the family, Laura! Isn't it the sweetest thing? Come on, Charlotte! Let's put a saddle on Tallulah and give her a spin!"

I can't breathe. My head hurts because it keeps jerking back and forth, like a broken toy. My hands are closed into fists by my side and I can feel the nails digging to the flesh.

Katie squeezes my shoulder.

"What's wrong?"

I look at her, mouth gaping. "What's wrong? She's just given Charlie a pony, Katie! Where the hell am I supposed to put it?"

She frowns. "I don't think—"

"Where is Jack?"

"I don't know, inside, I think."

"Jesus Christ," I mutter. "Typical."

"There you go, Charlotte."

She picks her up, with some difficulty, and hoists her on the pony. "You're a natural."

"Look, Mama!" Charlie squeals.

In a soft voice, but not so soft that I can't hear her, Bronwyn says, "Laura, sweetheart. Her name is Laura."

It's like a flash goes off in my head. I can't think straight, my vision has gone blurry, and next thing I know I am lifting Charlie off the pony and plonking her on the ground. I snatch the lead rope from Bronwyn's hand and pull the pony back to the van. "Pony's going home. Party's over."

Behind me, Charlie wails and I steel myself not to turn around. I hand the lead rope to the dumbfounded women and tell them that I'm sure there's a cooling-off period and we are returning the pony for good and they can reimburse Bronwyn directly, minus any costs. Whatever, I don't care.

Charlie is lying on the ground, hysterical when I get back, Bronwyn is crouched next to her, her hand on her back, consoling her. All the parents are shooting me dirty looks, grabbing their crying children, putting hands on their shoulders, and I'm thinking, what do they expect? Do they want a pony in their backyard?

I walk right up to Bronwyn. "What the hell is wrong with you?"

She stands up. "With me?"

"Yes! We can't keep a pony in the backyard!" I hiss. "But you know that. You did it on purpose, didn't you? You just want to make me look bad!"

"I think you're doing that all by yourself, sweetheart. Seriously. I was talking to your friend Katie before, I understand she's a psychologist. Maybe you should schedule a session or two, because you're not well, sweetheart."

"Stop calling me that!" I hiss.

She looks at me with concern, puts her hand on my shoulder. I shrug it off.

"I was only trying to help," she says.

"By giving her a pony that you *know* she can't keep?"

She frowns at me. "It was just for the afternoon, Laura."

I stop trying to pick up Charlie who is kicking me in the shins anyway. I stand up straight, study her face, try to figure out if I heard her right. "What?"

"For the party! You really thought I was buying her a pony? Where on earth would she keep it? Here?"

"But... you said..."

"What did I say?"

"You said, meet your new pony, or whatever!"

"It was just a turn of phrase!"

"But Charlie thinks it was hers to keep!"

She frowns at me again, but there's a ghost of a smile on her lips and I know I've been played.

She tucks her hair behind her ear. "I was about to explain."

My jaw is slack with shock, and for a moment I can't get the words out. Charlie is still crying hysterically. My chest is so tight I can barely breathe as I realize how stupid I've been. I should have waited. I should have called her bluff. Meanwhile, Charlie, still sobbing like the world has ended, manages to scramble herself up and turn to me, her face purple, her eyes blazing, and shouts at the top of her lungs, "IHATEY-OU!IHATEYOU!IHATEYOU!" Before running inside the house.

"I'd be more concerned about what Jack is up to than a stupid pony, if I were you."

"What do you mean?"

She cocks her head at me. "He's kissing her, Laura. They've been making out all afternoon. Where the hell have you been?"

I shake my head. "God, you are really something else, aren't you?"

"You don't believe me?"

"No, I don't! I know you're lying!" I turn around.

"Charlie?" I rush after her. I'm about to take the stairs two by two when I catch sight of a white fairy wing peeking out from behind the living room door, and when I pop my head inside, I find Summer leaning back against the wall, her hands behind her back. Further along the wall is Jack. He puts his finger on his lips. "We're playing hide and seek with the kids," he says.

"You have got to be kidding me," I snap. "Do you have any idea what just went on out there?"

I go up to Charlie's room, Jack follows, looking chastised. But Charlie won't speak to me; in fact, she'll scream if I'm in the room, so I leave Jack to it, my heart shattered.

———

"Nothing happened!" Summer says later when I've dragged her outside. The parents have whisked their children away, half of them in tears. She retrieves her bag from the garage, her big bag full of party things.

"Making out behind the door?" I hiss at her.

"We didn't."

She rearranges her dress around her breasts and I wonder if Jack slipped his hands in there.

"I didn't mean for you to have sex with him in the living room!"

"Oh, Laura please. Don't be ridiculous. Nothing happened." She gets her phone from a pocket deep inside the layers of her skirt and taps away.

"And anyway, you said to do something unforgivable. That's what you said."

"Actually, I said make *him* do something unforgivable, but okay."

"What was I supposed to do? Brush dandruff off his shoulder? If that's what you had in mind, you should have said."

"Oh, for Christ's sake. And anyway, you were supposed to do it in front of Bronwyn, that was the point, not in hiding!"

But just as the words leave my mouth, I realize that the joke, again, is on me. After all, it's me who's marrying Jack in two months. It's me, who is going to be walking down the aisle—sort of, it's not that kind of wedding—with all the guests watching on thinking, *Wasn't he shoving his tongue down some fairy's throat at that party?* before uploading pictures to their Instagram feed. Hashtag loser.

A taxi pulls up outside. "It's for me," Summer says.

"I got your cash," I say, reaching into my pocket.

She rolls her eyes. "Only if you want to." She takes it, gets inside the taxi, closes the door and flicks the window down. "By the way, who was it Jack had an affair with?"

"Who was it?" I shrug. "Nobody."

"Come on, must have been somebody to make Bron leave him like that."

"Please don't call her Bron."

"Why not?"

"Because that's what Jack calls her. It's weird if you do it. It's not like you're her friend. *Are* you her friend?"

"Of course not. So who did Jack have the affair with? You?"

"No! Why do you ask?"

"I'm just curious."

"Her name was Beth."

"Beth?"

"Someone from his work, I think."

"And is it over with Beth?"

"Jesus, Summer. What are you saying? Of course it's over."

She tilts her head at me. "It doesn't worry you? That he had an affair?"

"No! It doesn't worry me! He wasn't with me back then. It's ancient history."

She nods, like she gets my point. "Whatever you say, boss. I'll see you at work."

TWENTY-ONE

The rest of the weekend passes in a cloud of misery. I didn't tell Jack that I knew he'd kissed Summer and yet, obviously, I couldn't stop thinking about it. I convinced myself it didn't matter because it was about putting Bronwyn off, but technically it was me he was engaged to, so it was me he was being unfaithful to, if you'd count a kiss as unfaithful. Which I would, I think. But I didn't confront him about it. *You're such a pushover, Laura. Total wet blanket.* Instead, I slammed doors in his face—but not too loudly so as not to upset Charlie—and pretended to be angry because when I told him what Bronwyn had done, he didn't believe me. Although I was angry about that too.

"Don't you know," I said, "how sick she is? She's not right in the head, Jack!" I kept stabbing at my temple with my finger, vaguely aware I was the one looking not right in the head but unable to stop.

He took my wrists and held them tight. "You have to stop getting so uptight, Laura."

"Are you serious? She brought a pony to the birthday party and pretended it was a gift!"

"It was just a misunderstanding!"

"Yeah. right." I snorted. "I'm just trying to get through—"

I didn't hear the rest. I walked out, slamming—sort of—the door again. But Charlie wouldn't speak to me. At all. She wouldn't speak to Jack either, but he wasn't trying very hard. She spent the rest of the weekend sobbing on her bed, her face in her pillow, wailing for *Tallulah!* and it was all I could do not to kill Bronwyn. Bronwyn, of course, was fine. She lolled about the place, drinking G&Ts and eating ice cream straight out of the tub.

"This is your fault," I hissed into her face. "So you have to do something to help her. Go and explain, go and say something, anything, just make her feel better."

"Okay," she said simply. "I'll do it."

I gnawed at a fingernail as I contemplated how easy it would be to strangle her. I could do it right here, right now. I was so tempted I had to shove my hands deep down in my pockets. She walked out and I heard her going up the stairs. "Mommy's here, Charlotte, it's all right. Mommy will make it all better." And I rolled my eyes so far up my head they were in danger of leaving their sockets all together and bouncing around the floorboards. I waited a few minutes and hurried silently behind her, then spied on them through a gap in the door. They were lying on Charlie's bed, Bronwyn with her arm around Charlie's shoulders, awkwardly, like she'd never done it before and she didn't know how, while Charlie sobbed into her armpit. Bronwyn glanced up at me and I understood then that she knew all along I would be watching, and that was why she left the door ajar.

"You don't need to worry about Laura, Charlotte. Just ignore her. We all do." And honestly, at this point, a part of me wished her and Jack would get on it and just put me out of my misery. I mean, they shoot horses, don't they?

. . .

No one was hungry after a day of party food and birthday cake
and misery, so everyone made their own sandwiches. I made
one for Charlie—peanut butter and jelly, her favorite—with a
cup of hot chocolate and brought it upstairs, knocked on her
door.

"I don't like you anymore. Go away."

I bit the inside of my mouth, told her about the sandwich
and left it outside her room. She never ate it. In the kitchen,
someone had left the tub of vanilla ice cream on the counter.
Bronwyn, obviously, probably after she licked a spoon dipped in
it, which is the maximum amount she'll allow herself. I shoved
the tub back in the freezer and was about to close it when something caught my eye: a small white triangle of paper sticking out
between the frozen peas and an old store-bought cheesecake. I
tugged at it, unfolded it, smoothed it out against my thigh.

In large capital letters, the word, *MAMA*, had been
scrawled in blue sharpie, then crossed out with one single line
through it, and beneath that, in the same childish handwriting,
same blue sharpie, the word, *LAURA*.

———

But then, a miracle. Charlie comes downstairs to ask Bronwyn if
she could help with her math homework.

"What, now?" Bronwyn replies.

"Miss Lee says I have to practice divisions because I missed
the class," she says. Her tone has turned whiny. I peer around
the corner and through the gap in the door, I catch sight of
Bronwyn scrolling on her phone. She looks up at me and steps
back. "Charlotte, I'm busy. Ask Laura to do it."

Oh God. Yes, please. Thank you, Miss Lee.

By the time Charlie comes back to the kitchen, her steps
heavy, I'm loading the dishwasher. I make sure to look like I'm
completely absorbed in my task so that when she says, "I need

help with math homework," I jump, pretending I didn't hear her come in.

"Oh, do you?" I wipe my hands on a tea towel. "Okay, well, let's see what we can do."

She makes it clear she's not thrilled about the idea, but I don't care. She stomps upstairs with me behind her, then turns away from me, her arms crossed over her chest and sits at her desk and sulks.

"Where's your math book?"

"Why didn't you want me to keep Tallulah?"

Good, I think. Let's kick this pony right out of the park. I sit on the side of her bed. It would be so easy for me to tell her the truth, and I am so tempted I can taste the words forming in my mouth. *Tallulah was never yours, baby, it was just a joke Mommy played on me.*

"We don't have the room," I say. "Tallulah needs a big yard, lots and lots of space to run around." Her little chin wobbles but she nods, she gets it. She loves animals. She too wants Tallulah to have lots of room to roam. But still a tear escapes and rolls down the side of her nose. I hug her and tell her we can get a dog instead, which is something Jack and I had discussed except that I don't even know if Jack and I will be together much longer, but then I think screw it. Even if I'm not around, he can get a dog, surely. Bronwyn won't like it, so that's an extra bonus. And I know Charlie will love to look after it. She'll walk it, wash it, feed it. Jack won't have to do a thing.

"Really?" she says, face shiny with hope.

"Absolutely," I say. "Consider it done. You and I will get a dog next weekend. From the pound. A rescue dog. Don't call it Tallulah, though, that's all I ask."

She hugs me and my cup runneth over. We open the math book.

"I hate math," she says.

"You love math. You just don't know it yet."

We find a video featuring a bunch of angry cats that need to be separated into equal groups, so we use that for the basics. Then we buy enough pretend ice cream scoops for the whole class and divide them by the number of kids. We play magic tricks (think of a number, now divide by two, is it ten? No?) and I love her so much it's all I can do not to smother her. Then later, when it's time for bed, Bronwyn says she'll read her a story, and Charlie says can Laura do it, instead? And a rush of joy barrels through me, even with the tiny prick of disappointment at the use of my name, which is barely a toothpick's worth in the scheme of things. We read a chapter from *The Mysteries of the Universe*, then she tells me that Bronwyn doesn't always read stories, sometimes she looks at her phone and waits for her to go to sleep but she takes too long so she has to go.

"You can always insist that she read a story, you know. I'm sure she'd do it," I say, even though I'm sure of no such thing.

She shrugs, plays with a strand of my hair. "I don't care. I just like it when she's here."

"Oh, okay." Another little stab. More than a toothpick but less than a dagger. A sewing needle's worth. "So, what if Mommy came back to live with you and Daddy?" I blurt. "Would you like that?" And only then do I remember that there are times when asking a question you don't know the answer to, is about the dumbest thing you could possibly do.

"She already lives with me and Daddy."

"I mean, forever."

She looks up at me, eyes wide. "Mommy is going to live with you and me and Daddy forever?"

"Well, probably not with me," I say, my heart splintering. "There's not enough room for all of us, I'd be cramped in like Tallulah, so I would need to live somewhere else."

"Somewhere where there's more room?"

"Exactly."

"But you would still see us?"

Us. Many years ago, I used to cut myself and hearing her say "us" like that, excluding me from her "us" felt exactly like that, like something just sliced through my skin. Instant burn.

"I would like to, from time to time, come and visit." Whenever Bronwyn needed a free babysitter, most likely. "How would you feel about that?"

She shrugs. "Okay."

And something fragile and delicate inside me dies.

TWENTY-TWO

I go to bed early, anger zigzagging inside me. I wish Jack would take my side, I wish he'd see what Bronwyn is doing, undermining me at every opportunity. I long for him to come to bed and spoon me, tell me he loves me, we're getting married soon, she'll sign the divorce papers and she'll be on her way, and life will be better than ever.

But when he joins me, he falls heavily into bed, and I can smell the faint odor of Scotch on his breath, which I guess would explain why he's dead asleep the moment his head hits the pillow.

It used to be the other way around. I'd fall in deep slumber within minutes with Jack in bed next to me, and if I woke up, I'd find him gone. Sometimes I'd go downstairs to check and he'd be in his office, typing furiously at his computer. "Come back to bed," I'd say. He wouldn't look at me. He'd be hunched over, bleary-eyed, with only the light from the screen illuminating his face. "In a minute," he'd say, and I'd clock the bottle of scotch on the desk and know it would be a lot longer than a minute, but I wouldn't say anything. I'd go back upstairs and fall asleep again.

Jack starts snoring and I stare at the ceiling, remembering

Bronwyn's face when she said it. *He's kissing her, Laura. They've been making out all afternoon.* She wasn't even gloating. She was matter of fact almost, except when she said, *where the hell have you been?* She looked at me with disbelief mixed with pity. Like she couldn't understand how I'd been so oblivious. Had everyone else seen Jack and Summer together? Did they really kiss? Of course not. I tell myself that she misunderstood. Summer said nothing happened and Jack said they were playing hide and seek with the kids. I mean, sure, unlikely, when I think about it, Jack is not the kind of dad who'd kick a ball around the park with Charlie on a Sunday morning—God, she'd love that, maybe I should make it happen—but then again, it was her birthday party, he was making an effort to participate. A big effort. I think back to the moment Bronwyn brought out her cake, the sight of Jack and Bronwyn standing close together singing Happy Birthday to Charlie, Jack hamming it up in a loud tenor voice, Bronwyn... well, Bronwyn singing beautifully, obviously. Anyone would have thought they were a happily married couple gazing affectionately at their happy child at her eighth's birthday party, while I stood on the sidelines, sticking paper plates smeared with ketchup in a trash bag and picking modeling clay out of a little boy's left nostril.

So anyway, back to Jack and Summer, of course nothing untoward happened. Bronwyn's just jealous, which was the point of the exercise, so I don't know why I feel so bad. Maybe that's why she said it. *They've been making out all afternoon.* She *wants* me to feel bad. My thoughts race off in every direction like a bunch of feral cats and I think, wait. There's always an agenda with Bronwyn. She's trying to destabilize my relationship. If she really, really thought Jack and Summer were *making out,* she would have been upset about it. She wants me to believe it because she wants him for herself.

I hear a creak outside on the landing and immediately wonder if it's Charlie. I've bound myself in sheets tossing and turning and it takes a moment to free myself. I get out of bed without waking Jack, slip on my robe and go out to take a look.

Charlie is asleep, with her little moonlight on. I kiss her forehead, and on the way back to my room I notice Bronwyn's door is ajar. Her bedside lamp is on and her bed looks like it hasn't been slept in yet. The bathroom door is half open, dark, and I figure that it was her I heard earlier, and that she's gone out for a cigarette.

I haven't been in Bronwyn's room since she arrived and it is just as I would have expected. Pristine, neat, smelling of expensive perfume. Her bed is turned down, one corner opened diagonally like in a hotel and I wonder with a lurch whether her and Jack have made love in *that* bed while I've been at work, and I lift the corner of the sheet—white, one million deniers please, Egyptian cotton, organically grown and rinsed in filtered water—up to my face and smell it, but all I can detect is her perfume, and I flatten it back down the way it was. I glance at the dresser. It's covered with a million jars of cream and enough makeup to do the entire cast of *Cats*, all carefully arranged in rows, by type—beauty products on the left, makeup on the right—and size, with pencils laid down in a gold tray. The effect is not unlike a beauty display at a Bergdorf Goodman store. I open the top drawer of the dresser. She keeps her lingerie in there, but unlike my drawer, which looks like a grab bag of old cotton underwear from the local thrift store, hers is arranged in rows of matching panties and bras folded carefully together into neat little piles of delicate silk and lace, all unbelievably expensive no doubt and exquisitely feminine.

I'm not even thinking about what I'm doing it. I shove my hands in the drawer and rumple everything up into an entangled mess. Then suddenly I realize someone has opened—or closed—a door, and my ears prick up, trying to work out where it came from, and when I look back at what I've done, I panic. I try to put it all back the way it was, but there's a lot of black and a lot of red and it's hard to tell which panties go with which bra. My fingers touch something. A small Ziploc bag of blue pills. Where were they? I don't know. I push them at the back, keep folding her underwear into neat little piles, my heart hammering, and close the drawer.

As I turn to leave, I catch something out the window that makes me stop. A square of light illuminates the stone path, which means the light is on in my studio.

She's in there.

I'm annoyed now. It's twenty-five past one in the morning, and she has no right being there, in *my* studio. Ever since she got here, she has behaved like this is still her house, and she has silently recast me as the visitor. I wonder how long before she asks us to move out of our bedroom because it has a better aspect and a larger closet. I wonder what she's doing down there. Rearranging my art supplies? Moving the worktable back to where she had it before?

By now I'm heaving with anger. I walk down the stairs in my bare feet, find the door to my studio is wide open.

She has her back to me, standing in front of my worktable, dressed in a diaphanous lilac silk negligée, matching pointed-toe mules with a strip of soft feathers across the top.

I, on the other hand, am wearing my Terry-cloth robe which was white, once, and has a big orange stain on the front left pocket where Charlie dropped a felt pen that leaked for an hour before I noticed anything. I look down at my bare feet and wonder when I last had a pedicure. At this point I'm thinking it doesn't matter if she's in my workroom. I've got nothing to hide. I mean, sure, I wish I'd tidied up. I bet she kept it pristine when she lived here.

I quietly turn around to leave when she says, "Laura, who is Beth?"

I close my eyes briefly, my stomach twisting onto itself.

"Who?" I ask. I sound so fake even to my ears, I want to punch myself.

She turns around slowly. One of my cardboard storage boxes is on the table, the ones I store my paper and craft supplies in. I must have left it there after Charlie's party.

It's opened, and my heart feels like lead. When I look at her again, her face is white. She's holding something in her right hand, and it says something about how scared I am of her, deep down, that for a crazy moment I think it's a knife. But it's not. It's a small yellow notebook, the kind you buy in packs of five for a dollar from the corner store. This one is old, you can tell from the tattered corners and the fading cover.

"I don't know who you mean," I say.

"The woman who wrote love letters to my husband, remember her?"

She pushes a lock of hair from her forehead, fingertips brushing softly against powdery skin

"Did you know her? Is that why she borrowed your notepad?" She opens it to a page and shows it to me. Her hand is trembling. She looks like she's going to cry.

I put my fingers over my mouth as I stare at the page. I'd used the notebook to practice a different handwriting so Bronwyn wouldn't twig that it was me. I feel my cheeks burn as I stare at my own handwritten lines, mostly crossed out. They all say the same thing. *That was amazing today*. Over and over, in increasingly slanted script. At the bottom of the page I signed, *Beth x*, then I crossed it out, signed again, rinse, repeat. One kiss, two kisses, a practiced signature, each time with minor variations. I remember vividly when I slipped that final note in the pocket of Jack's jeans, the small one tucked against the right hip, knowing that it would be Bronwyn who would find it, because Bronwyn always went through Jack's pockets.

She looks slowly through other pages and I don't need to see them to remember what's on them. Shopping lists, canvas measurements. *Buy acrylic white!* And then more practice... *I love you,* crossed out, *I love you,* crossed out, *I love you. Beth xox.*

"Why are you going through my things?" I ask.

"I was looking for something to write on," she says, still glancing at the pages. "Who is she? Who is Beth?"

"Oh God. I'm sorry," I say softly.

"I don't understand."

I rub my forehead. I can feel my mouth pull down. My lips tremble when I speak again, in a whisper so low she has to lean in to catch it.

"It was me."

She jerks back, shakes her head over and over, her face clouded with confusion. "I don't understand, did you love him?"

"No! I mean... no, I swear, it had nothing to do with Jack, believe it or not." I rub my forehead again, I do it hard enough to hurt. "I feel so stupid. I'm so sorry, Bronwyn, let me explain." I glance behind me. "Can we go outside?"

"Why?"

Because I can't bear to look at you in this harsh light. You look so sad, so white, so confused. Because I'm ashamed. "Please?"

She gives me a small nod, carefully puts the notebook back in the box, and with slow, deliberate movements she puts the lid back on.

"I meant it as a joke," I say lamely.

She's sitting on Charlie's swing under the birch tree. Somewhere down the hill someone is having a party, but only the bass line makes it up here.

I walk barefoot on the cold grass and come to stand a few feet away from her. She doesn't look at me, just swings slowly, using one foot to push herself off the ground. "Careful with that," I say. "I don't know how solid it is for non-Charlie-sized people."

She looks up at me. I rub my forehead.

"Sorry. You probably know that already. You probably put it there." I lean against the back of the iron bench, facing her.

I'm cold, and my robe is heavier than hers, but while she's shaking, I don't think it's from the temperature. Her negligee—barely there—is open. Underneath she's wearing a pale silk nightgown. She pulls out a packet of Dunhill from a pocket, taps it out, lights a cigarette with a shaking finger.

"I don't understand," she says, pressing the heel of her hand on one eye, then the other. "Why would it be you? Did you *love* Jack? Back when he and I were still married? Was something going on between the two of you?"

"No! Oh God no, never, I swear! I was just..." She glances at me in the darkness, and I look away, trying to find the words to describe what the hell I was thinking when I did what I did, and I can't.

"I really need to understand, Laura."

"I know."

So I tell her the truth.

TWENTY-THREE

Why did I agree to paint Bronwyn's portrait? For the money, for sure, but as soon as I walked in, I knew I'd made a mistake. She had the perfect life, the perfect house, the perfect marriage. There are people who go through life behaving badly with no consequences, and she was one of them. She was lucky. I was never lucky, or I didn't think I was, back then. I always felt like I had to fight for my luck. Like life was one big hunger game.

At first, she behaved like we were old friends who had lost touch and how nice that we were catching up after all these years, and did I ever find out what happened to so and so? And so and so? And remember so and so? I had no memory who any of these people were. I'd spent that year with my head down, trying to make myself as small and invisible as possible. I didn't want to talk about the past, I just wanted to do the job, take my money and go.

Amazingly, I'd forgotten how insecure Bronwyn could be, under those layers of cool confidence. Which was odd, considering it was that same insecurity—although back then I thought of it as her sense of superiority, and after that her complete and total narcissistic personality—that had caused me so much grief all these years ago. Jack and I barely spoke back then, just polite interactions upon the stairs. Some days he would come home and she'd ask questions that made me blush for her. Where had he been? Who had he seen? And Jack would say something completely ordinary. He'd been at his office, at the gym, playing squash. Then one day she told me she had to fire the babysitter because she thought—and this she confided in me—that the young woman was sleeping with Jack and I thought, my God, you really are paranoid. I would have bet my bottom dollar the babysitter had done no such thing. Her only crime was to be younger and available.

I suppose sitting here now, my toes curling in the grass, I have to admit to myself that maybe I did hate her. I always say that I didn't, and that I don't, and that whatever goes on between her and Jack is between her and Jack, and our history is a bleep in the scheme of things, but in the cold dark of night, having to own up on what I did, I can't explain it, even to myself.

I thought I was being funny. Throwing a little spanner into her perfect life.

It was born more out of opportunity than malice. One day I used their ensuite bathroom because the guest one was blocked and Jack's suit jacket was laid out on the bed. I had my purse with me and for my own amusement I sprayed a little of my perfume on the inside of the collar. It was just a little prank, but when I returned the next day, I could tell Bronwyn had been crying. On the surface she posed the way she usually did, but every time there was a noise outside, her eyes would dart to the window, like a Labrador waiting for its beloved master. Finally, she blurted, "I think Jack is having an affair." Then she asked me what I thought she should do, if she should confront him. That was Bronwyn in a nutshell. She just assumed I'd be invested in her problems, maybe even make them my problems too and wrack my brain for a solution. But meanwhile, I'd found her Achilles heel and I was going to have some fun. I started leaving little clues, a trace of lipstick on his shirt collar, a little love note in his pocket, which I practiced in my little yellow notepad. I thought it was hilarious. Then Bronwyn would confide her fears in me and I couldn't get enough of it. She'd ask me, who the hell is Beth? And I'd say, someone at work maybe? And she'd say, what do you think she looks like? And I'd shrug and say, well, Jack is drop-dead handsome and he has very discerning tastes, so I imagine she's a knockout, and she'd look like she was in pain and nod, yes, yes, she must be a knockout, Jack only goes for knockouts, thereby giving herself a little boost. She did confront him and she'd tell me Jack was swearing to her till he was blue in the face that he had no idea who Beth was, and I'd say, well clearly he's lying. Are you going to let him take you for a fool?

And then, suddenly, and it really seemed very sudden, barely a month later, she moved out. I found out when I returned to the house to pick up some brushes I'd left behind. Jack was alone, red-eyed from tears and lack of sleep. He told me that Bronwyn had left him, accusing him of fucking other women and she couldn't deal with it any longer. My guess was that her ego couldn't handle it. She'd found someone else to seduce. Someone richer, an Italian millionaire surgeon, so that in the end she could say, "No, Jack didn't have an affair! He worshipped me! But we'd drifted apart. I met someone else. He was devastated of course but what can you do? Life is about love, and you have to follow your heart wherever it takes you."

I was thrilled, I won't lie. I'd broken her perfect life, and I wasn't even trying. Then Jack said she didn't even want Charlie. She'd left her behind, and I was shocked. Only then I felt guilty about what I'd done. I didn't think it was entirely my fault because whoever walks out on their family on the basis of a torn page from a cheap notepad has something else going on, but I wondered if I'd triggered it in her.

"A joke?" she says now, incredulous. "At my expense? At my family's expense?"

I don't know how to answer her because really, from this vantage point, there's nothing I can find to excuse what I did. I bring the sides of my robe closer together. "I thought you'd figure out it was me, and by then I'd be gone. I didn't think you'd act on it. I didn't think you'd leave your family because of it."

I say this last part with a dash of hope that she'd agree it's her who's the problem in all this. I may have been the catalyst, but I didn't pull the trigger because let's face it, I'm terrified right now. I don't know what she will do, or what she will say, and I want to punch myself for leaving that old notebook lying around. I should have put it in the trash back then.

"But why would you do that to me?"

"Why?" Memories of childhood humiliation flood through me. "I was angry with you, Bronwyn. For what you put me through at school. Oh God, come on! Please don't say you don't remember!"

At least I'm on firmer ground now. I have moved seamlessly from villain to victim. I remind her, in excruciating detail, of what she put me through. "Because of a *boy*!" I am fourteen years old again as I stress the word; he was just a *boy*, you were supposed to be my *friend*. "I spent an entire school year being ostracized, laughed at, sneered at, called names, older boys would leave dirty condoms in my schoolbag. No one would sit with me at lunch or hang out with me at recess. I spent a year being humiliated because of you."

"Jesus, Laura! Are you for real? You invented Beth as revenge? Because of some stupid thing I said about you when we were in junior high?"

I give a small, bitter laugh. "It was a bit more than a stupid thing, Bronwyn. And it was a really bad time for me. With my mother and all that..."

Her expression softens. "I know. I mean I know that now. I was just a kid, Laura, so were you. We were kids. I messed up, I started the rumor, yes, I own that, but they went off outside of my control."

"Oh come on," I scoff. "It was you, the whole time."

"No, it wasn't, Laura! I felt horrible about how bad things got, but it wasn't me. It was probably made to look like it was me, but it wasn't. I tried to talk to you about it once, about what we could do and you pushed me away, remember? You shouted at me never to speak to you again, remember? I still tried to stop them, believe it or not. I asked my mother to speak to the principal—"

"You did?"

"Yes, but she didn't take it seriously. She didn't care. I didn't know what to do." She smooths her hair. "It's no excuse. I messed up. I know that, but you know, I had my own problems back then. My parents were never there, they always seem to want to spend time away from me."

I nod. "I remember."

"Nothing like what happened to you, of course. I'm just trying to explain I wasn't as confident as I might have seemed back then."

It feels surreal to be having this conversation in such a grown-up, measured tone. I feel a wave of shame that I'm still stuck in the past, still fourteen and sad and miserable while the world has moved on.

"I get it," I say, trying really hard to get it. "I can see how confusing that must have been for you."

She shrugs. "It was a long time ago. The world moves on."

Except me, apparently. "How are they, by the way? Your parents?"

"My mother's still kicking, my dad died."

"Oh God. I'm so sorry. What happened?"

"He died in a car crash, years ago, long before you and I met up again."

"Oh, I didn't know."

We sit quietly for a moment. "I still miss him, you know? It's funny, isn't it? At my age? We were close, my father and I, as you know."

Were they? I have no memory of that. But then, I have very little memory of anything that happened in that year. "I don't think it's strange. I still miss my mother after all these years." Except I don't. It's hard to miss someone who didn't want you in the first place, although Charlie missed Bronwyn, so maybe that's just me.

I'm considering going back to bed when she says, "I didn't expect the rumors to take off like that. I didn't realize the damage it did to you or that you were still hurting all those years later—"

"I'm not!"

"I'm truly sorry, Laura. I mean that."

I nod, and suddenly I feel like crying. I rub a knuckle on my eye, as if to relieve an itch. "Yeah, well, as you said, we were kids."

"But you're right. Your mother had just died. You needed friends, not stupid bitches like me saying stupid things because I had a crush on some boy in eighth grade."

I chuckle at her self-description but she is dead serious and I rub my eye again.

"They're pretty formative years, I guess."

She drops her cigarette on the ground, grinds it with her toe. I wince. "I'll get you an ashtray," I say, pushing myself off the bench.

"Don't bother, I'll clean it up later." And I'm thinking, not likely, but okay. I lean back against the bench again.

"When I saw you again at the opening, I don't know... I felt sad we'd fallen out all these years ago. I thought it would be nice to reconnect. That's why I commissioned the painting."

I blink. "You didn't commission the painting. Jack did."

"I asked Jack to do it because I thought if I asked, you would turn me down."

"Really? But Jack tracked me down because I never called him!"

"*I* tracked you down, Laura. Also, I thought you could use the money, don't bite me but you looked like you could."

"Did I? Oh well, you know me, the eternal student."

She smiles. "And I thought we could be friends again."

"Really?"

She waves her hand. "Water under the bridge, as they say."

And I try to think back, and wonder how I could have got it so wrong. "I'm sorry for what I did," I say finally. "For being stupid Beth. That was unforgivable."

She shakes her head. "You really thought I left my family because of some mythical woman called Beth no one had ever seen?"

"Well..." I make a face. "Yes, that's exactly what I think."

She shakes her head again. "I left because this Beth happened on the back of what Jack did... with that girl. I'd had enough, Laura, I couldn't deal with his infidelities anymore. If it wasn't Beth, there would have been another one, I guarantee it."

I frown. "What girl? What did they do?"

She sighs. "We had a babysitter."

"I remember that. What happened?"

"Oh, you know, the usual sordid mess. I fired her when I found out she'd been fucking my husband behind my back."

"Oh no! I thought..." I was going to say, *I thought it was you, being paranoid, the way you were back then.* "No," I say firmly. "Jack wouldn't do that."

She looks at me under hooded eyes. "How long have you known Jack, Laura?"

I don't reply. "So did you know for a fact they were... having a thing?"

"Yes."

"How did you find out?"

"She told me. She said they were in love. I confronted him, he cried and begged for forgiveness, said it had meant nothing, she had seduced him. The usual... crap."

I can't believe what I'm hearing. She pulls out another cigarette. "Can I have one?" I ask. She puts the cigarette in her mouth and lights it, and I'm thinking that no, I guess I can't have one, but then she hands it to me. I remember with a pang that's what we used to do, back in high school. She'd steal her mother's menthols and we'd smoke them on our way home, and she'd often light mine, just like that.

"Thanks," I say.

She lights a second one for herself. "She was crazy. After I fired her, she'd send me the most vile emails."

"Like what?"

She blows out a plume of smoke. "Calling me names, telling me I was a cold bitch, that Jack hated me, that one day he would leave me and I'd die alone and miserable."

"Jesus!"

"I know. It was kind of scary. I blocked her email and I never heard from her after that." She shudders. "She was nasty. A nasty piece of work. So he never told you about Jenny?"

"No, I mean, why would he? That was before my time..." I resist the urge to bite a fingernail or rub my forehead. The truth is, I'm shocked. I never believed Jack had been unfaithful to Bronwyn, and part of me wishes he'd confessed that to me.

"Not that long before your time," she says.

I shrug again. "It had nothing to do with me. We don't talk about the past." As if.

"Well, he does like to keep secrets. He didn't tell me about you either, until recently."

"Yes, you said that. It's not the same thing, Bronwyn."

"No, I know that."

There's a pause, then I ask, "Do you mind? About me and Jack?"

"God no." She takes a drag of her cigarette, lets out a plume of smoke. "He's all yours, sweetie."

I let out a sigh of relief. And then, out of the blue, I ask, "When are you going back to Italy, truly?"

"I'm not."

"What do you mean?"

"Leon and I have separated."

My stomach does a little twist. "I'm sorry to hear that. I didn't know. Are you okay?"

She looks at me. "Not really, but I will be. I'm just sad, Laura, that's all."

"Can I ask what happened?"

She takes a breath. "Distance, mostly. Italy is a long way. I missed my little girl."

"Oh! Really?"

"Yes! Why so surprised? Oh wait, I have the maternal instincts of a brick."

"God, I'm sorry." I drag my hands down my face. "I was in a bad mood that day." She doesn't say anything. Just looks away. "The truth is, Bronwyn, I was under the impression..."

"That I didn't care? That I didn't want her?"

"No, no," I rush to say, thinking, *yes, yes, exactly that.*

"I missed her every day, Laura. But Leon... he was very possessive. He didn't like me talking on the phone to her. He certainly didn't like me coming over for a visit, unless it was with him. There's no way he would have let me stay here, in this house. I thought of bringing her over to live with me, but you know, a foreign country, the language..."

I am floored by what I'm hearing. "I am so sorry. I had no

idea." There's a question burning on my tongue, I wait a beat for good measure before asking it. "So where will you go?"

"I'm moving back to Seattle."

"Really?"

"Well yes, that's the whole point."

"Right, of course, makes sense." And I'm thinking, are you going to live here until you find a place? How long will that take? But I don't ask. I don't think I want to know.

We finish our cigarettes, Bronwyn says she's going back to bed.

"Yes, me too." I crouch down, pick up the butts, hold them in the palm of my hand. "Can I ask you..."

I stand up again. "Can you not say anything to Jack? About Beth?"

She tilts her head at me. "He doesn't know?"

"I haven't told him," I say. "I mean, it hasn't come up."

She shrugs. "Sure, whatever."

"Thank you."

I turn around and go back inside, put the cigarette butts in the trash, wash my hands. She touches my shoulder. "Let's put it all behind us, Laura, high school, all of it, okay?"

"Yes, I'd like that. And also... I'm sorry about the pony." I turn around, lean against the sink. "I really overreacted, didn't I."

"It was quite dramatic, yes."

"God, I feel so bad. Poor Charlie."

"She'll be fine. Anyway, I should have asked you if it was okay before hiring the pony. We're both to blame."

I tilt my head at her. "Thanks, Bronwyn." And at this point, I couldn't have felt any worse.

TWENTY-FOUR

I'm cold, shaky and lightheaded when I go back upstairs. I brush my teeth, rinse the taste of tobacco out of my mouth, slip into bed next to Jack.

Who is Beth, Laura?

I curl on my side. I feel so ashamed, I bring my knees closer to my chin and wonder where I could find a hole to crawl into and die. When Bronwyn held up the notebook, I saw myself back then. I thought I was funny, when in fact I was petty and vindictive, ungrateful. Then I think about how I reacted about the pony and it's hard not to think I'm the one shadow boxing through my life, looking for a fight where there isn't one, misinterpreting every gesture, every kindness and I wonder what else did I get wrong?

When I was fourteen years old, I came home from school one day to find my mother had died. She had jumped early that morning off the Snohomish River Bridge, although officially, the cause of death was accidental death. She had fallen, they said. Which I knew, and my father knew, and most people knew wasn't the case because she'd been seen climbing up the trusses alongside the east sidewalk of the bridge. She'd picked the highest spot to jump from. She didn't want to take any chances.

After the funeral my dad asked me to pack her things so we could take them to the goodwill store. He didn't want to see them. So I did. I went through her things, and I found most of them already gone. In the bottom of the closet, I found a suitcase I didn't remember. It was already packed with her best clothes, a pretty nightgown I'd never seen before, the little bit of jewelry she owned. I stared at the suitcase for a long time. It whispered that she was leaving us. It gaped at me with its contents neatly and lovingly folded, like a reproach. We weren't good enough anymore. I asked my dad later if she'd been planning a trip and he looked at me like I'd sprouted horns.

"Your mother? Going on a trip? Where the hell would she go?"

I remembered the phone ringing early that morning, I was still in bed, but I was awake, then the sound of the front door closing, the car starting. After I found the packed suitcase, I wondered if she had intended to leave with a man, if the pretty nightgown was for him. I wondered if he had called that morning to say he had changed his mind. Or maybe he had called to say he hadn't changed his mind, but she couldn't do it.

In the end it didn't matter what I thought. She left us anyway.

I shoved the rest of her things in black bin liners and we drove to the goodwill store downtown with all of it, suitcases included. I made sure nothing was left behind. Nothing at all.

Everything changed after that, in all the obvious ways, but in other ways, too. My father, who had been a brute, a loud, angry man who would smash his fist through doors and bellow every time my mother expressed an opinion, retreated into a kind of catatonic silence. I'd never been allowed to go anywhere, and suddenly I had more freedom than I knew what to do with. It was as if I was suddenly living alone.

Bronwyn and I were in the same class, but we didn't know each other very well, until I went back to school two days after the funeral. That's what we did back then. Emotions were for sissies. Everyone already knew, obviously, because bad news travels fast. Bronwyn was the first to come and hug me, that first morning in the school yard and I cried on her shoulder. She stayed by my side all day, holding my hand, patting my hair. Later, I thought she was just enjoying the drama but at the time I was just grateful someone cared. She was lovely to me, those first few weeks. We became best friends, I got less sad, we'd go to each other's house, sometimes she'd even lend me one of her bicycles—she had two—and we'd ride to the river and lay down on the grass and look at the sky and dream of what we'd do when we grew up, which invariably involved marriage, children, and volunteering for charities.

There was an older boy she liked, called Jimmy, who she thought could be husband material because his father worked in a bank. When Bronwyn's parents went away for the weekend, to their house on Orcas island—which is something they used to do all the time, go away without her —Bronwyn announced she'd have a party. I asked her why she didn't go with her parents and she just shrugged, said it was boring, she didn't like it. I found out much later that her parents treated these weekends away as *adult time* and said it was best if she didn't come along. Which to be fair, explained a hell of a lot about her. She invited half a dozen of our classmates and asked me to deliver Jimmy's invitation, because she didn't want to look too eager. So I did.

Bronwyn's house was amazing, huge, with all the latest mod-cons, and her room was like nothing I'd ever seen before. It was palatial and pink and soft, with enormous egg-shaped cushions you could disappear into and a four-poster bed with pink taffeta curtains all the way around. Before the guests arrived, she and I went downstairs and mixed whatever alcohol her parents kept in their living room bar into a silver bucket and called it punch. We brought it up to her room with tumblers and cups and an ice bucket, the other kids came, including Jimmy. She served him tumblers of punch and smoked her mother's cigarettes that she'd get him to light for her, take a puff and pass it over to him like it was a joint.

We played music, danced, Jimmy hung back on the edge of the party. I thought he was going to leave, and maybe she did too because she turned the music off, clapped her hands and declared we would play spin the bottle, but with a twist. If the bottle pointed to you, you got to say who you wanted to kiss. We sat cross-legged in a circle, and Bronwyn was the first to spin the bottle which wasn't really a spin, more a gentle twist until it pointed directly at Jimmy.

"Oh my God!" she shrieked. "Well? Who is it going to be, Jimmy?" She smiled shyly.

I was looking at her, so I didn't realize what was happening until it was too late. But suddenly Jimmy had tilted forward on his knees and was kissing me full on the mouth.

I gasped when he let go. There was a second of stunned silence, then Bronwyn burst into laughter. "Oh my God! That's so sweet!"

"No way," I said, wiping my mouth with the back of my hand, feeling my face burn. For a moment, I thought it was a joke at my expense, but Jimmy kept looking at me and then he said, "Will you go out with me, Laura?"

"Well!" Bronwyn said, clapping once. "I think that's the sweetest thing I've heard all day. Good for you, Laura."

"No, I didn't know... really."

"Of course not. Jimmy, I think that's so sweet that I got to bring the two of you love birds together. Would you like to sit on the couch with Laura?"

"Cut it out," I muttered.

"No! Why? You two make such a cute couple!"

Jimmy must have sensed something because he picked up his leather jacket, planted a kiss on my cheek and said, "See you Monday." Then Bronwyn put music on really loud and we all had to dance, and she laughed and danced like she was having the time of her life. At five pm, parents came to pick up their kids. I was supposed to stay over, but the moment we were alone she turned on me. Accused me of planning this whole thing, of humiliating her, calling me a slut, screaming she was embarrassed to be my friend, and then she told me to get out of her house, and I walked the two miles to my house in the rain.

That Monday I went to sit next to Bronwyn, the way I always did. I even brought a Dove chocolate bar which I put on the desk in front of her. She looked at it, curled her lip, and said, "That'll make you fat. But you're already fat, so you have it." She flicked it across the desk and it fell to the floor. I picked it up and when I went to sit down again, she'd put her books on my chair, then very loudly, she said, "Please sit somewhere else, Laura. My parents have told me I can't be your friend anymore. They don't want me to be friends with a prostitute."

A ripple of giggles went through the class, and I felt my cheeks burn. I sat at an empty desk at the back of the room, holding back tears. Pretty soon the rumor spread that I was a prostitute and for five bucks I'd show my tits behind the toilet block. The moment that rumor died down, another one would emerge. Days later it became that I was involved in orgies because I was addicted to sex. I came to school one day to find graffiti on the side of the toilet block that screamed, *LAURA IS A SLUT!* Sheets of paper were sticky-taped to the windows of the canteen with my phone number. *Call 555-7867 and Laura will suck your dick for free!* Although those were taken down quickly by the staff and I only got a couple of phone calls that consisted of heavy breathing before hanging up abruptly.

And still, as horrible as it was, it was still the fact that Bronwyn had changed from being my friend, someone I trusted, someone I loved even, to my arch enemy in the blink of an eye that hurt the most.

Eventually she must have tired of the games because gradually the bombardment eased, until it disappeared altogether. Then the following year her family moved away, and I never saw her again, except briefly in college where I avoided her like kryptonite, and then years later, that day in Bellevue, three years ago.

I lived with the memory of her being cruel and vindictive, and now I'm finding out she may have started the stupid rumors, but she wasn't responsible for the worst of it. Do I believe her? I'd completely forgotten that moment when she tried to talk to me, but it comes back to me now in vivid detail. She tried to take my hand, she wanted to sit with me, and I screamed at her and ran off.

Maybe it was just a stupid mistake she made, that got amplified by other kids, because let's face it, in terms of gossip, it was pretty titillating. I lie there, staring at the ceiling, contemplating the massive mistake I've made, when all these years I held a grudge so deep it caused me to do terrible things to a woman who did not deserve it, to the point that I am partly responsible for the demise of her marriage.

If I could hate myself any more, I think I'd die.

TWENTY-FIVE

I have a lunch date with Katie today, and I can't wait. I am dying to tell her about what Bronwyn said last night, about breaking up with Leon and moving back to town. I'm not dying to tell her about anything else that transpired last night. That should go without saying.

Summer brings me a cup of coffee, just the way I like it. She asks if I'm okay. I tell her yes, thank you. She looks unconvinced. Unsurprisingly, I think. I saw myself in the reflection of the microwave door earlier and I looked both disheveled and exhausted, although the disheveled part is only because it's humid today, and that's what my hair does. It frizzes. The exhausted part, however, is obviously because I didn't sleep much. It's starting to mess with my brain, this lack of sleep. I read somewhere you can bank sleep, store it up like camels store fat tissue in their hump so that when food is scarce, they can draw on those savings. I like that word, *bank*. It conjures up retaining walls, protective borders of earth, a cushioning. Safety. I don't think I've banked anything lately, except for my own stupidity. I've banked enough of that for a lifetime.

I keep replaying our conversation, analyzing it beat by beat.

I go back to the moment when she said, "We were kids, I messed up, I didn't expect the rumors to take off like that. I didn't realize the damage it did to you. Your mother had just died. You needed friends, not stupid bitches like me." It was like something dense and heavy was excised from inside me. Add to that my own confession about Beth, and the fact that she didn't punch me in the face, and this morning I have moments when I could almost laugh out loud. It helps soften the blow I felt about Jack and the babysitter, because let's face it, I'd never seen Jack as the wandering-eye type. When I first saw Jack and Bronwyn together, I genuinely thought they had the perfect marriage. Tight, shiny, smooth on the surface. A Botoxed marriage. Later, I understood that underneath it was wrinkled by Bronwyn's pathological insecurities. Zero trust, paranoia disguised as love. Except these insecurities had roots in reality.

Anyway, I tell myself she means nothing to me, Jenny the babysitter. I can only vaguely remember what she looked like. Fair hair, early to mid-twenties, sweet-looking.

Not unlike Summer, come to think of it.

"Are we okay?" Summer asks.

I look up abruptly. For a moment I'd forgotten she was still there.

"Sure, why?"

"You were annoyed with me, when I left. About Jack."

I think about it for a moment. "Did something happen?"

"What do you mean?"

"You didn't actually kiss him, did you?"

"No!" Then, with a pout, she adds, "not really."

Not really?

"It wasn't a real kiss, barely a brush of the lips against his cheek."

She says this while chewing on a fingernail, leaning against the doorjamb, her brow furrowed with worry. She looks so young, and again it occurs to me I need my head examined.

What the hell am I doing? Throwing this young woman at Jack? Asking her to flirt with my fiancé, the more the better, make it convincing, there'll be a hundred bucks in it for you.

"I don't understand," she whines. "I thought I was doing what you wanted me to do."

I rub my forehead. "Yes. I know. You're right. I should never have asked you to do such a thing. It's completely my fault. I apologize about that."

She sighs. "Okay... I really thought I was helping."

"I know."

"So we're good?" she asks.

"Yes, of course. We're good. Thanks, Summer."

"Good," she says with what looks like genuine relief. Then she adds, "You know, I don't think you need to worry about Bronwyn. For what it's worth."

"What do you mean?"

"I talked to her at the party. She said I was lucky to have you as a boss. Which I am." She half smiles. "She said you were a really good person, and it was nice to be back with her extended family."

"Oh really? She said that? Who's the extended part? Did she say? Am I the extended part?" I gnaw on a cuticle. She frowns at me.

"Just kidding," I say, even though I wasn't. I make a mental note to discuss this with Katie at lunch.

"Anyway, she said it was nice to see how happy Charlie was."

I have a headache. I press my fingers against my temple. "Was that before or after I kicked the pony?"

She gives me a sad smile. "You look tired. Can I get you anything?"

"No, thanks, Summer." I tell her again that everything is fine and I'm sorry I even asked her to flirt with Jack. I'm embarrassed, I don't know what's wrong with me that makes me come up with these harebrained ideas. I don't say that last part out loud. I just want her to go away, leave me to my tortured thoughts. I tell her I know she meant no harm, it's completely my fault. Which it is, obviously.

I ask her to call the freight companies and get quotes for sending the exhibition to each venue on the tour because that will take hours and I desperately want to be left alone right now.

TWENTY-SIX

I meet Katie at a café on Occidental Avenue. We sit by the window, order cheese omelets.

"You look tired," she says. "You okay?"

"Absolutely fine," I say, filling our glasses with water from the pitcher. "You look great, by the way." Which she does. She's had her hair done in a bob, with a short fringe. "I love the new hair. It suits you."

"Thanks!"

We talk about the twins, about Charlie, and finally I blurt, "I have a question for you."

"Yep, what is it?"

"You talked to Bronwyn quite a bit at Charlie's party. What did you think of her?"

Katie butters a piece of bread. "I'll be honest with you."

"I expect nothing less," I say.

"She was nothing like what you described."

"Oh?"

"Actually, I thought she was really nice."

I chuckle. "Oh right, well, there you go. Join the Bronwyn

appreciation club. I understand it's a bit of a lovefest. What did you talk about? Did she say anything about me?"

"We talked about Roman art, actually."

It's the second *actually* she's said so far, and I have to say, I'm not crazy about it. It makes her sound like she's jumped over the fence to the other side. I too was in the process of jumping the fence, although more like lifting one leg over it and waiting to see what it felt like.

"She knows a lot about the museums there, it was fascinating," she continues.

"Does she? I didn't know that."

"From what you've said, I expected her to be really cold, unfriendly, but she was the opposite."

"Yeah, well, I may have exaggerated in places."

She looks up. "Now that's a departure, coming from you."

"I know. I hate to say, but I'm warming to her."

"You're kidding! Oh wow, Laura, what happened to you?"

I point my knife at her. "I said warming. I didn't say I love her."

She laughs.

"Did she tell you she's split up with Leon and she's back for good?"

"No way!"

"Yes, way." I fill her in.

"So she's back for good? That's amazing. How do you feel about that?"

"No idea, I'm still processing."

"Coming from you, that's progress."

"Thank you." I push my fork down on my omelet like it's potato mash.

Katie tilts her head at me. "What is it?"

"I'm nervous about her moving back," I say with a sigh.

"In what way?"

I raise an eyebrow at her. I mean, it's not like we haven't had ongoing conversations about Bronwyn in the last few weeks. But her expression is serious, and I think about it for a moment. "She said the other day she was staying a few weeks, at least."

"You told me, I remember."

"You don't think she'd want to get back with Jack, do you? I mean, she hasn't said anything about that to you, has she?"

"Laura! You don't think I'd tell you if she had?"

"Yes yes. Of course. Sorry. I'm just... sleep deprived. It was a long night. So she didn't say anything about Jack?"

She gives a small shrug.

"Okay, what? Tell me."

"We talked briefly about our work—"

"I don't think she works," I blurt.

Katie glances at me. "She talked about her interior design practice. I told her I was a psychologist, and she asked me if I thought Jack was depressed."

"Really?"

She nods. "Do you think Jack is depressed?" she asks.

"No! But this is her pet project at the moment! She asked me the same thing! I suspect she's asking everyone!" I drop my fork on my plate, rub my face.

"She didn't mention you at all, Laura. I really think it was a genuine question."

"So what did you tell her?" I pour more water in our tumblers. Some of it sloshes over the rim and onto the table. I ignore it.

"That I hadn't seen much of Jack at all lately, but when I had seen him, I thought he seemed reserved, yes, but he could have had a lot on his mind."

"Exactly!" I say. "He's been looking for work for a year now, he's very stressed. Very stressed. We all are. So obviously, he's not at his best. But that doesn't mean he's depressed. That's just the kind of thing she'd say, to make me look bad."

She tilts her head at me. "I thought you were warming to her?"

"I am. It's just a slow burn," I say.

She smiles. "So if she's moving back, what does that mean for Charlie?"

"What do you mean?" I take a gulp of water

"Did she talk about custody arrangements? What her intentions are? Would she have Charlie half the time?"

I stop, the rim of my glass knocks against my teeth. I can't believe I didn't think of that. In my mind she'd live in another house, in another suburb, preferably miles away, and maybe come and visit Charlie every second weekend.

Katie catches the shock on my face. "But that would be good, right? For Charlie's sake?"

"Actually no," I say, putting my glass back down. "Not shared custody, not like fifty-fifty. I do not think that would be good."

"Why not?"

"Because she doesn't even know her. She thinks that Charlie should be a little doll with curly hair and pink dresses and frilly socks. Charlie is nothing like that! That's not what she's like!"

I must have shouted because Katie is staring at me, a shocked look on her face. She puts her fork down and takes my hand.

"Sorry," I mumble. "It's just that I miss Charlie. I live in the same house, but I miss her because Bronwyn monopolizes her all the time. I'm never alone with her anymore."

"Which indicates that she most likely will want to have Charlie half the time, if she's back in town," she says gently. "You have to be ready for that. And you of all people should agree it's a good thing. You know how difficult it was for you to grow up without a mother. You've said this since the beginning that Charlie needs her mother."

I did say that. Now I wish I hadn't. The back of my eyes sting. I disengage my hand from hers and wipe the corners of my eyes with my napkin.

"It's good, right?" Katie says. "It's good that Bronwyn wants to get involved with Charlie."

"You've asked me this five times now. If I say yes, you'll let me go?" I snap. She gives a small chuckle. I sigh, nod, pretend to agree with her, but my mind is going off on its own ride. My head fills with images of Charlie in a tutu going to some eye-waveringly expensive ballet school, Charlie at a beauty pageant with little frilly white socks and a tiara on her head, would she have a bedroom at Bronwyn's house? Of course she would. I can see it now, lots of pink cushions on a pink bedspread. I'm going to be sick.

"Of course it's good." I put my fork down. "I should go back to work."

The atmosphere is strained between us as we leave our table, and I know it's coming from me, but I can't help it. I resent Katie for taking Bronwyn's side, *actually*. I may be warming to her, but I'm not ready to surrender my perfect family over, even if it's part-time. Katie keeps saying it's fine, it's good, it's a good thing, so why do I feel like I'm losing my grip on them? Why do I feel like they're both slipping away from me?

While we wait to pay at the counter, Katie puts an arm around my shoulders. "You know what you need? You need a hot date with Jack. You've got a free babysitter at home, you should take advantage of that. Why don't you get yourself a new dress and book a nice restaurant?"

I nod, thawing.

"And why don't you pick up Charlie from school this after-noon? Spend some time with her, just the two of you. I'm sure Bronwyn won't mind."

"I'm sure of no such thing." I half laugh. "But yes, you're right. I'll do that. I'll get her number off Jack later and give her a call, ask if it's okay. No, I'll just tell her, that's what I'll do. We had a good chat last night. You're right. I'm sure she won't mind."

"I've got her number," Katie says, opening her bag.

I tilt my head at her. "You're kidding."

She pulls out her cell. "She gave it to me at Charlie's party. She's going to send me photos of the Alberici museum restoration project. It sounds amazing."

"Oh right, that's nice. You two really did hit it off. Ever heard of the internet? You could have looked it up, your amazing—" I make air quotes around the word, "—restoration project whatever. But I guess it's not the same as being in the amazing Bronwyn love circle, is it?" I cock my head at her.

She clicks her tongue. She looks hurt.

"Sorry," I say, but I don't mean it. My phone pings.

"I sent you her number," she says. I'm sure I'm imagining the note of irritation in her tone. Not.

"It's weird, I won't lie, that you're giving me Jack's ex-wife's phone number, but here we are."

She tilts her head, looks at me like I'm being unreasonable. "Go home, have a bath, pick up Charlie from school, plan a hot date with Jack."

"Sure, that sounds heavenly, as long as I'm allowed within touching distance of either of them, that should work." I'm snapping at her, even though it's obviously not her fault, but I just can't help it.

When it's our turn, Katie takes the bill. I put my hand on hers. "I'll get this."

"You're sure?"

"Yes, of course. Sorry I'm in such a foul mood." I reach into my bag for my wallet, I can't find it. I open it wide, check the pockets. No wallet.

"Great." I roll my eyes. "Sorry, Katie, I left my wallet at home. Do you mind getting this? I'll pay you back."

"Don't be silly," she says, reaching for her own wallet. Is she holding back a sigh? Am I imagining it?

"No, really, I will!" I say. "I wanted to."

"Just don't worry about it, Laura."

"Okay, thanks," I say, feeling like a child. And a complete idiot.

TWENTY-SEVEN

As soon as I return to the gallery, I ask Summer if she would mind if I left early. She doesn't mind. I text Bronwyn.

Leaving work early, thought I'd pick up Charlie?

Then I add, *Quiet day here.*

Which is a lie, but I'm still at the stage where I anticipate pushback.

She calls immediately. I am so surprised I stare at the screen, biting on a knuckle. I don't want to pick up. I'll pretend I'm busy. I'll text again, sorry I missed your call, I'll say. Then I tell myself to cut it out and I pick up.

"Hi!"

"I think that's a lovely idea," she says. "You haven't spent much time with her lately. I'm sure she'd love for you to pick her up."

And there is so much wrong with that sentence I don't know where to start, but I'm dying to. The words are already forming in my mouth, petty and resentful, itching to get out. *I don't spend much time with her because you won't let me, so I don't know why you make it sound like it's my fault. Also, please don't say things like 'I'm sure she'd love...' you don't know what she'd love. You don't know her like I do. Also, what are your plans regarding custody?* But then I think, for Christ's sake, Laura. You're warming to her, remember?

"Great!" I chirp.

"So if you do that, I think I'll go shopping this afternoon," she says.

"Great!" I say again.

Then she says, "Listen, I'm so glad we talked last night, Laura. I think we both understand each other a lot better now. I feel like we've cleared the air."

"Couldn't agree more," I say. "The air feels positively alpine from here." She laughs. It's a nice laugh, it reminds me of when we were friends, back in the dark ages when we laughed together. Surprisingly, it makes me want to hear it again.

I tell her I might take Charlie to the park on the way home. Good idea, she says. Charlie needs to run around in all that clear air we've just created, and I laugh too, feeling like we've crossed into a new dimension. Bronwyn and I having a friendly conversation about Charlie. We should try our hand at negotiating peace in the middle east next.

I'm standing outside the school gates and Erin comes up to me.

"Hi! How are you?" She says it with a frown, head tilted, and of course I'm thinking, birthday party, drama, pony, and feel a wave of shame burn in my cheeks.

"Good! I'm great. Thank you. And you?"

"I'm well. We're all well. We didn't see you to say goodbye, after Charlie's birthday party." She says this again, with a frown. "You seemed very upset."

"Not at all," I say with a tight smile. "Bronwyn and I had a small misunderstanding, that's all."

"I see. Speaking of Bronwyn..." She touches my arm. "I'm thinking of having drinks at our house. Just us, keep it small, simple. It would be so nice to see her again. I mentioned it to her, but we haven't made a date yet. The girls could have a play date. Can you talk to Jack and let me know? I know Rob wants to show Jack his new motorcycle. You know, boys and their toys." Then almost in a whisper, she adds, "Jack doesn't have a job yet, does he? Is he okay? Is he seeing someone?"

"Seeing someone?"

"Bronwyn told me about his depression." She shakes her head. "Unemployment is very hard on men, harder than on women, don't you agree? And it's been a very long time."

My face feels suspended in shock. "Oh my God! She told you that too?"

"Is that okay? You know we're friends, Bronwyn and I. You don't mind, do you? She's very worried about him."

"No," I say, repressing a sigh. "But it's not as bad as you think. Jack's fine. He will be. He's very busy, very very busy. I'll check with him and let you know when's a good day for us."

And then the kids come running out into the yard and Brielle skips over to her mother. Erin gives me a little wave and they walk off. I look around for Charlie. She is one of the last to come out of the building, and my heart sinks.

There's something different about her, and I don't just mean her outfit, although there's that. I didn't see what she was wearing this morning because I left before she went to school. She looks like a little fashion model in an ad for a luxury kids store, with wide, flowing red and black checkered pants down to her calves, black pumps with a low wedge heel, a silver buckle, a red top with a ruffled sleeves, a red felt hat with a ribbon around the rim and the most horrible part, a red velvet ribbon around her neck, like a choker. With a little pearl pendant.

I wonder how she feels dressed like that among her classmates who are in denim skirts and sneakers and tees. She sees me and smiles, but she doesn't come running the way she normally does. Her steps are measured, she looks more like an awkward sixteen-year-old than the eight-year-old bouncing with excitement Charlie I know.

She holds her schoolbag in one hand and walks up to me, with none of that exuberance she usually has, the way she'd normally run up and come to stand right in front of me like a little gymnast, feet together, face tilted up to me. And I know in my heart that whatever good intentions Bronwyn has, they're doing damage, and I absolutely have to talk to her about this.

"Where's Mommy?" she asks as I take her school bag from her.

"She went shopping. I was finishing early, so I thought I'd come and pick you up myself for a change."

"Okay," she says, taking my hand.

"I thought we could go to the park. And then maybe we could have ice cream after."

"No thanks," she says.

"Why on earth not?"

"I don't want to go to the park. I don't want to mess up my clothes."

"Oh, okay. Well, maybe we could do something on the weekend together. We'll make sure you're not wearing anything that can be messed up."

"Do what?"

"I'll think of something."

Jack is in the living room when we get home. Charlie goes upstairs to put her things away. Unheard of. It's like she's been kidnapped and replaced by a pretty poor copy.

Jack was scrolling on his phone, but he puts it away in his back pocket the moment I walk in.

"What's up?" he asks, stretching his arms above his head, fake nonchalant. I come to sit next to him, put my head on his shoulder. He gets up, and I hold back a sigh as I sit up.

He walks over to the bar. "I think I'll have an early drink. You want one?"

"No, thanks, I'm okay. Hey, listen." I turn to face him. "Why don't we go out for dinner this week? Just the two of us."

"Why?"

Okay, not the response I was aiming for, but I ignore it. "We've got a free babysitter at home. Why not make the most of it? It's been so long since we did something nice, you and me." He has his back to me. He waits a beat.

"What do you have in mind?"

"Oh, I don't know, what about we get a hotel room? Bottle of champagne, bubble bath, I could wear something sexy..."

He turns to me. "A hotel room? I thought we couldn't spend money!"

"I was only kidding," I say, even though I wasn't. I wish he'd been more enthusiastic to the possibility of a date with me, and who knows maybe even sex! God. Wouldn't that be a thing? But then I decide that's okay, Rome wasn't built in a day and my relationship isn't going to get fixed in a day either.

"I'll book us a nice restaurant, maybe Friday. Or Thursday. Okay? And we can talk about the wedding! God! The wedding! Remember the wedding?" I laugh. I sound like I'm snorting crack. I'm also thinking, *and we can talk about Beth!* Because I know deep in my heart that I need to tell Jack that Beth, it was me. And I can tell him that *Bronwyn didn't mind, and in fact according to Bronwyn your breakup had zero to do with Beth.* I won't mention Jenny the babysitter, obviously, or maybe I will. Maybe I'll say, by the way, I know about Jenny and I'm fine with it. Which I would be, obviously. *So yes, Beth, it was just a joke. It meant nothing. Bronwyn doesn't care, so why should you, right? In fact, Bronwyn and I are friends now, in spite of Beth. I'm in the love circle, can you believe it?*

He takes a moment to reply. "Whatever, Laura. Do whatever you like."

TWENTY-EIGHT

We lurch through the week, and Jack comments on how civil—his word—I've been to Bronwyn. The most interesting part of that comment, I think, is that he hasn't noticed how much nicer Bronwyn has been toward me. But I let it go.

And now it's Thursday and I left work early so I could buy a new dress I can't afford. I found one, red, swirling with big black flowers, cinched at the waist with a wide black belt. I've lost a couple of pounds lately, and it fits nicely. I charged it to my Visa card, and I didn't even wince at the cost because this has been a great, great day. When I got to work this morning, Summer greeted me with her trademark sunny smile and the *Seattle Times*, held across her chest. "Are you ready?"

"What?" I said, closing the door behind me.

She rolled her eyes. "What do you think?"

"Oh my God. The review?" I snatched the newspaper from her and dropped myself in my chair. I checked my watch. We still had an hour before we opened to the public.

"Have you read it?" I asked.

She was holding her hands behind her back. "I might have."

I licked my finger and scanned open the page. "Can I get a coffee?"

"You bet, boss."

And there it was. Kurilak's review of the Museum of Lost and Found. I read it with my heart in my throat.

Your Uncle Fred, One Roller Skate and Two Missing Engagement Rings.

   One of the best exhibitions you'll see this year, and probably the next.

Summer was reading over my shoulder and she laughed. I laugh too. We both read parts out loud, pointing fingers at particular words of praise. *Visionary... brio... wonderful... quirky...* He described the exhibition as holding a mirror to ourselves in delightful and unexpectedly touching ways. He talks about *Uncle Jeff, whose real name we'll never know, a man who had once been cherished and was rescued from the trash by a woman looking for a relative to love. How lucky can you be? How insistent a ghost must you be to spurn your own demise? Because that's what being human is about. We all want to be found. None of us want to be lost. We all want to be forgiven, not matter how unforgivable our sins.*

Summer and I glanced at each other and squealed, our eyes scrunched with excitement. I rested my cheek in my palm and kept reading. He described the violin that secured a young man the audition of his life and who became a famous musician because of it. He talked of grief and hope and bereavement and solace and of the people who have put something precious in our hands and trusted us to treat it with care.

And then, the last line.

One weak spot in an otherwise flawless experience: A Friday afternoon. An interesting photograph that plays well with

lights and shadows, but jars with the everyday objects that
surround it. The lowest point of the exhibition.

"Oh!" I turned to Summer. "I'm sorry."

She shrugged. "That's okay. It's an honor to be a part of the journey." She pressed her lips together into a tight smile.

So yes, I feel great when I get home. And since Jack and I are going out, I'll make a broccoli, spinach, cheese and egg bake for dinner. Charlie loves it, and it's a sneaky way to get her greens into her, plus protein. Win-win.

Bronwyn is upstairs with Charlie and Jack is out somewhere. I'm beating the eggs when he walks in, sweaty from his run.

"Guess what?" I say.

"What?"

I pull out my phone and read from the online version of the paper, and when I finish, I put it down, beaming.

"Congratulations," he says. "I'm really happy for you." And to his credit, he looks like he means it. He smiles at me, runs his hand through hair. "Okay if I have a shower now?"

"Sure."

Later, when I have the dish in the oven, I go upstairs and find Charlie in the bath and Bronwyn rubbing conditioner into Charlie's hair.

"Wow! I didn't hear a thing! No screaming! Who are you and what did you do with Charlie!" I fake a smile. I'd be lying if I didn't admit to a little pang of jealousy, no big deal, just a sewing needle's worth. Because if I was doing that to her, there wouldn't be any water left in the bath. She would have sprayed it all over me.

"Hi, m—, Laura," she says, her little face scrunched up, her eyes tightly shut.

I sigh.

"Mama's fine," Bronwyn says, smiling at me. I'm so grateful I find myself getting a little teary. I chuckle to cover it up.

"I told Charlotte how beautiful and silky smooth her hair will be after a treatment," Bronwyn says, squeezing the product down the length of Charlie's hair. "You know what they say in Italy? You must suffer for your beauty. Or maybe that's in France, I can't remember. But you understand the idea, don't you, sweetie?"

Charlie nods and I wince. Firstly, Charlie's hair is absolutely perfect as it is, crinkles and all. And secondly, I don't know that teaching Charlie about suffering for your beauty or whatever is the rousing inspirational speech Bronwyn thinks it is. But I don't say anything. I do see Charlie's eyes are covered with soap suds. I grab the washcloth and rinse it in the sink. I was going to put it in Charlie's hand, but instead I give it to Bronwyn.

"I think she needs to wipe her eyes," I say.

She takes it from me. "Ah yes, here you are, Charlotte."

"Thank you, Mommy," she says, in a tone so polite it's like she's morphed into a different child. She rubs the washcloth hard over her face and leaves it there, sighs into it.

"You two have fun, Laura, okay? That's an order," Bronwyn says.

I smile, tell them about dinner in the oven and go get myself ready, shaking my head at how grown up we've become, Bronwyn and I.

"This is nice, Jack," I say as the waiter brings our wine. We're a little awkward but that's to be expected, I think. "It's been a hell of a couple of weeks, right?" I say.

Jack smiles, nods, lifts his glass to check the wine against the light, tastes it. "It's good," he says. The waiter pours, leaves.

I raise my glass. "Cheers. You look nice, by the way."

"Thanks," then he adds, "So do you."

I smile. "There are a couple of things I wanted to talk to you about," I say. The image of Bronwyn, her back to me, *Who is Beth, Laura?* pops into my head, making me sweat. God, I wish I'd never conjured her up. It's not like I expected I'd end up with Jack when I invented her. Two little notes, that's all. Two little notes, a spray of perfume and a smear of lipstick, and now because of those small, stupid, actions I am tittering on the edge of losing my family forever.

"Forgive me?" I say softly, eyebrows drawn together.

He looks at me, frowning, head tilted. "What for?"

God he looks good. We've spent so little time together, I forget how good he looks. "You look great," I say with a sigh.

He smiles. "You said that, but thank you. And you do too. You look beautiful."

I reach for his hand over the table but he's turned his concentration to the menu so for a second my hand hangs there limply, so I loop to the bread basket instead and take a little roll, like that's what I wanted to do all along.

"So, should we talk about next week?" I ask. Because Beth can wait. "We're having that meeting at Sodo Park for the wedding, remember? Remember the wedding?" I laugh. It sounds forced. A pretend laugh. I want to swallow it back. I take a breath. "You know it's around the corner, right? How did that happen? One minute we had all the time in the world and the next—"

"Should we order our food first?"

"Yes, good idea."

I look around the room, smile at the other guests, touch my hair, then I tell myself to relax and read the menu. I make a selection among the least expensive items: a chicory salad with grapes and a prawn risotto, while Jack has no such qualms and orders sautéed crespelle and braised rabbit.

"Making the most of Charlie not being here," he says, closing the menu with a whack and handing it to the waiter, and I laugh, because I get the joke, which is that there's no way you could eat a dead rabbit if Charlie was in the room, and it gives me hope, this little joke. It's an *inside* joke. It conveys intimacy. I cling to that thought like a raft in rough seas and start again.

"Anyway, Jack, about the wedding, please don't worry about the money. I'm happy to get hitched on the cheap. Did you ask Mike about being DJ for the night? Although we probably should pick our rings!" I laugh. "My friend Ed, the jeweler, remember Ed? We went to art school together, remember? We could get him to do them. He'll do something simple and..." I was going to say, cheap, but at the last minute opt for "inexpensive."

"The thing is, Laura..."

"We don't have to do the rings. There's a JC Penny at Southcenter Mall, we can get them from there." I wait, my heart pulsing at the bottom of my throat. He scratches at something on the table. I can hear his fingernail on the timber.

I swallow. "What is it, Jack?"

He searches my face, like he's thinking about what to say.

"You still want to get married?" he asks, frowning.

I draw an audible intake of air and reach for his hand. "Of course I want to get married! Why?" And I'm about to ask, *don't you?* But he has drawn his hand away. He is rearranging the napkin on his lap, and I stop just in time because *don't you?* could easily be followed by, *I don't know. I'm not sure. Actually, no. I don't.* I flick the question away.

"I've been thinking..." he says.

"What?"

He takes a quick breath. "Maybe we should wait. The divorce isn't final yet, I'm concerned how long it's going to take—"

"Jack, she's signing in a few days, that's it. Why would you be concerned?"

"We don't have much money…"

"But we have *enough* money! We have my salary, you'll get another job soon! We've paid the deposit, and it's not like it's going to be an expensive—"

"I just don't think the timing is right, Laura."

"The timing?" I try to smile but my lips are trembling.

"For la Signora…" I look up sharply. The waiter puts down our plates, says thing that sound like they're coming through water. He retreats. I take a breath.

"Jack, honey, we're getting married in two months. People are invited, remember? Your mom and dad? Your sister Diane? Our friends? We're going to choose the music next week, remember? And the wines? It's going to be wonderful, Jack! You'll see, darling, I promise you."

He rubs his hand over his face. "It's just that…"

"Is it wedding nerves? Is that it? Because I think that's perfectly normal, completely natural. We can talk about that. Maybe we could—"

"Jack!" A man with a bald head and a round face puts his hand on Jack's shoulder. "I thought it was you! How are you, buddy?"

"Norman!" Jack says, getting up to shake his hand. "What are you doing here?"

"I'm with the guys." Norman points at a table not far away and it's like I'm not here, although Jack introduces me, but it's perfunctory.

Jack puts his napkin down by his plate and says, "Give me a sec, Laura, I'll be right back." And I'm thinking, is this really happening?

I watch him talk to his friends, people I've never met, when shouldn't he be talking to me? He stands chatting with one hand on the back of someone's chair, as someone else laughs. I'd forgotten what Jack is like at his most charming because it's been so long since he was like that with me, and it hurts to watch. He says he's starting a new consulting company, gives his spiel, and I'm thinking: *God, this is new, is it even real? I thought you were looking for a job?* Clearly, I am out of the loop. I lift my knife and check my face in the reflection. I look old and sad. Unwanted. Then Jack's phone buzzes on the table and I reach for it, which is not something I'd ever do. I am completely trusting of Jack, or I used to be, which possibly explains why my relationship is in such a mess right now, why I have no idea what's going on or if we're even getting married.

I lift the flap of the leather cover, just a little, barely an inch, and I'm thinking it's going to be Bronwyn. Of course it is. She must be pacing at home, wringing her hands, worrying we might be having a nice time and wondering how she could screw that up. Or maybe she knows I'm getting ditched. Maybe she wants to know, *have you done it yet? Is she crying?* Then I remind myself that I'm back in the love circle and kick myself for thinking unkind thoughts.

But anyway, it's not Bronwyn. There's a burst of noise at the next table, a sudden gaggle of laughter. I turn instinctively, my head swirling in a wave of vertigo and I wonder if they're laughing at me because I'm such a joke, and Jack is still chatting to his friends, and I'm still holding the flap slightly open and slowly I turn to take another look, to make sure, and I catch it just before it disappears.

Summer.

TWENTY-NINE

Jack is still talking to his friends, fake bonhomie oozing out of him like he's trying too hard. I grab his phone and slip it under the table. The text wasn't visible, just the name, and I don't know Jack's passcode. The screen tries to unlock itself with face recognition and fails. I reach down for my own phone, and with shaking fingers I dislodge his phone from its brown leather case and my own from its basic red case. It's harder than it looks and I break a fingernail but I get it done. I press my phone into his case and put it back on the table. Then I pick up my bag, walk over to where Jack is standing, put my hand on his shoulder.

"Sorry, babe," he says. He starts to introduce me to his friends but I just give a quick wave and bring my mouth close to his ear, so he has to bend down to listen. "Just going to the bathroom," I whisper, holding his phone, in my case, so that his face faces the screen.

"Okay sure," he says. I weave my way between tables in the direction of the bathrooms, my thumb swiping up the screen before it has a chance to lock itself again.

I shut myself in a cubicle and sit on the toilet lid. My hand is trembling, the phone is still unlocked. I should check the message now before the phone locks itself again, but for some reason I can't, and my shaking finger is poised above the icon. Maybe I misread the name. Maybe it's a different Summer. Maybe I am making a big mistake, and if I go back right now before he realizes the phone sitting in front of him is not his, maybe I can stop this insanity before it takes off like a runaway train.

But I have to know, and I click on the icon.

There is one unread text at the top of the list. The avatar is the default white S on gray background, but the sender name is Summer. I don't even have to open it to read the message, it's so short it shows up in the summary.

I miss you. Come over later? xxx

The shock takes the air out of me and I try to breathe, but nothing goes in and I feel like I'm drowning, until like a swimmer breaking through the surface, my lungs take over and I draw a great gulp of air, my heart hammering. Someone flushes a toilet, a door shuts abruptly. I open the message but there's nothing else. No other message from her, not a single read one, which tells me that he deletes them as soon as he reads them. I press the message to select it, click on the trash icon and flick the app closed. Then I press my fingers against my eyes until shards of pain erupt behind them.

I miss you. Come over later? xxx

I think about the afternoon we had at the gallery, Summer and I. How we squealed when we read the review. *It's an honor to be a part of the journey!* she'd said. And the other day, fifty times, *Are we okay?* She wanted to know. And me, like a moron, I said, Yes! Yes! Of course! We're fine! I even apologized to her for dragging her into my mess. I scream a silent scream and pull at my hair.

I picture myself walking back into the restaurant, hurling the phone at his face, *how could you?* I can see the scene play out like a movie, guests staring with wide eyes, forks frozen halfway to their mouths, waiters obsequious but insistent, *You have to leave now, Ma'am.*

But I also see with as much clarity how that particular movie would end. He would break off our relationship. He's been on the verge of doing that, I see that now. And right now, I would leave. But I know in my heart that Charlie is miserable and confused. I can feel it in every fiber of my being. I can't leave her, not like this. That's all I know.

At the vanity I put water on a paper towel and clean the makeup under my eyes. The paper is too thick, too harsh and chafes my skin. My heart is thumping with panic now. I have to get out of here, I have to get back to the table before Jack realizes I've swapped our phones. A woman walks in and goes straight to the mirror, pulls out a tube of lipstick. Our eyes meet and she frowns. "You okay?"

"Yes, thanks," I say. I throw the crumpled paper towel in the trash, stare one last time at my reflection and run shaking fingers through my hair, then give her a weak smile and walk out.

My legs are wobbly as I make my way back to our table. Jack is sitting down again, studying the wine list. I sit opposite, clock his phone—my phone—where I left it, the leather flap closed. "Have we gone through a bottle already?" I ask, although there's some wine left in my glass and I gulp it down.

"No," he says, "Just waiting for you. What did you do to your finger?"

I put the glass down and look at my hand. The tip of my index finger is bleeding, where I tore off a bit of nail. I stare at it, surprised that it doesn't hurt.

"I caught it in the tap, in the bathroom," I say, wrapping a corner of my napkin around the tip of my finger. When I unroll it again there's a red stain in the linen, like an ink blot. Jack's mouth curls with distaste.

The waiter takes this as his cue and appears to ask if everything is okay. We've barely touched our starters. Satisfied that I'm no longer bleeding, I take another slug of wine while Jack says something I don't hear. The waiter nods, takes our plates away.

"Those guys, back there," he says. Then he tells me how he worked with them on a big contract when he still had his company, and I get where this is going. Something about work they can throw his way, they're working on a big project, they were very interested to hear about his consultancy work. What consultancy work, I almost ask, or I would have if I'd been focused on this conversation, but I'm not really listening. My mind is back in the cubicle, staring at the screen in my hand. It's so vivid I can still feel the weight of the phone in my palm, the weight of wet cement in the pit of my stomach, the tears in my throat as I held back a sob.

"So anyway, sorry I took a while," he says now.

"That's okay." I try to smile but my face feels like it belongs to someone else. I am dying. I am wracking my brain for an explanation for when the inevitable happens: a call, a text, Jack picks up his phone and sees the photo of a grinning Charlie with her small-brimmed summer hat and red cheeks filling up the lock screen, and he'll know. *That's Laura's phone. Why is Laura's phone in my phone case?*

For a moment neither of us speak, I take another sip of wine, Jack gazes around the room, our waiter brings steaming plates of food which I think is for us, but then he stops at another table.

Jack pushes his chair back. "My turn. I'll be right back."

I look up sharply. He reaches for his phone but I slam my hand on his so fast he gives a shocked little gasp.

"Don't take your phone, Jack. Come on. What are you going to do, make calls from the urinal?"

I bet he would, too, I bet he'd call her. He gives me an apologetic smile. "Sorry, just a reflex. You're right."

Am I?

The moment he has his back turned, I pull both phones on my lap and swap them back into their respective cases. This time it takes no time at all although it makes my fingertip pearl with blood again. I put Jack's phone back on the table and fish around my bag for a Band-Aid, wondering why I didn't think of it before. I always carry Band-Aids in my bag. It's what you do when you have small children.

"You know what? Don't worry about the wedding," I say when he returns. The waiter sets down our mains. "We have all the time in the world. I'll cancel everything first thing in the morning, and we can make new plans when the time is right."

His body deflates and his whole face softens. "Thanks," he says. He reaches for my hand and squeezes it. "It's just for a few weeks, that's all."

"No problem, Jack. I understand."

Somehow, I manage to keep it together for the rest of the meal although I don't say much after that. In the end, I barely eat a thing, which probably explains why I feel very drunk by the time we leave. That and the wine.

In the car, Jack takes my hand and says, "I still want to get married, if you do."

I look down at his hand, pull mine away. He sighs.

On the way home, Jack is surprisingly solicitous. He keeps throwing glances at me. Tells me again that he's just asking for more time, that's all, and I wonder for a split second if I got the text wrong, but obviously I didn't.

I wonder how I could have been such a fool. I mean, I just about begged Summer to seduce Jack. I paid her a hundred bucks plus cab fare to suck his face off at my step-daughter's birthday party. It's hard not to conclude I deserve what's happened next, which is that she did seduce him, and he did like it, and now they're having an affair. I guess my brilliant strategy paid off. He and Bronwyn are still getting divorced, so there's that.

I wonder why he doesn't come right out and say it. *It's over. I don't love you. I've met someone else.* Until I think about it for a second. I pay the bills. I take care of Charlie—or I did a lot more pre-Bronwyn—I cook, I clean, I make the beds and wash his socks. What's not to like? Maybe one day I'll wake up and they'll all be gone, Jack to his own wedding to Summer, Bronwyn and Charlie to some new fabulous house somewhere, and there'll be a for sale sign on the front lawn and all the closets will be empty. Will I go around the house and make sure the baseboards are clean and the light fittings are dust free? Of course I will.

Back home Bronwyn is in the living room, sipping on something the color of honey, in a small glass. She's got a fashion magazine in her lap, classical music coming through the speakers. I realize with a weird sense of displacement how often I'd find her just like this, back when she lived here with Jack, in this house, and I was only a visitor who came to paint her portrait, and it occurs to me with a sharp twist in my stomach that I've never belonged here. I was just playing house.

"Did you two enjoy yourselves?" she asks, as if we were teenagers returning from prom night. Jack goes straight for the bar and I say I have a headache and I'm going to bed.

Half an hour later I'm curled up on my side, sobbing into my pillow. I don't know whether to hit myself for being so stupid or hit Jack for being such a jerk. I have a kaleidoscope of images in my brain, going round and round, of the past two years. How happy I've been, even through the hard times. How hard I've tried to make it work, to make them both happy. The sense of belonging I had never felt before. And it's been shattered in the blink of an eye, and I hate myself because it's partly my fault. It's my punishment for pushing Summer onto Jack.

Bronwyn knocks softly and comes in without waiting for an invitation. I sit up quickly, brush my cheeks. She gently closes the door after her and comes to lie on the bed next to me, props herself on her elbow, head in her hand. "Okay, let's hear it. What happened?"

"Nothing," I say, cracking a sob.

"Tell me." She tucks a lock of hair behind my ear, and for a split second, she's my fourteen-year-old best friend again, before all the drama, lying with me on my bed in my own bedroom at home. *Did you hear what Lucy said in History class? She's such a dill, I swear.*

I never think about what it was like when we were friends, only what it was like when we were enemies. But it feels surprisingly nice, and it reminds me how well we used to get on and how much I loved her before all the horrors. I find myself mirroring her position, my cheek in the palm of my hand.

"Where's Jack?"

"Watching some sports game on TV."

"Right."

"What happened?"

"He wants to postpone the wedding," I say, my mouth distorted with pain, picking at the bed covers. As if that was my main problem.

"Really?" She frowns. "Did he say why?"

"It's not the right time."

She makes a face, thinks about it. "I don't think it's that big of a deal, Laura, it might be a good thing to wait until he has a job."

I laugh. Sort of. "Will he ever have a job?"

"Of course he will. You worry too much. You always did."

I shrug. I consider telling her what really happened. I'm so close, I can feel the words rolling in my mouth. *He's fucking the girl I work with, remember her?*

But I don't. I've spent so long maybe not *hating* her, but certainly disliking her profoundly, rekindling our friendship feels a little like steering a tanker in the Suez Canal after realizing you've missed the exit. It's going to take some time.

I wipe my face with a corner of the sheet. "How was Charlie tonight? Did she enjoy her dinner?"

"She loved it. We watched Gossip Girl, the reboot, and she went to bed."

"Oh. Did she like that?"

"What's not to like?" she says, and I'm thinking it's so unlike Charlie, I wonder if she's at the stage where she'll say anything to her mother to live up to expectations.

"You're going to be okay? You want to sleep with me in my room?" she asks.

I chuckle. "No, thanks. But don't tell Jack how upset I am."

"I won't."

THIRTY

That night Jack sleeps close, his arm thrown over my chest, holding tight. I stare at the ceiling, at the moonlight filtering through the branches.

Who are you, Jack?

I think back to how we got together. I'd left a box of painting supplies. It took ages for me to go and get it, I don't know why. I went to pick it up maybe three weeks later, and Jack was alone, eyes rimmed red from crying. I'd never seen a man cry before. Not even my dad, after my mother died.

She left me. It was not long after I'd finished her painting, he said. She even had someone come and hang it in the living room and the next day she was gone.

He needed help to look after Charlie, I said I would. I barely left that house after that. Two months later, we were lovers.

How well did I know him? Not well at all. I was dazzled, it must be said. Jack was in another league. And I don't mean because of his looks. I've never gone for looks in a man. I find handsome men intimidating. But he seemed so... grown up. Confident, successful, rich. Who did I think I was? Did I really think he picked me for my scintillating conversation? I doubt it. I was there, I was free. I was good to Charlie. I would do until another, better offer came along.

I wait until he's snoring, then slowly push the covers off me and slip out of bed. Because one thing that's harking at my brain is, when did this affair start? I pick up my phone from the bedside table and step quietly out of the room, grabbing my robe along the way. I close the door behind me and pad softly down the stairs.

I never go into Jack's office these days, mostly because he's always in there, but also because it's a sad place. He used to keep it tidy, with his engineering books and reference books arranged neatly in the bookshelf, the desk clear, paperwork either filed or sitting in a neat pile. Not anymore. There's an empty bottle of scotch on his desk, a tumbler that looks like it's been here a while.

I turn on the computer, type in the password—Charlie's birthday—and I'm in.

I open the mail application and search for Summer's name. I know that the odds are pretty slim, why would they email each other? But I have nothing else to try and I need to try *something*. The skin around my thumbnail is dotted with speckles of blood, and yet I keep gnawing. My heart is pulsing in my throat. I expect the worst, I won't lie, and when nothing comes up I wonder if he uses a different name for her.

I scan through the emails, my vision blurry. I check for anything that looks like it's from her and while I find nothing on that score, there are other emails that stop me. They're all seem to be in response to job applications, and some of them are quite positive.

Thank you for your time yesterday, Jack, we've been impressed by your experience and have put you on the shortlist. Expect to hear from us next week to schedule a second interview.

But then, days later, a change of mind.

Jack, upon further reflection, we've decided that you are not the right fit for the company.

It's amazing how many of these rejection emails there are, and how meek his replies. *I understand. Of course I understand. Appreciate your time. No problem. Let me know if you change your mind.*

I keep scrolling back to the time he started looking for a job, and find an email from someone called Emily at Garner Technical Staffing, that says:

Dear Jack,

We have received some strange and disturbing emails, from a person who calls herself Jenny Smith. She alleges that you sexually harassed her when she was in your employment as the babysitter. She is in the process of filing for damages in court because you caused her to lose her job when she complained about the harassment. She also asserts that this is not the first time it's happened with women in your workplace.

I'm sorry to bring you this disturbing news, but I'd appreciate if you could let me know the state of affairs. At this time, considering the legal implications, our management has instructed that it is not in our best interests to continue working with you.

I stare at it for a long time, my hand clasped over my mouth. There's a reply from Jack a day later.

I am so sorry about that, Emily, I'll try and get to the bottom of it.

And that's all, he doesn't explain, and he doesn't refute either.

Jenny Smith. The babysitter.

I type her name in the search bar.

An hour later, I've just about forgotten about Summer. I am completely in shock at the myriads of threads from jenny-smith1998443@ aol.com. Jack has saved the emails that came directly from her into their own folder. The oldest one is dated around the time I was painting Bronwyn's portrait, and my heart breaks a little more, if that was possible, because she was right. The affair was real.

The very first email is innocuous compared to the others. It says, *We should talk. I dont care she fired me. I just want to see you.*

His reply: *Jenny, I don't think so. I'm really sorry about everything that's happened, but I really don't think that's a good idea. I hope you understand.*

Her: *Your sure Jack? I could tell her a lot more about what happened between us. Do you want me to do that?*

Him: *I don't know what you're talking about. Again I'm sorry about everything that happened. I wish you the best.*

Her: *You want to catch up for coffee?*

That's the last one he responded to as far as I can tell: *Again Jenny I don't think that's a good idea. I'm sorry. I'd appreciate if we didn't correspond anymore.*

That's when her tone goes right up. *I dont give a shit what youd appreciate Jack. Im going to tell her everything that you did to me. By the time Im done shell have you arrested.*

And then ten minutes later.

I'm sorry I didn't mean that. I just miss you.

I think of the emails Bronwyn told me she received and how she got off easy, compared to what Jack had to endure. In his case, they come every second day, sometimes every day, sometimes ten times a day, and sometimes there is a gap of a week and I don't know if it's because he hasn't saved them or if she hasn't emailed. But Bronwyn was right. She's completely insane. Her tone ranges from begging to see him and apologizing, saying she hasn't been well and she doesn't know what she's doing, but she misses him so much and she dreams about him. And then the next one will be absolutely horrifying.

> *I've called all your clients. I've put out reviews of your business on all these websites I could find. I said dont hire him hes a psycho. He is a sex addict. He tried to rape me. I'm taking him to court. You should not enable men like that.*

And it goes on and on. She forwards copies of emails she has sent to at least a dozen engineering companies in the state, with the same kind of claims.

> *I am suing Jack Blackman for sexual harassment. Do not trust him, do not contract him, do not employ him. You will regret it. He is not to be trusted he is a double-crossing piece of shit. Just ask his wife. He's done it before, to other girls he worked with. I lost my job because of him. That's why I'm suing him.*

And then: *You think I give a shit about your wife you piece of shit? I saw on her Instagram that she left you. She is with another guy now. You have no idea how happy that makes me.*

And then a few days later. *You wanna catch up? Your free now.*

And then: *I want money you piece of scum. I wont stop until you give me money.*

And then: *You shouldnt have messed with me. Youve only got yourself to blame.*

It's shocking. Horrible. A barrage of hatred from a deranged, unstable, unpredictable young woman. I understand why Jack has been so reluctant about putting anything on social media. Why he has not been able to get a job. Why he is constantly on his phone, constantly barricading himself in his office. He must be monitoring review sites and trying to stay ahead of whatever she might be telling prospective employers about him, and, clearly, it's not working.

I think back to all those weeks when he was distracted, absent. Staying up late and not getting up till noon, when every attempt on my part to do something together as a family was met with an impatient rebuke, like I was wasting his time. How he'd sit at his computer till all hours, his eyes red from looking at the screen, and every time I walked in, he'd close the browser, the document, the email, whatever it was.

Every time I'd suggest dinner out, he'd say we couldn't afford it. If I suggested a weekend away camping—we could afford that, surely—he'd say he was too busy, even though he wasn't busy, not *weekend-busy*. And yet he loves hiking, fishing, camping, which is where Charlie gets it from. If you asked Charlie today, right now, what her perfect day was? She'd say camping in Curly Creek Canyon. Or Sweet Forest. Go hiking, see some wildlife. Find some animal footprints on the trails. About a month ago, I came home early to find him sitting in front of the TV, scrolling his phone, a tumbler of bourbon on the coffee table, not even on a coaster. He'd just found out he missed out on another job, he'd said. I sat down next to him and put my head on his shoulder. "Let's forget about all that for the weekend. Let's go to Vashon Island. It's not far. We can stay in the cabins where we stayed last time." And when his shoulder twitched I wasn't sure if it was on purpose, to make me sit up, but he didn't stop me when I did, and when I looked at him he'd curled his lip like I'd just suggested a trip to the hazardous waste facility. But then he caught himself and smiled. "I'd love to, Laura, but I'm too busy this weekend," before going back to his phone.

I scroll to the end of the email trails. There's a lull that begins about six months ago. Again, I have no idea if he deleted other emails or if she gave up, but the last one is from a month ago.

I saw her today, that bitch your fucking

Is that me? Am I *that bitch your fucking*? A prickle of fear makes me shudder.

———

Later, as I slip back into bed next to him, I wonder how he can bear to sleep with yet another young woman, considering what the last one put him through. Jenny Smith is dangerous, that's obvious. What if she finds out? What if she comes after his family?

Then I wonder with a start, is it me, *that bitch your fucking*? Or... No. It couldn't be Summer. They didn't know each other a month ago. It couldn't be.

Could it?

THIRTY-ONE

I spend the night planning in my head how I'm going to fire Summer. I imagine what I could say. *The problem, you see, is if you stay, I can't guarantee I won't kill you. I saw your text, I know what you're up to. You're not even going to deny it? You think you're special? I thought I was special. There's always an agenda with Jack.*

Maybe it's best if I don't tell her the real reason. I'll say the workload isn't as big as I'd expected and I've decided I can handle it by myself. I wonder if she'll believe me, considering I'm either leaving early or when I'm there I'm so distracted I barely get anything done.

I get up early so I don't have to see Jack, knock back a cup of coffee and grab a granola bar which I shove into my mouth in one go. When I drop the wrapper in the trash I notice some of the broccoli bake I made last night. If there were leftovers, I don't know why Bronwyn didn't put them in the fridge. She could have had it for lunch. I use a chopstick to poke through, and it's not just *some* of last night's bake. As far as I can tell, it's all of it. And yet she told me herself Charlie loved it. Of course she loved it. It's one of her favorites.

"Good morning, how are you feeling?" Bronwyn says behind me. She puts her hand on my shoulder, glances at the trash.

"Ah." She daintily bites on a fingernail.

"Did you throw out the food I made? Why?"

She sighs. "Laura, I'm sorry. I just thought..."

"What?"

"Well, Charlotte is getting a little chubby."

"What?"

"You know how it is with girls her age. If you don't snuff it out quickly, they'll stay like that forever. I just thought... all that cheese..."

I feel my chin wobbling, and she clicks her tongue. "Laura..."

I don't understand what I'm doing wrong, why everything I do ends up in the trash. Why I'm not even good enough to make dinner for my step-daughter.

"She's not chubby or fat or anything! She's perfect!"

I can hear myself shrieking but I can't help it. Bronwyn looks at me with alarm, then puts her arms around me.

"I know. I'm sorry. I shouldn't have done it. I apologize."

But I'm sobbing now, fat tears blasting out of my eyes. I brush them off with my hand.

"Hey! I'm sorry! I won't do it again! I promise." She holds me at arm's length, frowns. "Did you get any sleep?"

"No," I whine. "I have to go to work."

"Okay, I'm here if you need me. Okay?"

I nod. "Thank you."

On the way to the gallery, I try to remember what I'd decided I would say, and I can't. My head hurts, my mind is a fog. I've got Jenny Smith's emails racing around my brain like dogs on a track, the image of my broccoli and cheese bake in the trash. The way Bronwyn looked at me, with so much pity. I have to stay focused. All I know is that Summer has to go, and she'll probably be upset because she thinks I'm going to put on a show of her photographs one day. I know she does, even if she has never said it out loud. And her piece in my exhibition is *the lowest point* and it should never have been there, and just for that she should go.

Just before nine am, I unlock the front door of the gallery, turn off the alarm, flick on the lights, and then she comes in.

"Good morning!" she chirps, as happy as a bird, and I have to say, it takes a certain kind of person to behave like that, to live a lie without so much as a flicker of shame.

"Summer, I need to talk to you for a moment."

But before the door has a chance to close, Bruno, Gavin and another man I have never seen before enter.

"Gavin! Hello! Nice to see you." I say this brightly, but his response is curt and he looks at Bruno. A little stab of anxiety twists inside me when Bruno introduces the man as Mr. Dore, from the insurance company. He offers his hand.

"Call me Andrew, please."

"The insurance company? Why?" I blurt.

"Andrew needs to go over a few things," Bruno says gravely.

"But it's all over, isn't it? The police were here, we made a report, it was a robbery. The claim is being processed!"

"Why would you think that?" Gavin asks. I feel my cheeks redden. I turn away, shrug, mumble that I don't know, I just assumed.

"Should we go out the back?" Summer asks. She turns to me. "Can it wait? What you wanted to talk to me about?"

I'm still wearing my coat and I take it off just so I don't have to look at her. I spot the Seattle Times on the desk and hold it up to Bruno with a fake smile. "Did you see the review, Bruno?"

"Yes. I'm very pleased. Shall we go this way?" He indicates the corridor.

"You go," I say, licking a finger and unfolding the paper, as if finding the review again was important right now. "I'll open up the gallery."

"We still have half an hour, Laura," Bruno says.

Andrew Dore isn't just from the insurance company, he is an *assessor* from the insurance company, which I interpret as an *investigator* from the insurance company. Bruno takes his place at the table and pulls out a chair next to him for Summer. Andrew Dore stands at one end, I sit opposite Bruno and Gavin hesitates, then takes the obvious seat next to me, but I get the weird feeling he'd rather not sit there.

Andrew Dore spreads out photographs over the table, big close ups of the old, scratched up, lock. I don't even remember someone from the insurance company being there that day, taking photographs, but then I don't remember much about that day. Just a blur of panic. I do remember what I did, however. In fact, I remember that part so well that it engulfs me, making it hard to breathe.

"Okay if I record this?" Andrew Dore says, putting his phone down on the table. Everyone says, yes, except me. I say it eventually, just later than everyone else.

"So one point we'd like to clear up today..." He taps on his iPad. "We spoke to your security company and they say the alarm never went off."

Gavin and I look at each other. "Well, it wouldn't have," I say.

"What do you mean, Laura?" Andrew Dore asks.

I can feel my heart beating in my throat. "The alarm. I didn't turn it on." I turn to Gavin. "You said you were coming back."

Gavin raises both hands, palms out. "Whoa, hang on, Laura! I said I *might* come back! I said I wasn't sure, remember? We went over this, Laura! Remember?"

"Yes, I know, but you said..." I let the sentence die. But it doesn't matter what he said. He's right, we went over this when the police were here. The point is, I was the last one here. I should have set the alarm on. Even knowing Gavin was coming back, I should not have left the gallery without setting the alarm, even for fifteen minutes. The truth is, I forgot. My mind was on Charlie and... I don't know. I just forgot. Just like I forgot about having the lock fixed.

"I just want to be clear here," Gavin says, as if he hadn't been clear enough. He turns to Bruno, then to Andrew Dore. "This has nothing to do with me. I wasn't even here, okay? I left at lunchtime to go to the printer—" He starts counting on his fingers "—to go over the exhibition catalogue, then to the post office, then I went to the bank—"

"I know," I interrupt. "I didn't mean to imply..."

That's also what I said last time, when we went over this with the police. *I didn't mean to imply...* Except then, as now, I do mean to imply. I feel the same wave of resentment I did then that I am left to shoulder the responsibility for what happened, when in fact, *you were supposed to come back, Gavin! That's what you said! None of this would have happened if you'd come back as you said you would!*

"Good," Gavin says. "So don't *imply.*"

"I wasn't."

"Okay," Andrew Dore says. "I'm not sure why that didn't make it in the initial report. The other thing I'd like to discuss is this." He taps on the photographs. "The lock. It wasn't just tampered with; our experts believe it was made to look that way. This is why we have reason to believe this was an inside job. We're looking into that now. The police are aware of it also, so don't underestimate what I mean by an inside job. It's still a robbery. It still attracts a jail sentence."

I am boiling, and my hairline prickles with sweat. I rub my face and groan that this is insane! Bruno argues that it couldn't possibly be an inside job. *It's just us here, Gavin is my nephew, Laura is a long-term trusted employee, there is no way on earth either of them would do such a thing!*

You can almost hear the click of the cogs turning in the collective brains in the room, and all three men turn to look at Summer. I don't.

She laughs. "I didn't do anything! I was just there! Waiting for Laura! It's not my fault the door was open!"

And I'm thinking, *shut up! Just shut up!* I will her to look at me, but she doesn't, her eyes are darting between Andrew Dore and Bruno, her voice rising with panic. *I have nothing to do with this!*

"No, of course not," Bruno says, squeezing her shoulder.

Then Summer does the most horrible thing. She leans forward and cranes her neck to stare right at me across the table, across Bruno, her eyes pantomime-wide in an expression that screams, *Aren't you going to say anything?* And I am reminded how young she is, so young that she believes her message is discreet. That she thinks it's nothing to have an affair with your boss's boyfriend. That the world belongs to her and everything in it is hers for the plucking.

Bruno rubs her back and says, "It's all right, Summer. We trust you. Don't we, Laura?"

Before I have time to answer, he taps his finger on one of the photographs. "Nobody thinks *you* did this."

"No, of course not," I say. "I mean we *do* trust you, completely."

"I really don't think it's fair to put this on Summer," Gavin says. "Summer came at nine o'clock because that's what Laura told her to do. She didn't know no one would be here. It's Laura's fault she was late."

I look at Gavin with surprise, but he won't look at me. I am reminded of the many times I tried to make overtures with him, start conversations, ask for his opinion on a particular piece of art. More often than not he would grunt something in reply and now, I finally articulate what I've always suspected: Gavin doesn't like me.

Summer sits back hard against her chair, her arms crossed, her eyes narrowed. I am dying. I clench my jaw, my nostrils flaring. *Don't you dare.* But I'm painfully aware that if Summer thinks she's being suspected, this changes everything. I am one small, petulant sentence away from getting arrested.

I saw her.

Bruno asks us to sign prepared affidavits where we get to swear we know nothing about the robbery, nothing about what happened to the artwork, we have no idea who was involved, and if we ever find out we will report this information to the police as well as alert the insurance company. Andrew Dore pulls them out of his briefcase and hands them out, telling us in a stern tone that withholding information is a criminal offense. I have no idea if that's true, and I wonder if everyone can see, as I do, Summer's hesitation in signing hers. My own pen shudders when I sign mine and it barely looks like my signature. And then the meeting is over.

They leave clutching our affidavits that are not worth the paper they're printed on. After they've gone, Summer turns to me. "You could have said something!"

"I did," I blurt. "I told them we trusted you." I couldn't even bring myself to say *I* trusted you.

"They think I took it! *The Inverted Garden!*"

"No, they don't," I insist. And I'm thinking, if only. It would solve a lot of my problems if they put her in jail for it. Maybe I should consider it. "Of course they don't."

"Bullshit! You saw the way that guy was looking at me! You have to tell them, Laura! You have to tell them what you did!"

She's so upset it takes me an hour to convince her it's not so bad. We signed the affidavits. That's all they want. Everything is fine.

She presses her lips, shakes her head, sits down to work at the computer and I can feel the resentment oozing out of her. It's in the way she chews on her bottom lip, the quick jerks of her head, the muscles in her neck like cords.

"What should we do now?" she snapped.

I excuse myself to go to the bathroom and stand at the basin, my face gray. I throw water on my face. I stare at my reflection and rehearse excuses to get away. I'll say I'm sick, I have to go home, she'll probably put it down to the fact I've been ditched like yesterday's trash. There won't be a wedding after all, not mine anyway. My mind goes off on its own journey and I follow along. I thought we were in love, we had problems, sure but show me a couple who doesn't. I thought we were happy, happy enough anyway. I was happy. I was the happiest I've ever been. I think about Charlie. What's going to happen to her now? Jack will be off with Summer, who knows? Maybe they'll get married! After all, he'll be free in a few days.

I spent the rest of the day interacting with visitors while pushing down the rage I felt at Summer's betrayal which was not unlike swallowing razor blades. She kept tugging at my sleeve, asking me in hushed whispers, her eyes swimming with fear, what would happen to her if I didn't confess, and I winced every time she used that word. I did my best to reassure her, soothing her in dulcet tones that *everything will be okay!* until I couldn't take it anymore and said I was going home early.

"Again?" she snapped. Because screwing Jack was not enough. She had to be rude too. "So what if Bruno and that guy come back? What if they want more information? What should I tell them?"

"They won't come back," I said, and still she argued, so that I spent the next twenty minutes cajoling the woman who was screwing my fiancé behind my back into not sending me to prison.

THIRTY-TWO

Jack is in the backyard with Charlie, pulling at weeds. The remnants of their wildlife monitoring project laying untouched on the dining room table, looking sad and forlorn. After that initial burst of enthusiasm, Jack had simply lost interest.

"You okay?" Bronwyn asks from the doorway of the living room.

I wish she wouldn't ask me that all the time. No, I'm not okay. I want to tattoo it on my face. *I'm not okay!* "Yes! Thank you," I chirp, but the back of my eyes are burning with repressed tears. "I'm just going upstairs for a minute."

In my bathroom I throw water on my face, stare at my reflection in the mirror. I look so old, ugly. An old prune. No wonder Jack wants to fuck other women. My hair is thick in all the wrong places, strands of gray like bits of old wire. I grab a pair of scissors and start hacking at every bit of gray I can see, biting the inside of my cheek so hard I can taste blood, and suddenly Bronwyn is there and I breathe through my nose hard and I wish she would go away, leave me alone, just once.

"What on earth are you doing?"

I stare at my reflection again and burst into tears.

"Jesus, Laura. Don't quit your day job. Give me that." She takes the scissors from my hand. I expect her to put them in the trash or somewhere out of my reach, but instead she guides me to the edge of the bathtub and sits me down, puts a towel around my shoulders.

"What's going on?" she asks, gently running her fingers through my hair. Her fingers are cool against my hot scalp.

Even if I wanted to keep it in, I couldn't. I just don't have the energy anymore, so I blurt it all out.

"Oh, honey," she says. "That's terrible. I thought something was going between those two."

"Yeah," I snort. "You want to know how they got together? Because that's a story too!" I'm unstoppable now. I tell her of my bright idea to get Summer to flirt with Jack because I was afraid Bronwyn was making a move on him.

She clicks her tongue. "God, you're a character, Laura. Seriously who thinks like that? You should have asked me straight up! I would have told you I'm not remotely interested in Jack! Jesus, he's all yours, I mean that."

"Yeah, well, I'm an idiot, so..."

"I promise you, I don't love Jack anymore. I haven't for years. I don't want him."

I wipe my nose on my sleeve. "I didn't believe you, when you first told me about his affair with the babysitter. I really thought Jack would never cheat on you."

"Yes, well..." she pulls back to admire her work. "He's just a man. Tell me about Summer. How did she come to work for you?"

"She came to the gallery, she applied, that's it." I mean, it's not really, there's the small detail of her watching me... how did she put it? Hack that lock like I was trying to kill it. But I don't bring that up.

"I see. Was she qualified?"

"Bruno really liked her." I snort a laugh. "He pressured me

into putting her work into my exhibition too. I'm such a pushover, honestly. Even she says that."

"What's the work?"

"It's the photograph, the black and white one of a man's back, with the poem underneath. It's about her boyfriend Dexter supposedly, I'm not even sure he exists."

She stops cutting my hair. "I remember that photograph."

"Really? According to the best art reviewer in town, it's the low point of the exhibition."

"So it's Summer's... Wow. That is so interesting. Did you notice..." She lets the question die.

"What?"

She shakes her head. "No, nothing."

I turn to look at her. "Tell me."

"The freckle." She touches her own shoulder.

"No? What freckle?"

"Top left, near the shoulder blade?"

"What about it?"

She holds my shoulders, makes me turn around. I lift my legs, so my feet are inside the bathtub. She resumes cutting my hair. I can barely feel it.

"It's shaped like a star. Just like... the one Jack has. I don't know." She takes a breath. "I think that's a photo of Jack. I really do."

The room tilts. I press my fingers against my eyelids. A photo of Jack? Lying down in bed? It's just a freckle, for Christ's sake. What is she saying? It's just a coincidence. It has to be. "She didn't know him until they met at the opening," I say, but then I remember the email from Jenny Smith, dated more than a month ago. *I saw her today, that bitch your fucking.*

Oh God. And something else snags at the edge of my brain. *I met you on a Friday afternoon...* That's when we have our openings, on Friday afternoons. Which is when I first saw Summer. *Carrie Saito, photography. Domestic Scenes.* She'd brought her portfolio, I barely glanced at it. It was a busy night. Gavin wasn't well, he wasn't here. Somebody had to serve the drinks, Charlie was at a sleepover. I asked Jack to help me. *Do I have to? Can't Bruno do it?* Bruno owns the place. He'd never tend bar. Jack did it in the end, reluctantly. He stood behind the trestle tables draped with white linen cloth and refilled glasses of champagne and wines for the guests. I have an image of Summer talking to him at the bar; It was a hot day; she wore a short red dress that left very little to the imagination. Jack handing her a glass of champagne. I didn't think anything of it, why would I?

I had to stay back and clean up afterwards and Jack left, but when I got home he wasn't there. I was warming up dinner when he came back an hour later. *I went for a drive.*

I found my love on a Friday afternoon...

How did it go after that? Something about being in his arms, never letting him go.

"They've been screwing for months?" I whisper. I've made it sound like a question.

"Maybe I'm imagining it," she says. "About the freckle."

"Oh my God. I don't think you are." I can't breathe. I push her away with my arm. "Stop, just stop." I turn around, try to get up but the room is spinning. I rest my forehead on the heel of my hand. I have to think. He's been cheating on me for months. She applied for the job because of him, why? Did she want to see me up close? Laugh at me? Is that what they do behind my back?

I get up but she's crouched in front of me, holding my hands.

I pull away from her. "Leave me alone."

"Where are you going?"

"To pack. I have to get the hell out of here." I'll stay with

Katie. And I have to talk to Bruno. I have to tell him the truth about the lock, I don't know why I didn't do it before. I'll tell him the truth and deal with the consequences and Summer can go to hell.

"Stop. Listen to me," Bronwyn says.

"I can't right now, okay? Feel free to laugh at me by the way, seriously. Knock yourself out. I deserve it. I'm the biggest fool there is."

"You can't leave! Are you crazy? What about Charlotte?"

I stop, look down at her, crouched in front of me, and feel the corners of my mouth pull down. "She's got you now," I say, brushing my fingers on my cheeks.

"She needs you. Jack needs you."

"Like hell he does."

"You have to hold your ground and fight for him! Confront her! Fire her! Talk to him! Fight back, Laura!"

"You must be kidding," I say. "Why would I? He's been cheating on me for months! He was cheating on you for months too! What happens if he ever gets a job and we need a babysitter? Will I have to warn them to stay away from my creepy husband? Only old ugly witches need apply? Will I be suspicious every time he tells me he's going for a ride, a run, a drive? Hardly seems worth it."

"Don't rush into leaving, please. It's just a phase, that's all."

"I don't even know what that means."

"He's not the first guy to fall for a young woman half his age—"

I snort. "She's twenty-five, but okay."

"She probably seduced him. Maybe he ended it and that's why she took a job with you. To get him back."

I try to think. That's what her poem is about.

> Why did you leave and take my heart with you?
> I lost my love on Thursday afternoon.

But I found you again, my love.

"Deal with her, get rid of her, confront her, confront him! If you must, but fight for him, Laura. Fight for Charlotte. At the very least, think about it."

"Why are you even saying that?" I ask. "What do you care if Jack and I are together? You're back, you'll share custody of Charlie..." I pause. Press my fingers against my eyes. Then I laugh. "Sorry!"

"We're a family, Laura. All of us together."

"Jesus, Bronwyn. You're starting to sound like a Hallmark card."

She smiles, stands up. "Oh, sweetie..." She pulls me up and puts her arms around me.

"Thank you for being so nice to me," I cry. And let's face it, if someone had told me even three days ago that Bronwyn would be the one to console me out of my state of despair, I would have thought they were smoking crack.

"That's okay. We're friends."

"I haven't been your friend," I say, wiping my cheeks. "I've been horrible to you."

"No, you haven't."

"Yes! I have! I'm so jealous of you! You're so perfect, and everybody loves you, and nobody loves me because I'm such a loser."

"Cut it out."

"And if I hadn't invented stupid Beth you'd still be married to Jack—"

"Stop it. You know that's not true."

"I really thought you wanted him back, you know."

"I know. You told me. That's because you're an idiot."

I snort a laugh, pull my sleeve over my knuckles and wipe my nose. "At least I got a haircut out of it. Is it a nice haircut?"

"It's lovely." She rearranges a few strands here and there. "Go and have a look."

I walk over to the mirror. My eyes are red and puffy from crying. "Thank you. It's a very nice haircut," I say, and she laughs.

THIRTY-THREE

That night I find an Ambien in the bathroom cabinet and swallow it without water. I fall into a deep sleep. I dream of Charlie. She's screaming because she's trapped, suffocating in layers of purple tulle and I'm desperately trying to free her, hacking at the dress with nail scissors, but the tulle just keeps growing back and I can't reach her. And when I open my eyes, I think the nightmare is real because she's here, her hands shaking me, her little face etched with worry.

"Mama!"

"What? What's happened?" I sit up, my head woolly, my tongue thick and furry.

"I can't find my soccer things," she whines.

"Soccer things?"

"I've got soccer practice!"

Oh God. Soccer practice. I realize that she's wearing her soccer uniform: blue tee with the club logo and shorts. But they won't let the kids play without their shin guards.

I swing my legs out of the bed. The room spins. "What time is it?"

She hands me my phone from the bedside table. Nine am. Jesus. It's Saturday. She's got soccer practice at ten and I completely forgot. "Where's Daddy?"

"I don't know."

"What about Mommy?"

"She's downstairs. She doesn't know where they are."

Her mouth turns down, and her little chin wobbles.

"It's all right, Charlie. They're in the garage." I run my hands over my face. "Why are you so upset?"

"I don't want to be late!"

"You're not going to be late. We've got a whole hour."

"You're coming now?"

"I'm going to have a shower and then I'll get your shin guards."

"You have to come now!"

"Charlie, that's enough," I say. "We've got loads of time. I'll be right there."

This is the first soccer training session since she's gone back to school, which is why her shin guards are still in the cardboard box where I stored them at the end of the last season.

Our garage has a wall of metal shelves full of boxes, milk crates, Jack's old electronic measurement instruments, broken radios, sports things.

Charlie stands next to the step ladder, jumping on one foot, then the other. I keep talking to her to calm her down, but for a moment I don't remember where I put her soccer gear and every time I open the wrong box she gets more upset. I tell her again to calm down, return to my task, but I can hear her breathe behind me. "It's okay, Charlie, really." I spot the box with the Christmas decorations—that one is helpfully labeled, now why didn't I think of that?—and push it back, but it snags on something, and I realize there's something behind it. I stand on my toes, push the box aside.

No. Please, God. No.

My heart somersaults and the room tilts, and I feel the step ladder wobble under me. For a moment I think I must be dreaming, but I know I'm not. I rest my forehead in my hand for a second, try to quieten my heart. Because what is wedged behind the box of Christmas decoration is a plexiglass box, the size of a paperback, with a miniature scene by Claire Carter. *The Inverted Garden.*

I shove the box of decoration back in front of it, I just want that thing out of my sight right now, but I've done it too hard, and I hear the plexiglass scrape against the brick wall.

My heart is pounding, I almost give up on the shin guards, but then I spot the right box and pull them out. I walk down the two steps on the ladder and hand them to her. She lets out a sigh of relief.

"Can you take them to your room please? And can you ask Mommy to come see me?"

She nods, disappears inside the house, and I close my eyes, rest my forehead against the edge of a metal shelf.

"What is it?" Bronwyn asks. I turn around. She's frowning at me. I didn't even hear her come in.

"Can you take Charlie to soccer training?" I tell her the time, where to go, take the car, I say. You know where the spare keys are.

"Of course, everything okay?"

I drag a milk crate and sit down, drag my hands down my face. "I'm in trouble, Bronwyn."

Bronwyn had heard about the robbery, although not about my insanely stupid reaction to finding the door open, and this time I tell her what really happened.

I'm pressing my fingers against my eyelids. "What am I going to do? Summer saw me, you see? And she asked me out right if I'd stolen it and faked the robbery, but I didn't. It was just a stupid mistake, and I've let it go for so long, I can't admit to it now. Nobody would believe me. I assumed someone took it because they had the opportunity. They saw the door was open, they realized what that meant, they walked in, took one work and walked out again. But now they'll say it's me, that I did it, and I don't know what to do! What am I going to do?"

"Where is it?" she asks.

I hold on to the ladder to stand up, go up the two steps and retrieve the plexiglass box.

Bronwyn's hand flies to her mouth. "That's it? the artwork that was stolen?"

I nod. It's scratched all over from where it scraped against the wall. My hands are shaking when I take it down. "She's setting me up," I say.

She takes it from me, studies it. "You think she stole it and put it there."

I nod, gnawing on the corner of my thumbnail. I can just see her, that very first time she came into the gallery. *That's my favorite*, I told her. *Oh really? Let me make a note of that.*

"She watched me when I was trying to get out of the gallery. I wanted to get to Charlie, I was frazzled. Phone, keys, hands, sign on the door. She would have seen that I didn't lock the door properly. Or maybe she walked past after I walked away. It was still early in the day, around three. She walked away, came back late at night dressed like a cat burglar and took *The Inverted Garden*. Because let's face it, there's only so many possibilities. So many people who could possibly have put it there on that shelf. There's only one person who might have had access to the gallery after I left that day, and who later came here, for Charlie's birthday party." I think of her that day, with her magic wand and her big bag of tricks like Mary Poppins. She didn't even need the step ladder. She could have stood on that milk crate and she could have reached that shelf.

"Do you think Jack knows about this?"

"I don't know. I'm so confused!"

"I know, I understand, but look. God knows I've had my own problems with Jack, but I can't imagine him doing something like this to you. It doesn't make any sense."

I pull away, wipe my tears. "I don't know what to think anymore."

"Is it expensive? If he wanted to sell it? Could it be why they took it?"

I wipe my cheeks with the back of my hand. "It's worth fourteen thousand dollars which is a lot of money, but who would he sell it too? There are collectors of Claire Carter's works out there, but they'll know instantly that's the one that got stolen from Bruno Mallet, and if they were prepared to overlook that detail, they'd want to pay below market value for their trouble. Ten thousand dollars, maybe? Five? I can't imagine it's worth the risk, do you? And then he'd have to find these collectors. How would he do that? I mean, does he have contacts in the underworld stolen art scene? Is he some kind of criminal mastermind?"

She makes a face. "I doubt it."

"Exactly."

She picks it up again. "I don't think Jack knows about this. I know him, and I just can't see it, Laura. I think it's just her."

I nod, press my fingers between my eyes. "I hope so."

"I know so. What are you going to do?"

"I don't know. Hide it somewhere. I have to, because the only reason she would have left it here is to frame me. She's going to dob me in at some point. Call the police, tell them she's seen it. They'll come and raid the place and I'll get arrested. I'm amazed she hasn't done it already.

Bronwyn puts her hands on my shoulder while panic

zigzags through me. Am I going to jail? Is that what's going to happen? Why? What the hell did I ever do to her? And it occurs to me that I have no idea who she is because when I gave her the job, I didn't check her references, I didn't even go through her resume because she wasn't my first choice, offering her the position was a spur-of-the-moment decision. And now I'm thinking I don't know her at all. And yet I was quite happy to bring her into my relationship drama. *Here's a hundred bucks, go seduce my fiancé and make it good.*

"Listen, I'm going to take Charlotte to her soccer game, and you're going to pull yourself together, okay? Be strong. You'll get through this, Laura, *we* will get through this together. Go and hide that thing, don't tell me where. Don't tell anyone. And when I get back, we'll sit down together and come up with a plan, okay?"

I nod, hook the sleeve of my shirt over my knuckles and wipe my nose. Then I hug her. "Thank you."

"You're welcome. I love you."

I laugh. "I love you too."

"We're in the eye of the love circle. Remember that."

I chuckle, wipe my cheeks with my fingers. "I will."

After she and Charlie are gone, I brush myself down, take a breath. She's right, of course. I need to pull myself together and confront this situation head on, whatever that means. Easier said than done, though. Summer could be ringing the police right now. An anonymous tip. *It could be nothing, but I thought you should know, remember that robbery at gallery Bruno Mallet? Check her garage.*

Maybe I should tell Bruno the truth, but just as the thought pops into my head, I kick it right out. There'd still be a police investigation. A witness—Summer—will say she saw me break the lock. The artwork turned up in my garage. I'll be carted off to jail before I have time to say, *I've been framed!*

No. I need to hide this thing and then figure out what the hell Summer wants from me. And if it's Jack, then I'll tell her, honestly, I don't know why I thought you had to go through all that trouble. *All yours, babe,* as Bronwyn would say. You can have him. We don't want him. Not anymore.

I walk to the top of the stairs and drag an ottoman from my bedroom. I climb on it to reach the cord that opens the trap door to the attic. The trick is to hold the trap drop with both hands and let the ladder slide out slowly, otherwise you could well accidentally decapitate yourself. The attic is the perfect place because nobody ever goes up there. It's a classic gable-ended space with exposed timber rafters, dormer windows covered by spider webs. It's dim inside, dusty from disuse and I trip on a roll of insulation. I am reminded of a time when Jack was full of enthusiasm and full of ideas, and he was going to convert the space into a light-filled office and workshop before Jenny the Babysitter sent him into spiraling hopelessness.

When I made changes to the décor of the house, we moved some furniture up here that Bronwyn had chosen and might like to reclaim one day. Angular dining room chairs, two dressers in brushed stainless steel with drawers I could never work out how to open, an antique, inlaid wardrobe that stands alone in the middle the room, and beyond it, in the far corner, a slate colored, steel sideboard—Bronwyn was going through a big steel and slate phase back then—with curved doors, shelves, and drawers. There's an open cardboard box of tools that Jack left behind, balancing on stacks of timber, and I briefly consider it as a hiding place, but then decide that the sideboard is better. I walk over, floorboard creaking under my feet, brush past the wardrobe and as I glance sideways behind it, I stop. What happens next feels like it's unfolding in slow motion. I am so shocked by what I see that for a second my vision blurs and I let go of *The Inverted Garden*. It falls, slowly, and lands on a corner, smashing into pieces, spewing out its lilliputian insides —bits of columns, peacocks, trees, shrubs—in every direction. And as my vision clears and the room rights itself, I know, as clear as day and without a shadow of doubt, that Bronwyn doesn't *love* me.

She *hates* me.

THIRTY-FOUR

I remember Jack saying he'd stored my portrait of Bronwyn in the attic, but I don't remember ever seeing it the few times I've been up here, but then again, I wasn't looking for it.

It's here, propped against the wall, and I am on my knees, blood thumping behind my ears. The canvas is torn in myriads of places, small cuts, wide cuts, like someone has taken a knife and stabbed it over and over. It is covered with lime green graffiti, and my knee bumps against an old spray paint can, sending it toppling. She must have found it among Jack's tools, and used it to scrawl in big angry letters, *FUCK YOU BETH* and under that, *BETH IS A SLUT*, and below that again, over two lines, *LAURA IS A FUCKING SLUT*.

She has vandalized her own portrait because I'd painted it.

I have a sudden and visceral memory of being fourteen years old and arriving at school to discover that I am a slut, and for those who didn't already know, it had been painted in garish red letters on the side of the toilet block. I never, ever think of that hideous year, not if I can help it anyway, and it's a testimony of how effectively I've put it behind me that I only now remember the school principal, an older woman—she was probably in her early fifties, but every adult looks old when you're fourteen—with a helmet of blond hair and thick-rimmed glasses, gathering all the students together in the school hall and demanding the culprit come forward, thereby ensuring my humiliation was absolute and irrevocable. Nobody came forward, that should go without saying. But everyone sniggered behind my back, and sometimes in front it too. The next day a maintenance worker came and painted over it, but you could still see the faint outlines under the cheap, public school regulation paint.

I think back to how Bronwyn swore to me the other night that she had never done any of those things. She started the rumors, yes, she'd admitted to that, but things got out of control, and she was powerless to stop them. "But I tried!" she said. "I felt terrible! I got my dad involved and I tried to talk to you, remember that? I never meant for these shocking rumors to go this far."

And I believed her, for the simple reason that I wanted to. But now I realize I always knew it was her who sprayed the school wall that night. I knew it in my heart, but seeing these words again, I know there's no use pretending. It's in the way she does her As and her Ts. It's just the same as she did them back then. Same handwriting, same hatred.

I move closer to the painting, slowly, my hand outstretched and touch it. There's a lot of fine dust in this attic, but none on the painting and none on the spray can on the floor, so I know this act of violence was done recently. And anyway, this is about me confessing to being Beth and she only just found out about that the other night.

Who is Beth, Laura?

Two notes. Two stupid love notes torn out of that stupid notepad. It's not like I bought a burner phone and sent naked pictures of my tits. It was just a joke, I thought she understood. She told me she didn't care.

My heart is bouncing against my ribs like it's trying to punch a hole through. I pick up the small pieces from *The Inverted Garden* scattered around the floor but my hands are shaking so much I keep dropping them again. I tell myself the damage is not as bad as I'd thought, except it's pretty bad, although the pieces themselves seem to be whole. Maybe Claire Carter can put it back together.

Once I've put everything I could find in the bottom of the plexiglass box, I go back down the ladder and shut the door behind me.

I have to get out of here. I have to get away from this house and from the painting in the attic before she comes home with Charlie because I couldn't bear to look at her right now. I have to think how to handle this.

I have to get rid of *The Inverted Garden*.

I leave a note on the kitchen table to tell her that I've had to go to the gallery and I'll be back soon, but my handwriting is shaky so I crush it and stick it at the bottom of the trash and do it again. This one is better. It will do. I grab a brown paper bag from where I keep them in the pantry and shove the artwork in all its pieces into it. I grab my leather jacket, my keys and my purse and I run down the street to the taxi rank and give directions to the gallery, because let's face it, I still have to hide *The Inverted Garden*, and it occurs to me that the gallery is the last place anyone would look for it. The driver shoots me odd looks in the rearview mirror and I figure I must be breathing too loudly, which is something I tend to do when I'm stressed, although I can't imagine I'm alone in that.

It's Saturday, therefore our busiest day, and yet I'm still surprised how busy the gallery is. Visitors flocking to see the exhibition because of Kurilak's review and others equally as praising. I thought Gavin would work today, but my stomach

drops when I realize Summer is here instead. She has her back
to me, she is chatting to an older couple in matching windbreak-
ers. I have to walk past her larger-than-life photo of Jack's back
to reach her, and it's all I can do not to grab it and yank it off the
wall. But I do stop. I can't help it. I stare at the poem, the words
dancing in front of my eyes, blurry and ugly and twisting upon
themselves.

You gave me your heart
Keep it forever, you whispered, and I will keep your heart
For we must never be apart

I turn around slowly, and for a second, I imagine strangling
her. I can see myself doing it, my hands around her pretty neck
as I scream into her face, *You've been screwing Jack for months!*
But none of that happens. Instead, I go to stand next to her,
smile, my face so tight it feels like it's encased in plaster. I touch
her elbow.

"Hi," I say softly, give the elderly couple a quick smile. "I
don't want to interrupt, I'm just going to catch up on some
emails." I wave toward the corridor.

"Hi!" But she frowns at me for a minute too long, shifts her
gaze down my front, and I realize with a start that my jeans are
stained from kneeling on the floor of the attic and my tee-shirt,
which is visible under my unbuttoned jacket, is covered in dust.
I brush myself down with my free hand, mumble something
about Charlie, I don't know what, I'm not making any sense, I
just figure you can usually blame everything on small children.

"Laura is our curator," Summer says with an outbreath. She
smiles at the older couple. They give me a strange look and I try
to smile too but I feel sick. I imagine telling them, *And this is the
woman who is fucking my future husband!* But I manage to flash
some teeth and hurry to the back, feeling her eyes on me the
whole time. I do my very best impression of 'professional

woman in a hurry,' but my legs are wobbly so I probably look like I'm drunk.

I stop in front of the tool cupboard, fish my keys out of my pocket, unlock it, scan the shelves for an adequate hiding place and when I get to the bottom shelf, I see Summer's bag tucked in. Nothing unusual in that, it's where she usually leaves it, but she's left it unzipped and I catch the glint of metal. Keys.

It happens in a flash. I've bent down, swiped her keys out of her bag and shoved them in my jacket pocket. As a decoy I grab a pile of paper cups from the top shelf and lock the door again. Then I fish out her file and write her address on the inside of my forearm. *425 23rd Ave S, Apartment C125.*

I drop the paper cups by the sink in the kitchen and catch sight of my reflection in the microwave door. No wonder they were staring at me out there. I look insane, hair sticking out, eyes wild and bloodshot.

"You're leaving already?" Summer asks as I walk past.

"I have errands to run. I'll be an hour or so."

Then I walk out and hail a taxi.

THIRTY-FIVE

Summer lives in one of those large modern condominium buildings cladded in bright primary colors that are all clustered together, with retail units on the ground level. I get out of the taxi and walk to the glass doors of the building.

I expected it to be locked, but it's wide open. I wait for the elevator, scanning the wall of letter boxes for her name and don't find it. I feel sick. I hold my paper bag tight against my chest, feel the sharp corner of the box against my rib. My plan is simple in its conception, tricky in its delivery, but it goes something like this. Since she stole *The Inverted Garden*, she can have it. I'm going to hide it somewhere in her apartment. Under her bed. In a closet. Under the sink. I don't care. I just want it out of my house. I want to see her face when she calls the police and sends them to my garage, and they find nothing. Then I want them to search her apartment and find evidence of her affair with Jack while they're there.

The elevator smells of fried food. It makes my stomach lurch. I walk down the carpeted corridor to Apartment C125.

Her apartment smells like her, and for a crazy moment I

think she's there. It's more than her perfume, it's a feeling, a presence. But she's not obviously, it's just her evil spirit.

The living room is lighter and larger than I'd expected. My eyes are instantly drawn to the black and white photographs on the wall. So many of them, all from the same series as the one in the gallery. Light and shadows, a man's back, a shoulder, the back of a head, a dozen of them at least. How long has this affair been going on? Judging from this shrine to Jack, a very long time. I need to focus. Breathe. I look around for a space to hide the artwork. I check out her things: candlesticks, placemats, paintings on the wall, indoor plants, books, CDs, crockery. I open kitchen cupboards, sideboards, riffle through bookshelves. The key is to find a hiding place where she won't look. I open the only other door off the living room and glance into the bedroom. She's made her bed, pink bedspread, matching pillowcases.

I'm about to close the door again when I hear a toilet flushing, and I'm thinking that the walls must be really thin in this place if you can hear your neighbors flush their toilet and sound like they're in the next room. Then as I turn away, my gaze lands on a different set of photographs, framed, lining the shelves. These are completely different. Vacation snaps from a skying trip, Summer in a restaurant, Summer on a terrace somewhere in a European city. They're mostly selfies, but in all of them there is a man by her side. They are posing cheek to cheek, laughing together, and I recognize that man, and that man is not Jack, he's the man in the photo she showed me on her phone, and his name is Dexter.

"Who the hell are you and what are you doing in my house?"

As I turn toward the man behind me, the one who just spoke and whose name is Dexter, my eyes sweep over the wall of photographs, the black and white ones, and I realize with a shock that they look nothing like Jack, and why I ever thought they were of Jack, is a mystery.

"You're Dexter," I say. "I'm Laura, I work with Summer." I then mumble a story about Summer sending me over to get something, and I rang the buzzer but didn't get a reply.

"Oh, right, shit, I wish she'd told me! You gave me a hell of a fright! Nice to meet you, Laura." He extends his hand. I take it, barely, a kind of half-limp handshake.

"Yeah, sometimes the buzzer doesn't work. There's a building maintenance guy around, but you never see him."

I turn back to the black and white photographs on the wall. He follows my gaze, sighs.

"Yeah. That's me." He stares at them for a moment, like he's puzzled to see them there. He scratches his chin. "At least it's not my face." He grins. "But you already know that. There's another one in your gallery. What did Summer need anyway?"

I can feel my cheeks burning. "Nothing, I mean, it's a... book." I pat my paper bag. Something sharp pokes through and pricks my hand. I wince. "I should go."

"You okay?" he says behind me. "You don't want a glass of water or something?"

"No, thank you. I have to go."

I don't wait for the elevator, I run down the stairs, lean against the side of the building and fold myself in two, my head in my hands, and wait for the dizziness to pass and for my heart to slow down. I feel so stupid. I saw that photograph in the gallery many times. I saw it up close, and I've never, ever thought it was Jack. It looks nothing like Jack. Why did I believe it was? Because Bronwyn told me. Bronwyn who saw it for half a minute in a room full of people. What else did she make me believe? That Jack and Summer were making out in the living room at Charlie's birthday party. That they seemed close, creepily so. She just opens her mouth and I swallow whatever lies come out of it—hook, line, and sinker.

Eventually, I push myself off the wall and flag another taxi, and because this is not my day, I find out my Visa card has maxed out when I try to pay. I don't know why I'm surprised. I fumble for the right cash in my purse and hurry to the gallery.

Summer watches me enter, her eyes wide with confusion, bewilderment, her mouth gaping. I clock her cellphone in her hand.

"Can we talk?" I blurt, closing the door after me, but someone catches her attention, and she is too polite to fob them off. It's a good thing. It gives me time to drop her keys back in her bag and shove the paper bag down the back of a shelf. I wait for her at the desk at the back, my hand pressed between my eyes.

"What the hell is going on, Laura? Dexter just called me, he said you let yourself into my apartment?"

I swivel on my chair to face her. "Sit down, please." I point to the other chair.

"Why?"

"I need to ask you something. Please."

She hesitates, but she drags the other chair. I motion for her to sit closer and take her hands in mine. She tries to free them, but I hold on. "Listen, I know this is going to sound very strange, but I have to ask. Have you ever texted Jack?"

I study her face closely. "Your Jack?"

"Yes. Have you ever texted him?"

"No! Of course not! Why on earth would I do that? I don't even have his phone number! What's wrong with you, Laura? You're scaring me, you know? You've been acting really crazy."

I keep nodding until she stops speaking, and then I put my hand out. "Would you be really angry with me if asked to have a look at your phone?" I ask, because I have to be sure. There is no room for doubt. Somebody is messing with my brain, and I need to be absolutely sure that it's not her.

"Would I mind? Damn right I would! You're going to tell

me what the hell is going on? And how did you get in my apartment anyway?"

"I can't explain everything right now, but I am asking, please, to unlock your phone and open your texting app and show me."

"You have no right," she snaps.

"I know, I'm asking. Please."

She relents with a sigh, probably because she thinks I've lost my mind and I need to be convinced that she's telling the truth. She taps angrily on the screen and thrusts her phone at me, opened to the messaging app.

"Thank you." She's still holding it as I scroll through her past messages and sure enough there are no texts to Jack. There were no texts sent on the day we were at the restaurant together that read, *I miss you, come over later?* No texts in her history that look remotely like they were for Jack. There are a hell of a lot of texts addressed to Dexter, though, and some of them are racy enough to make me blush.

"Thank you," I say, handing it back. "I really appreciate it."

She snorts, gets up and almost slams her chair back against the wall.

"You actually thought I was screwing him? Is that why you went to my house? Did you think he was there? What the hell, Laura! Seriously! Do you have any idea how insane you are? I should never have gone along with your stupid schemes. I was doing you a favor, and you know what? You're a nut job. You really are."

She goes on like that for a while, making me wince, and I mumble that I know, yes, she's absolutely right, it was stupid to ask her to get involved and I can understand why she thinks I'm a nut job. Her voice is getting progressively louder and higher, and I glance over her shoulder to see if any of our visitors are noticing. They are. People are beginning to crane their neck.

"Please, if you could keep your voice down, Summer..."

"You're going to tell me what the hell is going on?"

"Not yet, but I apologize for everything. I really do. I'm an idiot."

"Yeah, you won't get any arguments from me on that score. And you know what else?"

I shake my head.

She flaps a hand in front of her face. "Forget it. Go home, Laura."

I don't go home, not yet. She walks back to the front of the gallery, high heels clacking against the timber floor, and I sit there for a moment, then shakily grab the mouse and load up the video of the theft from the security provider dashboard.

I've watched the grainy footage before, but this time I watch it in slow motion with my fingers pressed hard against my temples, but it's the same as every other time I've watched it. A person dressed in black with a hoodie obscuring their face walks in, walks out with *The Inverted Garden* in their arms, and that's it. I watch it again, squinting at the screen till my eyes hurt and this time I catch something that makes me sit up. It's fleeting, and it's something I've noticed before but it didn't seem important. It's when the figure turns right, away from the gallery door, the cuff of his sleeve pulls up, quarter of an inch, enough of a gap for the streetlight to catch a flash of metal.

And just like that, I know. And it makes so much sense, I don't understand why I didn't figure it out before.

THIRTY-SIX

I walk home to give myself time to think things through. The main *thing* being, what the hell is Bronwyn doing? I go over all the conversations we've had since we *let the past go* and *forgave each other*, since I was allowed *back into the circle of love*, but I can't figure it out. On the surface, it looks like she wants me to think Jack is having an affair. Is that it? Is that the end goal? Because she doesn't act like she wants me to give up on the relationship and move out. She also doesn't act like she wants to move back in and be Jack's wife and Charlie's mother again. In fact, she insists she doesn't want him back, that I should *fight for my relationship! Fight for Jack! Don't give up on him!*

The only conclusion I can come to is that she does want all these things. She wants Jack and Charlie and her beautiful house and her nice life back, but she's not finished with me yet. She's feeling nostalgic for the good old days. I haven't been humiliated enough in this round. Which makes me think, there's a lot more to come.

It's two o'clock in the afternoon when I get home. I spot the Lexus parked in the street because opening the garage door is one step too far for Bronwyn. When we loved each other again, when we were in the eye of the love circle, I would have been happy to do these things for her. Now, I can taste the resentment like bile rising up inside me, and I know I'm going to have to watch myself. I repeat a mantra in my head. I love Bronwyn, I am deliriously happy we are friends again, I am grateful for her support.

Charlie is in the living room watching a documentary about coyotes and even taking notes. Bronwyn is in the kitchen, standing on one side of the kitchen island, stirring a spoonful of powered chai latte into a cup.

"Laura. How *are* you?" she asks, eyebrows drawn together.

"Exhausted!" I say. I drag out a stool and sit on the other side of the kitchen island. "Jack's not home?"

She shakes her head. "Not yet." Then quietly she adds, "But I wouldn't read too much into it."

"No, no," I say, nodding. She gives me a funny look. I rub my hands over my face, hard. "I think I'll go and lie down."

She reaches for another cup from its hook and pours steaming hot water from the kettle. "Where did you go?"

"To the gallery. Summer lost the keys to the workroom, so I had to bring her my set. How was soccer?"

She shrugs. Pushes the cup of chai latte she just made in front of me. I take it with both hands.

"I don't know," she says with a sigh. "Soccer was soccer. I always think they should give them a ball each so they won't have to fight for it. But Charlotte seemed to enjoy it."

"Oh, good."

She glances toward the living room. "Did you hide it?" she asks softly. I nod.

"Good, good." She raises a hand. "Don't tell me where, please."

"I won't."

"Listen." She picks up her cell from the counter, taps on the screen, fingernails clicking against glass. I take a sip of my tea, try not to shake the mug.

"I know I said we'd put our heads together and figure out what to do about the—" she glances toward the living room, then cups her hand around her mouth and whispers, "burglary..." and it dawns on me with a sharp twist in my stomach what a phenomenally stupid idea it was to tell her about the lock. "But do you mind terribly if I go out for a couple of hours? There's an open house I want to go to. Check this out."

She turns her phone toward me. "Oh my God!" I blurt, putting my cup down. Just from the exterior, you can see how huge that house is. It'd better be. It has a price tag of four point nine million dollars.

"You want to buy that?" I also note with a twist in my gut that it's only a few blocks from here, on Fifth Avenue North.

"God no. I couldn't afford it, but I'd love to check it out. You want to come? We can take Charlotte too."

Well, obviously. She's eight years old. I'm not leaving her here on her own all afternoon. "No, thanks." I yawn. A fake yawn if I ever saw one. It's impossible to fake a yawn, I remember that now. I tilt my head this way and that as if stretching my neck. "I'm so tired I could cry. I think I'll grab an hour of sleep."

"Okay. As long as you're sure. Okay if I take the car?"

"Sure. Help yourself."

I sit with Charlie. She drops her pen and paper next to her and puts her head on my lap. I caress her hair. It is indeed silky soft and smooth and crinkle-free, and I hate it.

"Did you enjoy soccer?"

She nods on my lap.

"Did you have fun with Mommy?"

A tiny hesitation followed by another nod. I'm about to ask

more, but the front door opens and Charlie springs off the couch.

Daddy's home.

I've also sprung to my feet, so eager that I'm shaking. I want to grab his hand, drag him away. *We have to talk*, then I realize how different he looks. He's dressed in a suit and tie. He picks up Charlie, hugs her tight. Everything about him is different, and it's not just the clothes. Charlie giggles, squeals to get away. He lets her go and she runs back to the couch, and I study him, try to figure out what it is about his energy that is so striking, and then I get it.

He's happy.

"What happened?" I ask.

He grins, lowers his head but still looking at me, he says, "I got a job."

I've made sure Charlie is happily settled in front of the TV with her note-taking and a glass of orange juice. I'm sitting on the edge of our bed, one leg crossed over the other, hunched over, biting at my bottom lip. Jack loosens his tie. He's grinning so hard it almost reaches his ears.

"You got a job on a Saturday?" I say, my heel bouncing against my shin. "Where?" And I'm literally thinking he's going to say, at the gas station, or packing shelves at the grocery store, but instead he says,

"It's a small firm, but they're getting big contracts." He crouches in front of me, takes my hands in his. "They're the guys from the restaurant. They called me in yesterday and again this morning. I didn't want to say anything, didn't want to raise our hopes up, but they've got a big project starting Monday, so they were pretty desperate. I've just been there all morning, we even had lunch." He laughs. "They gave me the job, Laura!" He presses his lips together and wipes his forehead with his hand. "I just hope nothing goes wrong."

"Oh Jack, honey." I put my hand on his cheek. "That's just fantastic news! I'm so happy for you!"

He opens his mouth to speak, but I stop him. "Sorry. We can talk about that later. I need to show you something first."

I take his hand, walk out to the attic trap door. "Bronwyn has gone to an open house nearby, she'll be back any minute, so we have to be very quick. She cannot know we've been up there, okay?"

"Why?"

"You'll see."

It's easier to open the trap door with two of us, and we manage to open it quietly. We walk up the step ladder, into the dusty space. I take his hand and slowly, quietly, guide him to the far end, past the antique wardrobe.

"There," I say. I look at him as I point to the painting.

"What?"

"What do you mean, what?" I turn to the painting.

It's not there. There's nothing there. Nothing at all.

I search around the attic, but I know it's useless. She's moved it. She's hidden it somewhere else. Does she know I've seen it? I don't know, but the thought is making my chest throb with fear.

"It was there," I say. "But you know that. You put it there, right?"

"I don't know, Laura, I don't remember what I did with it."

"But you told me you put it in the attic!"

"Did I? I thought Bron took it away."

"No! It was hanging in the living room when she left, remember?"

He nods gravely. "Yes, of course I remember."

"And you put it in the attic!"

He nods again. "Yes, yes. I think I remember that."

"You think? It was there, Jack."

"Okay, yes. It was there. So, what about it? What did you want to show me?"

I raise a finger. "Wait." I hear the car pull up outside. "Oh God. Get back down, now."

He doesn't understand what the problem is, and I have to push him down the step ladder. We've only just closed the trap door when Bronwyn appears up the stairs.

"What are you two doing?" she asks, cheerfully enough, but it still makes my stomach twist onto itself.

"I was telling Laura about my new job," Jack says with a grin.

There's a beat of hesitation. She's still smiling, she turns to me. "On the landing?" she says.

"I was on my way to Charlie's room. I got intercepted," I say. Then I laugh. I don't know why. I'm delirious. I sound like I'm snorting crack.

"You've got a job?" she says finally. "Jack! Honey! Wow! That's wonderful news. Congratulations! I want to hear all about it!"

"Let me get changed first," he says. "I'll meet you two downstairs."

"How was the house?" I ask, pouring myself a glass of wine and knocking it back in two gulps. "You're buying?" My heart is knocking around my chest. I'm astonished she can't hear it.

"It was fabulous. You should have come." She frowns at me. "Did you get a rest?"

"Yes, no. Not really."

"She hates me," I say to Jack. I'm shaking, biting on a fingernail. We're in the bedroom again. Jack told us downstairs about the new job over a glass of wine, or another one in my case. Bronwyn listened, enraptured, while I tried to. He said something about a conference he needed to attend next week, that he'd be hitting the ground running, that this was exactly the kind of firm he wanted to work for. I try to feel excited for him, I really do, but all I can think about is the painting, and the fact that it's gone, and a slow coil of anxiety wraps itself around my chest, because I don't know if she knows I've seen it.

"She doesn't hate you," he says.

"Yes, she does, Jack."

"She's been really great during this visit, don't you agree? You said so yourself."

"Because I didn't know she hated me back then, see the difference?"

He winces. "She doesn't hate you."

"You didn't see the painting."

He rubs his hands over his face. He looks tired. "Are you sure you saw the painting, Laura?"

"I'm not crazy, Jack. If that's your question. Also, it was hard to miss. She had sprayed green paint all over it, insults. I'm a slut. I told you all that. I didn't imagine it."

I come to sit next to him. He puts his arm around my shoulder. I let out a long breath.

"I have to tell you something," I say. "Oh God. Actually, I have to tell you lots of things. But the main one is, I think Bronwyn is trying to break us up."

"Laura…"

"She sent you a text, Jack, pretending that the text was from Summer—"

He frowns. "Summer? The woman you work with?"

"Yes."

I tell him what I asked Summer to do. "I thought Bronwyn

wanted to get back together with you. I mean, I still think she wants to. I don't know. I'm confused. I'm sorry."

"You did what?"

There's an edge to his tone. I study his face. "I'm really sorry, I know how stupid that was..."

"Laura! For Christ's sake! Are you insane? Do you know how that makes me look?"

"Well, yes, I understand that now, I'm really sorry!"

"I kept trying to get away from her!"

"Let's not get carried away," I say wryly.

He groans into his hands. "I cannot believe you did that!"

"I know. I can't either, trust me, but listen, Bronwyn saw how... close, Summer was with you. So she sent a text pretending to be from Summer, to your phone, while we were at the restaurant. I saw it when you were talking to your friends."

"You're not making any sense." He grabs his phone from the bedside table. "Show me that text."

"I deleted it," I say, chewing on a fingernail.

He looks at me, his face clouded with confusion.

"I know how it sounds, but please, you just have to believe me!"

"Okay, so there's a text from Summer sent by Bronwyn, but it doesn't exist and you're the only person who's ever seen it. How am I doing?"

"Don't do that. I'm telling you the truth."

"Did it say it came from Summer? You saw her name?"

"Yes."

"So her name will be in my contacts. Right?"

"Yes! You're right!" I look over his shoulder as he scrolls through his contacts, up down, types Summer's name in the search bar. No results.

He throws the phone on my lap.

"She's not in my contacts."

"She must have deleted it."

"Do you hear yourself, Laura?"

"You don't believe me."

"No! I don't! You know why? Because you've been acting crazy for weeks. Look at you! You're a mess of nerves! You barely speak to me, you *hate* Bron, you accuse her of all sorts of crimes I don't even understand, then you're friends again, you ramble on about some love circle, then you tell me she's desecrated the painting you did, even though we can't find it! You tell your colleague to flirt with me? Entrap me?"

"No! Jack, not entrap, I promise. It's not like that! And I know how it sounds but you have to believe me!"

He sits next to me, runs his fingers through his hair. I put my hand on his back. "Bronwyn says—"

I pull my hand away. "Bronwyn says what?"

"That you've been acting real strange, Laura. She's worried about you. And I have to agree with her."

"Oh my God!" I stand up. "Don't you see? That's what she does! She sets up these situations to make me look bad!"

"Stop saying that! Nobody is trying to make you look bad!"

"Yes! She is! And you won't believe me! You will believe her instead of me! Do you know how that makes me feel?" I'm shaking, my hands locked into fists by my sides, already half-drunk, or at least drunker than I'd wanted to be. It occurs to me that we've never had a fight, Jack and I. Not a big one, not a real bad one. And why would we? I'm amenable to everything. Where we live, where we go on vacations, whether he has a job or not, whether Bronwyn can come and stay in our house. I am allergic to confrontation. I am the quintessential pushover. I am a wet blanket. So here we are in our first ever big fight and I feel like a B-grade actor in a straight-to-TV movie as I pummel his chest with my fists, hissing rather than shouting into his face because while I may be boiling with rage, I'm also acutely aware of Charlie downstairs, as well as Bronwyn. We fight in hushed tones, he holds my wrists, repeating my name over and over but in a voice that is supposed to calm me, like I'm the nut job that broke out of her straitjacket and he's the reasonable, long-suffering doctor.

"Hey you guys!"

"Jesus!" I've jumped away from Jack, my heart somersaulting in my chest. Bronwyn is standing at the door, her hand on the handle. "You didn't hear me knock?" she asks, her face a picture of innocence.

"No, we were talking," Jack says. He runs his fingers through his hair.

I'm breathing like I've been running. She raises an eyebrow at me, and I'm thinking maybe it's not so bad. I mean, obviously she doesn't believe him, she can tell we were fighting, and that just feeds into her narrative. *He's having an affair with the woman I work with. We're having a fight.*

"Well, anyway," she says. "I was wondering what to do about dinner..."

A first, I almost say.

"What about Chinese?"

"Great idea," I say, "Let's go downstairs."

On the way down, she slides up to me. "I didn't interrupt anything, did I?"

"No, of course not."

"I did knock."

"I get it." But I know she didn't knock. And now I wonder with a hammering heart how long she's been standing there, listening.

I drink too much over dinner. I'm angry with Jack for not believing me, for thinking I'm crazy, for believing that Bronwyn is a decent person who's *been really great during this visit, don't you think?*

But everybody else is in a great mood, especially Jack. He

tells us about his new job, I try to follow but I can't, except for the part where he tells us he's going to Portland on Monday for a conference on composite materials.

"Like I said, I'm hitting the ground running. I'll be briefed in the morning and we're presenting in the afternoon, and I'll fly back that night."

Later, he takes Charlie to bed, reads her a story. Bronwyn wants to chat, but I tell her I'll be right back, then go up to my bathroom where I puke a mix of wine and Chinese food into the toilet bowl, brush my teeth and go to bed.

I wake up again when Jack comes in. He takes a shower and I wait for him. My head is pounding. I feel sick.

"There's something else," I say when he returns, a towel wrapped around his waist. I prop myself on my elbows. I'm slurring my words. I think I'm still drunk. My left eyelid is twitching.

Jack leans back against the dresser, arms crossed against his chest. "What?"

I tell him about the emails from Jenny Smith that I found on his computer. He stares at me, his face distorted in pain.

"I didn't do anything!" he says. "You have to believe me!"

"Oh well, now that's interesting. Because a few hours ago, I was begging the same of you." I sigh. "I do believe you, Jack. Of course I do. Bronwyn told me it was a one-night stand."

"Is that what she said? No! Nothing happened!" He turns away, grabs a fistful of hair. "I feel like I've spent years saying that!" He stops, faces me. "Charlie was having an afternoon nap. She woke up crying, and I went in there to console her, and Jenny was already there. Charlie went back to sleep, and we both stayed and watched her for a few minutes. I guess we were standing very close together, and Jenny turned to me and moved to kiss me. I pulled away. I asked her not to do that, she got really embarrassed, she apologized, and that was that. The next day, she was gone." He takes my hands. "I swear to you,

Laura, on my life, that's what happened, and that's all that happened. Nothing else. Then Bron told me Jenny had confessed that we'd had an affair even though we didn't! She showed me emails Jenny was sending to her, full of lies! And she'd started emailing me too! And my clients!" He rubs his hand over his face. "But you know that. You saw the emails."

"You should have told me."

"You're kidding? I'm barely coping, Laura! I keep praying that she'll stop! It's like being targeted by a campaign of psychological violence, and every time I think she's given up she starts up again." He turns to me, eyebrows knotted together in pain. "I can barely handle it. I didn't want to bring Jenny into our relationship. I didn't want to lose you too."

"Oh, Jack. You wouldn't have lost me. I would have helped."

My heart breaks as he tells me how relentless and terrifying it's been. He spoke to two different lawyers, he spoke to the police. They all said there was nothing they could do. It was a case of *he said, she said*. He tells me how she ruined his employment prospects. I know, I tell him. I read the emails, both from her, and from his potential employers.

"But you just got a new job. What changed? Do you know?"

It's the guys he spoke to at the restaurant, he says. They knew him from when he had his own company. They've worked closely together. They heard the rumors about him but never believed them. When they called him on Friday morning, the day after our dinner at the restaurant, he told them straight up about Jenny Smith's campaign of lies. But it's been two years now, and despite her threats there's never been a court case, not even an official complaint. They're prepared to take their chances.

"She knows about you," he blurts. "She'd stopped emailing me. I didn't hear from her for months. Then suddenly out of the blue she sent a new email." He looks away, drags his hands down his face. "That's why I had to postpone the wedding,

Laura. You understand? I desperately want to marry you." He laughs, in a sad way. "But I'm terrified of what she'll do."

The realization dawns on me, like a revelation. I am so stunned that I sit there, gaping, unable to form the words.

Jack narrows his eyes at me. "What?"

"Oh my God! It's her!"

"Who?"

I get out of bed, come to stand in front of him and put my hands on his chest. "Have you spoken to Jenny since she started doing this?"

He shakes his head. "I tried early on but her cellphone number has been disconnected."

I nod. "Have you seen her? Met up with her?"

"No! She asked me to, many times, but always for a drink or a coffee as if we were... friends! No way!"

I walk away, biting on my thumbnail. My heart is thumping as I pace, the pieces coming together in my mind.

"It's what she does. She spreads rumors, then she accuses someone else of doing it."

"What are you talking about?"

"It's not Jenny sending these emails, it's Bronwyn."

"What? No!"

"She found out about Jenny somehow. She must have been incensed about what happened between you two, even if it was just a kiss or whatever. Trust me, Jack, I know her."

"That's ridiculous."

"Is it? Think about it. How would Jenny know who your old clients were? How would she know to contact employment agencies that specialize in your field of work? And Bronwyn didn't know you and I were a couple until you told her we were getting married. Would that be around the same time Jenny suddenly reappeared?"

He sits down on the edge of the bed. "No. It can't be." He shakes his head forcefully. "Jenny was horrible to her too."

"Jack..."

"She used to leave little notes from someone named Beth for Bron to find. Little handwritten notes that made it sound like I was having an affair."

———

I had to tell him, obviously. I wasn't ready for it, and it was one of the hardest conversations of my life because he looked at me like he didn't know who I was.

"Bron left because of you." He said it quietly, like he was spent.

"No, she didn't leave because of me, or Beth, or Jenny. She left because she wanted to. She didn't leave Charlie because of a couple of love notes in your jeans pocket. She left because she's insane, and she's sick, and she wanted to punish you. And she's not finished yet. And you have to believe me. About the painting, about the texts from Summer. You have to believe me because if you don't, I don't know how we can go forward."

We talked for a long time. We argued, we cried, but he agreed in the end. He looked pained. He said he couldn't get his head around it, he couldn't make sense of all the things I'd said, but he took a leap of faith.

I breathe out. "Thank you. And once you've signed the divorce papers, she has to leave, okay? The next day, I'm not joking. She can stay in a hotel if she needs too. God knows she can afford it."

"Okay. Deal."

"When is it, by the way? That you meet with the lawyer?"

"Tuesday."

"Oh, thank God. Not long now."

"No," he says, kissing my shoulder. "Not long now."

THIRTY-SEVEN

While Jack is prepared to believe me about the painting, he refuses to consider that Jenny's emails might have been coming from Bronwyn.

But I know I'm right. I know it in my bones, and I am terrified.

This morning I wake up with the sun, my head pulsing with pain, my throat parched. I put my pillow over my head, but it's no use, and I get up, go to the bathroom and gulp water from the tap.

Downstairs, it's just Charlie and I having breakfast. Jack and Bronwyn are both still asleep. Charlie is wearing pink pajamas with a picture of a tiara-wearing bunny on the front. She plonks herself on a kitchen stool without saying a thing and drops her chin in her hands, her legs swinging, hitting the bar. My head hurts and the sound she makes is like the clank of a hammer on a scaffold, metal on metal. I rummage through the cupboard for a Tylenol. I ask her how she slept and she shrugs. I ask her what she wants to do today and she shrugs. I pretend not to notice her mood as I serve porridge. She wrinkles her nose and draws shapes into the thick oatmeal with her spoon, the side of her head in her hand.

"Where's Daddy?"

"He's still asleep."

"Where's Mommy?"

I try not to shudder. "She's still asleep too."

"What are we doing today?"

I try to think. It occurs to me I've been trusting Bronwyn with Charlie blindly all this time and now I want to punch myself in the face for my stupidity. "I don't know," I say. "What would you like to do?"

She shrugs. "Are you going to work?"

"No, it's Sunday. I don't work on Sundays. You know that."

She doesn't reply. She dips her spoon in her porridge, right to the bottom of the bowl and opens her hand wide, like she's releasing an insect. The spoon tilts slowly and comes to rest against the side of the bowl. She hops off her stool, leaves the bowl where it is and stomps up the stairs. I pick it up, throw its contents in the trash and put the dishes in the dishwasher.

I go upstairs and find her in her bedroom, crouched by her bed. She has laid Bronwyn-themed clothes onto her bedspread —pink, striped and feathery stuff—and she holds up a pair of yellow tights and a sparkly blue skirt. "Can I wear this?"

I bite the side of my thumb. "You can wear whatever you like."

She frowns at the clothes, puts them back on the bed, picks up a yellow dress with a bow at the shoulder, holds it up. "Or this?"

"Whatever you prefer." I watch her pull items out of her closet, holding them up against herself and checking herself in her mirror. I lean against the doorjamb and glance around the room. There's a full-page ad for the *Sex and the City* reboot above her bed, titled *And Just Like That*. Coming Soon To HBO.

Charlie has never watched *Sex and the City,* for the simple reason she's too young and wasn't even born when it was a thing. What interest she could possibly hold in the reboot amounts to minus one trillion. And yet there they are—minus Samantha—hovering above her pillow in their expensive clothes and glossy hair. Then there's a picture of a smokey-eyed, red-lipped, thin-waisted but busty blond in a gold sequin dress lying on a boardroom table, torn out of *Harper's Bazaar* or *Vogue,* and which has absolutely nothing to do with what an eight-year-old might like or relate to, let alone tomboy Charlie. I have no idea who the woman in the picture is, and I'd bet my bottom dollar neither does Charlie. But I know what she's doing. She thinks if she can show interest in these magazines, if she can show Bronwyn she *gets* it, that she's a chip off the old block, then maybe Bronwyn will love her.

"Or that?" She holds up a red corduroy skirt and a fuzzy pink jumper that looks like it's made of cotton candy.

"I tell you what," I say, pushing myself off the wall and reaching into her closet. "Since it's chilly outside..." I pull out a pair of jeans, and a green long-sleeve tee with a cartoonish picture of the earth and the slogan, *There Is No Planet B.* "Why don't you wear those?"

She hesitates, looks up at me, her hands reaching out but not quite. I nudge the clothes forward.

"Because it's chilly?" she says, taking them from me.

"Because it's chilly. And you know what I think we should do today?"

"What?"

"We should go to the aquarium and—"

"We're going to the aquarium?"

She looks up at me, her face alert, expectant but hesitant. Before Bronwyn, you could tell Charlie every day that we're going to the aquarium and every time she'd scrunch up her whole little face and bring her little fists near her eyes and do a little jig on the spot, and she'd raise both arms high and shout,

THE AQUARIUM! YES! These days, thanks to Bronwyn, Charlie doesn't know what she likes anymore. She lives on eggshells, afraid she'll get whatever the question is wrong, as if everything is a test that's hers to fail.

"We're going to the aquarium," I repeat. "Go brush your teeth." And suddenly, she smiles, her face—open and smoothed out of worry—turned up to me, before doing a little skip down the corridor. *It's going to be fine. Everything is going to be fine. We are going to be just fine.*

———

The aquarium is packed. It turns out we're not the only ones with the bright idea to come here on a cool, rainy Sunday. Charlie has her face pressed against the glass and she's waving at the diver. Later she'll tell me that that was Kelly or Mark or Samantha and I have no idea how she knows since they're always suited up in their identical red suits and yellow masks and breathing gear and they literally all look the same.

We spend time with sea otters, then walk through to the underwater dome for a bit of shark spotting, where Charlie tells me that sharks have cartilage instead of bones and did I know that they have eyelids and that they can only swim forward? Then she hugs me, suddenly, her face buried against my belly.

"I love you, Mama."

"I love you too, sweetie." I kiss the top of her head.

Outside, we walk to a bench on the waterfront. She leans against me and I put my arm around her.

"Mommy might not be staying with us much longer," I say.

She looks up abruptly. "Why?"

"No reason. She's looking for a house to move into. She'll still be close by."

"Does that mean you're not leaving us?"

"Leaving you? No! Who told you that?"

But then I remember with a twist in my heart that it's me who said that, after the incident with the pony.

"No! I'm never leaving you, Charlie! Never!"

"You promise?"

"I promise," I say. I promise fifty times. She puts her arms around my neck and stays there a while. Then she tells me on the way home that Mommy doesn't like her. It sends a stab of pain into my heart.

"Why do you think that?"

She shrugs. "She's always angry with me."

"What do you mean?"

It comes in spurts. The myriads of ways Bronwyn is annoyed, or disapproving, or outright hostile. It's because Charlie is too slow, too messy, she doesn't take care of her new expensive clothes. She likes the wrong things.

Just a couple more days, I whisper. We just have to hang in there until Wednesday and then it will be over.

I don't tell Jack what Charlie told me. Later, I will wonder why I didn't because if I had, everything would have turned out differently. But in this moment, I am afraid he won't believe her either.

Later that afternoon, Jack and Charlie sit at the dining room table and finish the urban wildlife monitoring project. Whatever that is.

At least the dining room table is clean again, so there's that.

THIRTY-EIGHT

Monday. Jack got up before dawn to catch his flight to the conference in Portland. I watched him from the bed as he got ready and I could tell how excited he was, in spite of the weirdness of the last few days.

He kissed me on the way out. "My flight back lands just before nine tonight. I should be home by nine thirty. I love you." And he was gone.

———

Just one more day. That's what I tell myself all the way to the gallery. It's Summer's day off, so I'm by myself today. I spend the day catching up on all the work I should have been doing the past few days. After lunch I text Bronwyn, tell her I'm picking up Charlie. She doesn't text back.

I almost expect to see her at the school gates, but she's not there. Erin is there, though. She's talking to a woman I recognize, another mother. They shoot me odd looks and it occurs to me they've never been welcoming, and I wonder what lies Bronwyn has spread about me. Then Erin comes over to say hi.

"Oh God, Laura. Honey. I'm so sorry. I should have called. You okay?"

For a moment I don't know what to say. "Why do you ask that?"

She leans closer. "Bronwyn told me about you and Jack. I didn't want to sound like I was prying..."

"What did she say?"

"Well, you know... she probably shouldn't have told me, it's none of my business, but she knows Brielle and Charlie are best friends and I was asking about you and that just... came up."

"What did she say, Erin?"

She does that horrible thing people do when they're pleased about something, but they don't want to show it. She presses her lips tightly together to stop herself from smiling, but it's in her eyes. She tilts her head. "That you and Jack are breaking up, that Jack canceled the wedding, that he's seeing someone else. And honestly, I was so shocked, Laura, I mean you never see these things coming but still, you two always seemed solid. I did think it was odd she told me... and she asked that I don't say anything to you because you'd be upset... but I should have called. I'm sorry, Laura, I should have checked in. I've thought about it many times, but I didn't know how to broach it. You know how it is."

And I'm thinking, is that Bronwyn's big hidden agenda? For Jack and I to break up, then to spread gossip about me, alienate me from my friends? Is that it? And then what? Does she want him back? Or will she just disappear, secure in the knowledge she's ruined my life? Again.

"We're working through it," I say, biting my tongue. I have a suspicion that whatever I say might find its way back to Bronwyn.

Then she says, "Bronwyn said he got a new job. Let's hope this time..."

"This time what?" I ask.

Erin leans forward again. "The babysitter doesn't ruin it for him."

I walk into the house with my sunglasses still on. We find Bronwyn in the backyard, smoking a cigarette, dropping ash on the grass, a copy of Vogue on her lap. I stand at the back door, Charlie leaning against me, she looks up.

"Well hello, you two!" she says brightly. "Give your mommy a kiss, Charlotte! How was school?"

Give your mommy a kick in the shins, Charlotte.

Charlie does as she's told with about as much enthusiasm as a trip to the dentist. I mouth to Bronwyn, *bad mood*, and roll my eyes. Bronwyn gives me a little *Oh,* of understanding.

I jerk my thumb behind me. "We stopped to buy a chocolate cake. To celebrate."

Bronwyn looks puzzled. "Celebrate what?"

And I'm thinking, isn't that obvious? Jack's new job? But then I wonder, am I supposed to hate Jack or not? I don't remember. I rub a spot on my neck. Charlie has come back from kissing her mother hello, and as she walks past me and back into the house, I tilt my head in her direction. *For Jack. Her idea,* I mouth exaggeratedly enough that she'll get it.

"I'll get started on dinner," I say.

"Sure, I'll be there in a sec." And for a crazy second, I think she means to help with dinner, which sends a jolt of panic zigzagging inside me, but then she stretches her arms above her head, closes her eyes and says, "I think I'll have a nice long bath."

My hands are shaking when I make Charlie a snack. If she notices, she doesn't say. She takes it to the living room to watch TV while I unpack the groceries and when I open the freezer, moving bags of frozen vegetables around to make room, I find them: a dozen squares of paper in different sizes, different colors. I gather them together, sit on a stool and open them one by one. They all have the same single word in big capital letters.

MOMMY.

On some of them, Charlie has pressed the pen so hard it went through the paper, as if she'd clutched it in her fist. My heart splinters. I want to sit with her and wrap her in my arms and say, it's going to be okay, it's almost over, I promise you, just one more day, but I know I can't. I crumble them in my hands, biting down on my own teeth and stick them at the bottom of the trash.

I grab my phone and go into Jack's office. I glance up as I reach the next landing and hear nothing. She must be in her bath.

In Jack's office, I check the dates of the emails from Jenny.

The first one is dated over two years ago, when Bronwyn was still living with Jack, and I was still painting her portrait. Had she fired her then? I don't remember the exact dates. I scan through the rest and the more I read, the more convinced I am that Bronwyn sent them, and it's making my heart tumble around my chest, bumping against my ribs.

But I need proof. I need something I can show Jack. Something irrefutable.

Bronwyn told me at the time she was very thorough in her interviews when she searched for a babysitter. There must have been application forms, references, interview notes. I search through his files. You can almost see the physical separation between *before* Bronwyn left, and *after* Bronwyn left, just from the neatness of the files and how organized they are. The before Bronwyn left have neatly-printed labels, although now slightly yellowed with age. As time went on Jack started scribbling on folders. *Tax. Bills. Applications.* Then he stopped labeling them altogether, just shoved receipts, invoices, rejection letters, manuals for electronic equipment, unopened bills into them.

There is one older file carefully labeled *babysitters*. I flick through its contents and my heart races when I find Jenny's application for the job. There's even a cellphone number. Before I call I push the door of the office so it's almost closed, but not completely, then sit down at Jack's desk, and punch the number. I try to think of what to say when she picks up. *Hello, I'm looking for the person who's been ruining Jack Blackman's life. Do I have the right person?* But it doesn't matter anyway, the number is not in service.

I check the file again. Jenny's address is in West Seattle. Maybe I should go there tomorrow. Then I see that she's listed her next of kin, *parents*, with a phone number. I listen for Bronwyn. If she was walking around I'd hear footsteps from here, and the fact that I don't tells me she's still in her bath. I try the number listed for her parents. It rings once, twice. Someone picks up. They don't say anything, just a pocket of dead air.

Then a female voice, older. "Hello?"

"Mrs. Smith?"

"Who is this?"

I make sure to keep my voice low. "My name is Laura, I'm looking for Jenny Smith."

A sharp intake of air.

"I was hoping you'd be able to give me a phone number." Then I rush to say, "Or I could give you mine, if you could ask her to ring me? I have a cellphone for her, but it's disconnected."

"What did you say your name was?"

"Laura."

"Are you a friend of Jenny's?"

I hesitate. I almost say yes, but I change my mind. "No. I'm looking for a babysitter, someone recommended Jenny."

"I don't know who told you that. Jenny died almost two years ago in a car crash."

"Hi! What are you doing?"

I pull the phone away from my ear like it's on fire, stab it with my finger to end the call. "Jesus, Bronwyn!" I drop my head in my hands and let out a sound, somewhere between a breath and a laugh. "You scared me!"

"Why?" She's wearing a loose white top and black yoga pants, her feet bare. Her hair is wrapped in a white towel. She's smiling at me, head tilted.

"I didn't hear you come down, that's all," I say, one hand on my chest.

"Oh, I see. I didn't mean to scare you." She rearranges the towel on her head, tucks in a lock of hair. "Who was that?"

"What?"

"On the phone?"

"Katie," I blurt. "I forgot to call her back before." I grab the mouse to hide my agitation. My hand is shaking as I close the mail application and shut down the computer.

"It didn't sound like Katie," she says, and my heart thumps in my chest so hard I can't believe she's not hearing it. I wonder if she's been listening at the door, and for how long.

"Should we eat?" she asks.

I stand up. "Right, yes! Good idea! I'm starving!" I laugh. I sound like a hyena.

"I thought I'd make pasta," I say, rummaging through the pantry.

"Lovely! And I got us a bottle of Chardonnay." She pulls it out of the fridge and opens it, and I'm thinking, I don't want to drink tonight. I need to keep my head clear until Jack comes home.

"I don't know," I say. "Maybe not. I'm pretty tired. It'll put me to sleep."

"Laura! You're always tired! It's never stopped you before!"

She takes two glasses from the cupboard and fills them both, hands me one. "Here you are. To us!"

"Okay!" I say, half laughing. I'm so nervous my hand is shaking. "To us." I take a sip. A phone rings somewhere upstairs.

"Oops, that's me. I'll be right back." She disappears with her wine.

I put my glass down. Grip the edge of the sink. I need to call Jack and tell him about Jenny, but then I change my mind. I sure don't want Bronwyn to overhear our conversation.

I pick up my glass. I'm about to take another sip but then I think, screw it. I really don't want to drink tonight. I pour my wine down the sink then reach into the fridge for Charlie's apple juice which I mix with a little water. Close enough. She'll never know.

Dinner is an exaggerated chirpy affair, on my part anyway. I am the guy who warms up the crowd before the TV show host comes on. I tell stories about my day that didn't happen but sound funny, like seeing a man I knew on the bus but wracking my brain, trying to remember where I knew him from, until I couldn't stand it anymore and I walked up to ask him and it turns out he's the guy in that commercial who sets fire to his house and calls his insurance broker, remember that one? Anyway, that was the guy. It was so funny. But the whole time my stomach is twisted and my heart is thumping in my throat like someone punching me from the inside.

Charlie plays with her food, Bronwyn just smiles at me, as if there was more and she was waiting for it. I knock back the rest of my watered-down apple juice.

I want Jack to come home. I want to tell him about Jenny. I desperately wish he were here.

I want her out of my house.

After dinner, Charlie goes back to the living room and watches more TV—she's allowed to wait for Daddy as a special treat. Bronwyn goes outside for a cigarette.

"You want one?" she asks at the door, holding up the packet. I glance at the clock on the wall as if it held the answer. It's a quarter to eight. Assuming there's no traffic, Jack will be home in just under two hours.

"I think I'll clean up first," I say. "Then I'll join you."

"Sure."

I load up the dishwasher, because that's what I would normally do and I feel that now, more than ever, I need to project normality. Only once everything is tidy and clean do I allow myself to go back to Jack's office to get my phone.

But it's not there. I thought I'd left it on the desk. I retrace my steps in my mind's eye. I hung up the call when Bronwyn appeared, then I fiddled with shutting down the computer and we went back downstairs together. Only when I was in the kitchen did I realize I'd left it on Jack's desk, but I didn't want to arouse suspicion by getting it when we were about to sit down.

I check the top of the storage cabinet, the shelves, even inside the drawer where he keeps his files, but it's not there.

Back in the kitchen I check everywhere, but I can't see it, and I begin to feel uneasy. I go into the living room, Charlie is asleep on the couch. I point the remote at the TV. I had no idea she was so tired. I scan the coffee table, the couch. My phone isn't anywhere to be found.

I look down at Charlie and smile. She is so still, so perfect. I caress her head. "Come on, sweetie, let's get you up to bed."

She doesn't stir.

I perch myself on the edge of the seat, lean down and kiss the side of her head. "Charlie, wake up. I'll take you upstairs."

Nothing.

I shake her shoulder gently. "Charlie? Honey? Stop playing, please. It's not funny." But panic is racing through me and I can't breathe. I shake her fully. "Charlie? Honey, wake up! Wake up, Charlie! Charlie!" I can feel my face distort with panic, my heart exploding, my mouth opening and I'm screaming over and over and I can't stop.

"Charlie!"

"Oh for fuck's sake, Laura, will you shut up? You're going to wake the dead!"

THIRTY-NINE

I lost my vision for a second and when it came back it was like a
badly tuned TV channel. I'm on my knees; Bronwyn is
towering over me. My cheek is burning where she's slapped me.

"What have you done?" I wail, crawling to Charlie. I pat
her face. "Oh God! What did you do to her?"

"Stop crying! Jesus, Laura, she's only asleep. She'll be right
as rain in the morning."

"Oh God." I look at her. "She's asleep?"

"I may have overdone it with the sleeping pills. They never
give you the dosage for kids, that's the problem."

"Sleeping pills? What did you give her?"

"A couple of things. Can't remember. Temazepam, for sure,
and something else... Now what was it? Xanax maybe?"

I put my hand on Charlie's forehead. "I thought..."

"You thought she was dead? God no. Laura, please. I'm not
a monster."

"We have to get her to the hospital. We have to call an
ambulance." I scramble to my feet to look for my phone, but my
legs buckle and I stumble.

"Oopsies! Looks like you're not doing so well yourself! I

may have overdone it on the temazepam dosage, or is it the Rohypnol?"

I've scrambled back to Charlie, grabbed her hand. "You gave her Rohypnol?"

She tilts her head at me. "No, Laura, I gave you Rohypnol. And the rest." She wags her finger. "You should have turned down that glass of Chardonnay! You're too much of a people pleaser, Laura! It'll be your downfall!"

Chardonnay?

Bronwyn drags an armchair to the center of the room. I check Charlie's pulse, put my finger under her nose, check that she's breathing. I force myself to focus. I close my eyes for a moment. My head is pounding, swathed in waves of vertigo. Have I been drugged too? I try to remember if I drank any wine. No, I didn't. Yes, I did, but just one sip.

"There." She brushes her hands together, satisfied.

"What are you doing?" I ask.

"Just getting the scene ready... Yes. That should be fine. You want to come and sit down, Laura? You look like you need it!"

"Why?"

"Because I'm asking."

"I don't understand what you're doing." I wail. "We have to call an ambulance! Charlie isn't moving."

"Charlotte is just fine. She's having a nice long sleep, that's all. You okay? You don't look so good. Get off the floor, Laura. Come sit down."

"I need to find my phone." I try to stand but I don't have to pretend to be drugged. My legs feel like they are made of ribbons. "I have to call Jack."

"I've got your phone. Don't worry about your phone. And Jack will be home in..." She checks her watch. "An hour, give or take. Here, let me help."

I've managed to stand up and I'm holding on to a bookcase.

She takes my arm, guides me to the chair. "What is happening?" I say.

She's staring at me, eyes narrowed. I have to concentrate. I have to act like I've been drugged. I move my mouth slowly, like I'm speaking in slow motion. "What are you doing?"

She smiles, satisfied. "There, that's better, isn't it?" She looks around the room and grabs a cushion from another chair, a small one, puts it on my lap.

"Why are you doing this?"

"Well, thank you for asking because I've been dying to tell. Now, Beth. Do you mind if I call you Beth? Jesus, you look terrible. You're drooling. Maybe I shouldn't have added the Rohypnol. What can I say, I was experimenting. Stay with me, Beth, don't fall asleep on me, we have much to do yet."

"Beth? Is that what this is about? Oh God. You can't be serious! I'm sorry about Beth. I really am."

"And I forgive you! In fact, it's a good thing you told me about Beth. You see the plan was for Jack to overdose on OxyContin because heck, that man is depressed, let me tell you. In fact, I have. I've told everyone how depressed he is. I've also told everyone how worried I am that you are not taking his condition seriously, and when they find his suicide note, they'll remember that."

"Overdose?"

"Yes, I got some pills online from some dodgy dark web place. You'd be amazed what you can pick up on the dark web. They're probably fake, but it doesn't matter. If anything, it's better. More likely to kill you, I'm told. Oh wait, you already know about the pills. You went through my drawer. I had them hidden inside a cute bra I got from Victoria's secret, and you put your grubby hands on everything, including the Ziploc bag."

I grab her hands. "Please don't hurt Jack, I'm begging you, Bronwyn!"

She pulls them away. "Stop that. Jack won't be committing suicide anymore."

"You're not going to hurt him?"

"No!"

"Oh, thank God."

"You are."

She walks to the sideboard and opens a box. "You see, thanks to you, Beth, I've been having money problems. I was on a good ticket with Jack. I had the perfect life, the perfect man, total freedom, lots of cash, beautiful home." She looks around the room. "Until you ruined it. You have such ordinary taste, Beth, truly parochial." She sighs. "There's always someone who wants what you have, have you noticed that? First Jenny—"

"They'll know the emails didn't come from Jenny. I talked to her mother, she said Jenny died in a car accident."

"Yes. I know. I was there. Ramming her car off the road."

"Oh my God."

"Oh my God, what, Laura? I mean, Beth? Actually, I'm exaggerating. I didn't *ram* her car, I just nudged it. At high speed. But what do you expect? She kissed my husband, Laura. Full on the mouth. I saw them on the security cam which I *always* turned on when I went out so I could take a peek at what he was up to. And a good thing I did too. I confronted her about it, she cried, like the sniveling child that she was. She said it was just a kiss, she was very sorry blah blah blah. Anyway, long story short, I tricked her into meeting me for a drink, I made sure she drank too much, which was easy because kids like Jenny do whatever they're told by people in positions of authority. By the time I bumped her car down the embankment at seventy miles an hour, she had a blood level of oh point eight. Case closed. But I digress. Where was I?"

"They'll know it was you, the emails from Jenny…"

"No, they won't. Do you think I'm stupid? I had someone install some very interesting software on my laptop when I was in Italy. Every one of these emails looks like it was sent from within a twenty-mile radius of here. So, in fact, if anyone was to *really* look into it, trust me when I say they'll be more likely to believe that *you* were impersonating Jenny Smith rather than me. I'd keep my mouth shut about that one if I were you. But I don't want to talk about Jenny anymore. Let's talk about Beth."

"Beth..." I whisper the name to myself. "It was a joke. I didn't mean..."

"Yes, I know, you told me. What did you call it? A prank? It paid off nicely, for a prank, you didn't lose any time getting your claws into him. Hats off to you, by the way, credit where it's due. I thought you were a whining little mouse with zero ambition and abandonment issues. I stand corrected."

"It wasn't like that..."

"I thought Beth was real, Laura!" she barks. Her face is tight with sudden fury. She takes a sharp breath through her nose, lets it out, then runs her hand through her hair. "I tried to make him tell me, so I could, you know, have a chat to her, but he wouldn't tell me. He kept saying he knew nothing about her. Now I understand why, but I didn't then. I decided to teach him a lesson. I had an affair with Leon, and I was sure Jack would beg me to come home, but he didn't." She shakes her head. "By then Leon had fallen in love with me, and Leon is worth a hundred Jacks, trust me, that man is wealthy. So, all was well. And you know, Italy's nice. But..." She sighs. "I got too confident. I thought he couldn't live without me, you see? I got... sloppy. He walked in on me screwing Felipe—very sexy Italian gardener—in *flagrante delicto*, and he threw me out with nothing. Finito. I got to keep the jewelry he gave me, I sold some so I'd have some cash, but you know... So I came back to this dump, and figured the only way to recoup a little bit of cash would be to kill Jack—"

"But why?"

"I need the money, Laura, I thought I was making that clear.

I have nothing! Nothing at all! My mother hates me, so I know for a fact I won't get anything from that old bag, not even when she dies, and a girl's gotta live." She smooths her long hair all the way down to the tips. "We're not all like you, Laura," she says with a sigh. "Some of us have standards. At least with the house I'd have a buffer until I figure something else out. Don't look at me like that. We're still married, remember? If Jack dies before we get divorced, then Charlotte inherits everything. This house, which is worth three point two million, by the way, can you believe it? I thought it was a little on the high side, but the agent assures me it's the market. And there's a life insurance policy although I wasn't completely sure Charlotte would benefit if he died by suicide. And I wasn't going to ram his car off the road, was I? How would that look. I got away with it after Jenny and... Anyway, then you told me you were Beth." She bends down, hands together between her knees, her face inches from mine. "Really? Laura? You steal my man? Again? It's getting on the obsessive end of the spectrum, don't you think?"

She stands up straight. "I'm sorry I ruined your painting, by the way. Sorry not sorry. I did think it was a risky move, leaving that painting up there, after you said you needed a hiding place for your stupid artwork thing. I went back up to the attic and I found something. A little peacock, tiny little thing made of glass. How did it get up there, I wonder?

"Anyway, that painting is now at the bottom of a dumpster on some construction site somewhere, and I can't say I'll miss it. But bad luck for you, though, Beth, because before I knew you were Beth, I was going to let you off the hook for the simple reason you mean nothing to me. I barely know you exist. But then I thought, wait!"

She returns to the sideboard, puts white gloves on and takes something out of the box, examines it.

It takes a moment to focus on what she's holding, and when I do, I start to cry because what she has in her hand is a gun.

"So you see, it's like this. You bought this lovely little Sig nine millimeter—" She turns to me. "I had to borrow your wallet, by the way, I hope that was all right, I didn't leave you in the lurch, did I? It was only for a day, so I could use your ID because, unfortunately, they need ID! The nice man at the store didn't even check if your driver's license matched my face, although I was wearing a beanie and I made myself as ugly as I could, just like you. He wrote down the details so he could do his background check, which I had to pay *extra* to speed up." She turns the gun in her hands. "I paid with your Visa card. I hope that's okay too. It was a little on the expensive side, but what can you do?"

She brings the gun to me, hands it over. "Don't worry, the manual safety is on. How does it feel?" I don't move, so she wraps my fingers around it, maneuvers my index finger on the trigger.

"Stop it!" I shout, trying to push her away. "Stop!"

"So when Jack comes in that archway here..." She points in front of me. "You'll—well, I'll be squeezing your finger on the trigger, but you're the one holding the gun, technically, I'm just holding your hand—and we will shoot him!"

"No!"

"Yes, Beth! I need that gun powder on your hand and your fingerprints on that gun! You know the drill. It will be a team effort! I'll hold that cushion here, in front of the gun so Jack doesn't see it right away. And honestly, I can't imagine anyone will be surprised you killed Jack. You've been acting very strange lately, Laura. I mean Beth. I mean Laura. I mean Beth. You're imagining that Summer is having an affair with Jack, which is ridiculous! But I have to say, it's been fun. I mean, I just mention some imaginary freckle and you're all over it. I still can't believe you thought that was Jack!" She laughs and laughs and laughs. "And the poem? Oh my God, you're priceless. I hope you confronted her, by the way. I'll be testifying to that of course, but I could use a little backup there. And you've been *paying* her to flirt with him because you were so sure he and I were in love again! God, you have a suspicious nature. When all we wanted to do was be good co-parents to little Charlotte." She tut-tuts, shakes her head.

"You sent the text," I say. "That night at the restaurant."

"That's right! I sent that text. You gave me one Beth, I raised you one Summer." She cocks her head at me. "I only did to you what you did to me, you can hardly complain. But yes, I got a burner, put the number in Jack's phone under Summer's name. Don't look at me like that. I was with him for six years, you think I don't know his passcode? I made sure the texts were set to be visible even when the phone was asleep, and when you went to your romantic dinner, I sent it. I could just see you two, kissing over shared pasta and then *ping*! And you'd look down, and he'd look down, and there's Summer. And he'd argue and bluster and you wouldn't believe him because let's be honest here, there's you, and then there's her, and you know who he would pick, right? I bet you told Katie about her. And about me, didn't you? Essentially, you've been acting crazy all around and you look like hell, and look, I'm not saying everyone will immediately say they should have seen it coming. They'll be shocked, for sure, but once they'll think about it, they'll agree things have been building for a while."

I'm folded in two, my face in my hands. "You're insane. You're completely insane."

"That's what my mother says."

I look up, pleading. "It won't work, why would I take temazepam if—"

"And Rohypnol."

"—I intend to shoot Jack, what if I fall asleep?"

"I didn't give you enough to fall asleep, Laura. I gave you enough to be compliant. But sure, when we've done the deed, I might give you extra, but yes, I see that I didn't explain that part." She bends down again to be closer to me. "You're trying to kill yourself. It was supposed to be a murder suicide, and you didn't have the guts to shoot yourself, so you took a cocktail of drugs. But, like everything else you do, you screwed it up. You didn't take enough. You'll live. You're going to jail for the remainder of your miserable life." She takes the gun back. "So? What do you think?"

"It doesn't have to be that way. You can have the house, Jack will give it to you, I know he will! He will give you whatever money you want! Please, Bronwyn, stop this before it's too late!"

"It's too late. Also, don't be stupid, Beth." She checks her watch. "We have another forty minutes or so, so you get comfortable. It will be over before you know it. Then when it is, I'll tie you up, then go upstairs and call my friend Amelia, I'll tell her I'm up in my room, in bed, about to go to sleep. Yes, it's very early, but I am so bored alone with you downstairs, berating me about Jack all the time. And then I'll say, oh my God, what was that? Did you hear that? And she'll say, no... and I'll say, it sounded like a gun shot. More than one, actually, because you're not aiming very well, and you're not taking any chances. I'll panic, drop the phone and run down the stairs and I'll untie you, call nine one one and scream and tell them that I was in my room and heard the shots and ran down as fast as I could, and you tried to shoot me too, but I disarmed you. What do you think?"

But my head has lolled forward, and I've closed my eyes. She bumps my head.

"Wake up, Laura."

I moan, my head lolls to the side, my mouth drooping.

She slaps me once. My head hits the side of the back rest on the armchair. I don't flinch.

"Shit," she whispers. "Maybe I overdid it. But that's okay. You'll be awake when the time comes."

FORTY

She leaves the room. Only when I hear her footsteps going up the stairs do I dare open my eyes.

I press my fingers on my temples, take a shuddery breath. I have to focus. I don't have much time. I have to get help.

Harold. He's our closest neighbor. If I can get to Harold, he will call for help.

The quickest way to get to Harold's house is out the front door, but it means going through the hallway and past the stairs, and if she happens to look down she'll see me. The French doors. They lead to the deck. I can get to Harold that way.

In two strides I'm there, pulling at them. Except they're locked.

I feel the tears burn the inside of my nose, the back of my eyes. I'm wasting too much time. I take off my shoes to be quieter, look back at Charlie. Her lips twitch. Okay. That's good. She's asleep. Concentrate. Then I see with a start that Bronwyn has left the gun on the sideboard. I snatch it and for a split second I wonder what to do with it. I try to imagine confronting her, demanding my phone, but I don't know if I can pull it off. Can I shoot her if she comes for me? I don't know, and in my mind's eye she's laughing at me.

I walk over to the hallway, glance up the stairs, my heart somersaulting in my chest. Floorboards creek above my head. Very quietly, my hand flat on the edge of the door, I turn the handle and open it.

It's raining. I run down the path to the gate. Harold's house is completely dark and I wonder if he's asleep. For a split second I consider going back inside, grabbing his spare key from where we keep it in the kitchen drawer, but I can't. It's too late. I take a step, a leap, I'm already running when a bolt of pain shoots through my legs and I trip, land hard face down, my chin hitting the ground, blood pouring inside my mouth.

"Harold!" I cry.

"Can't you see he's not there?" Bronwyn snaps behind me. She's holding one of Jack's golf clubs. She uses it to point to Harold's house. "Are you blind, as well as stupid? The house is completely dark, Laura!"

There's dirt and pebbles digging in my knees, I clock the gun on the ground and grab it, point it at her, my hand shaking like a branch in the wind. "Where is he? What have you done to him?"

She leans on the golf club like it's a cane. "He's in the hospital." She makes a sad face. "He had a fall down the stairs. Luckily, I was there when it happened. I went there to personally invite him to drinks on Sunday. I've invited a few people, by the way. Just a friendly neighborly get-together. And no, I didn't push him, in case you're wondering. I was nowhere near him. I did, however, slap some cooking oil on the top three steps, which I cleaned off before the ambulance arrived."

I'm going to be sick. I'm still pointing the gun at her. "Give me my phone."

"For Christ's sake, Laura, you just don't give up, do you? There are no bullets in that thing."

"I don't believe you." I point the gun away from her, press the trigger, but nothing happens. Then I remember her saying something about the safety latch. I fumble with it but my hands are shaking too much.

"I told you. There are no bullets. Here."

Before I have time to react, she's yanked it out of my hands. Then, in one smooth motion, she has pointed the gun at me and released the latch.

I scramble backward, raise one hand. "No!"

But she's already pressed the trigger. "Click!" She smiles, then drops her arm. "There. Happy? Come on, get up. Let's go."

I push myself off the ground and come to kneeling. "Listen, listen to me. Just one second. Give me one second. It's not too late to end this madness. I won't tell anyone, I give you my word." I bring my hands together in prayer. "I'll convince Jack to give you the house. We'll move out. Just end this here, right now. I'm begging you."

She narrows her eyes at me. "Huh. I guess I didn't put as many pills in that wine as I'd thought. Interesting."

"Listen. Please, just end this! You can have the house and anything you want! I swear to God, and I won't tell anyone what happened here."

"Whiny whiny whiny. Jesus, Laura. You sound just like your mother."

I don't say anything for a moment. My brain has snagged, frozen on the word, *mother*. "What did you say?"

"She whined and cried and begged just like you are."

"My mother?"

She bends down, hands together between her knees, her face inches from mine. "Did you really think I *wanted* to be your friend? Have you looked at yourself, like, ever? It never occurred to you that, when you came back to school after your mother's funeral, maybe I had an ulterior motive in befriending you? Or did you actually believe your well-being was paramount to me? I guess the question is: did you actually believe I gave a shit about you?"

"I don't understand!" I cry.

"No, you were never the brightest star in the firmament, Laura. That's your problem, but let's face it, it's been my strength. Okay, let me spell it out. I wanted to be close to you, Laura, so that if there was even a whiff of a rumor that there was someone else on that bridge that day, I'd be the first to know."

"No. No no. No. You can't... No. Please, it's not true. It's not true."

"Oh, but it is! I overheard my dad on the phone one day, talking about their plans. Where they'd move together, what the house was like, whether it was close to schools. Yes, that's right, my father and your mother were in *love*. My father was walking out on my mother, and I couldn't fault him there, to be fair, I'd have done the same if I could, and your mother was leaving your father, and they were starting a new life together, and if that wasn't bad enough, they were taking you with them, but not me. I was to stay with my mother. That's right, Laura. You, boring, plain old you, were going to live with your mother and *my* father. And I wasn't."

She stands up straight and pulls out a cigarette from the pocket of her skirt. Lights it, the flame briefly illuminating her face.

"I'd known for a while," she says, blowing out a plume of smoke. "I wasn't going to let it happen. So, early that morning I called your house and spoke to your mother. I said I knew everything, and I was on the bridge and I was going to kill myself unless she came to explain herself. I said if she spoke to my father, I would jump. She believed me, she came. Alone. There's no traffic on that bridge at that time of the morning. I was right up the top of the trusses. She begged me to come down, she sounded just like you just now. Listen to me! Don't do anything! Please, please, please! She climbed up to get me. She didn't look like she liked it much, but she did it."

"No! Bronwyn, no!"

"I pushed her off. She tried to hang on, though; she was feisty, way more than you. I had to kick her before she let go. Then I slid along the top all the way to the other end and I came back down. And then, I became your friend."

She drops her cigarette on the ground. I can't speak. I can't even take a breath.

"And then years later," she continues, "I told my dad. I'd gone to see him at his real estate agency late one night, he was always working late, drinking by himself. I wanted money, he said no, we had an argument. He was drunk, I told him I knew what a slimy creep he was and what I'd done. He was shocked, well, he would be. He grabbed his coat, his keys and he got in his car. I followed him, and I nudged him off the road. You know what the roads are like up there. That's how I got the idea to do the same to young slut Jenny. Oh don't look at me like that, Laura. What do you expect? She tried to fuck my husband! She only brought it upon herself. You fuck with me, you have to die. I don't make the rules."

"You're insane!"

"Whatever." She kicks my foot. "Come on, Laura. Let's go inside. We could kill Charlotte now if you like. Don't look at me like that. You realize Charlotte has to die too, don't you? You have to kill her, because then I get everything: the life insurance, the house, everything. I'm the only one left, you see? She couldn't die if Jack committed suicide, but now? Why bother letting her live? What would be the point? But we couldn't use the gun yet, in case someone heard the shots. But you could strangle her."

My vision has gone blurry, black dots dancing in front of my eyes. I claw at her blindly, dig my fingernails into flesh, scramble to get a purchase. And all the time she's laughing.

"Enough. Come on." She grabs my hair and yanks it, and suddenly I'm upright and she has a clump of my hair in her fist. There's a look of surprise on her face. "Oh my God! You didn't drink the wine!"

But I'm burning with rage. In that moment, when she's still realizing I'm not as drugged as she thought, I've wrapped my arm around her throat and we both fall to the ground. I'm like a drunk, blind fighter, unable to tell if my fists are connecting with any part of her, but I'm kicking and biting and there's blood in my mouth, dirt in my eyes, and I'm no longer in control of my body or my mind. All I feel is pure fury raging inside me. Fury without consequences. But then she manages to free herself from my grasp and now we're both standing. I think of Charlie, the way she used to ram her head into things when she was upset, and I before I know it I've put my head down and I run into her, feel my shoulders make contact with her chest, feel the air go out of her, feel her body move as she flies backward, arms flailing, and disappears into the darkness.

The world tilts and I fall to my knees and the pain that erupts in my head is so violent that for that split second before I pass out, I wonder if she shot me.

FORTY-ONE

But nobody shot me, as I find out when I wake up in the hospital thirty-six hours later with probes in my skull and tubes in my arms, like a broken marionette. Traumatic head injury, they said. I passed out and hit the ground, they said. I was kept under sedation until the swelling in my brain subsided. I could have died, they said. I have no memory of what has happened, so I don't laugh.

Jack is holding my hand. His face looks different, gaunt and pale, creased by rivers of tears.

"What happened?" I ask. But my mouth isn't moving properly, like it's been pumped full of Novocain.

"Shhh. Go back to sleep."

I go back to sleep and I dream of Charlie; she's six years old, she's wearing a yellow raincoat Jack got for her two sizes too big. She's grinning at me, a cheeky grin, kicking puddles of water in her unicorn-patterned rain boots. She runs to me and wraps her arms around my waist, her face turned up to mine, her yellow hat fallen back, her eyes squinting against the rain. It's the first time she's hugged me.

I dream of Jack, of our first kiss, our bodies pressed together against the wall outside Charlie's bedroom, I can feel the stubble of his day-old beard against my skin, the sweet smell of him, teeth knocking, his hips pressing against mine.

"Laura. Baby."

My eyes are glued shut. No, they're not. It's the effort of raising my eyelids, it's too much. A sliver of light.

"Where's Charlie?"

"She's okay. She's sleeping. She's safe."

He gives me water in a cup with a straw and I take a sip. I sit up, wincing

When Jack found Charlie and me, he called the ambulance and rushed us to the hospital. He didn't look for Bronwyn beyond inside the house. She lay on those stairs for close to fourteen hours before she was found, with a broken back.

Alive.

But she's in bad shape. Well, you'd hope so, I guess. She's in the ICU and Jack tells me that when they brought her in, she was conscious long enough to tell the police what had happened. I've been planning to kill them all. I've gone crazy, I'm insane. I'm jealous. I'm sick, I bragged that I bought oxycodone online and was going to use it to fake Jack's suicide. The police found the bag of pills taped behind my bedside table, just where I'd told her they were. But I changed my mind, I'd decided to kill them all and kill myself. I bought the gun, I was waiting for Jack to come home so I could kill him, I tried to kill Charlie, I tried to kill myself. The only reason we're all alive is because of Bronwyn. It's Bronwyn who lured me out of the house, away from Charlie. She fought me for the gun. She didn't know it wasn't loaded. She's not sure what happened then, only that I pushed her. But she saved Charlie's life and almost died in the process.

And that's when I remember. Memories burst inside my head like flashes going off. They are so violent and freakish that at first I don't think they're real. Me screaming at the sight of

Charlie unconscious on the couch. Bronwyn slapping me. Me in the armchair, holding the gun. Me crawling outside, shouting for help.

"No, no, no!" I'm pulling the wires off me, shouting, pain exploding behind my temples, an ocean of noise in my ears and finally I realize what he's saying as he holds my wrists.

"It's okay!" He stares into my eyes. "I know you didn't do it. I know. It's all right, Laura. We know what really happened."

It's Charlie who saved me. Charlie, Jack, and the urban wildlife monitoring project. I didn't know what the monitoring part of the project was. I never asked. I was too busy going crazy.

The monitoring part involved small, motion-triggered cameras that Jack and Charlie hid outside, nestled in trees along the crumbled stairs, where there was enough vegetation on the hillside to attract a squirrel or a raccoon, or maybe even a coyote.

Our entire interaction on those steps was captured by those cameras and stored on a server somewhere. All of it. Bronwyn describing how she killed my mother, her own father, what she did to Jenny, what she wanted to do to Charlie, to Jack. It's all there. She's under arrest now, with a police guard outside her door. They say she'll probably never walk again. She certainly will never hurt anybody again.

And then Jack cries. He cries with his forehead on my shoulder. He is sorry he wasn't there. She didn't want you there, I say. That was the point. She wouldn't have done it if you were there. He is sorry he didn't believe me sooner. But you believed me in the end, that's all that matters.

FORTY-TWO

It's Thanksgiving weekend and I'm in a different art gallery, opening a different package. This gallery is my own. I am dressed in overalls, painting the walls white, or I was until the courier came.

Am I thinking of Bronwyn? Yes, although I try not to think about her anymore. I'm getting better at it. It's been two years now. In that time, we sold Jack's house in Queen Anne, the house Bronwyn had planned to kill us all for, and moved to Carmel, where we bought a beautiful house by the sea. Then a year ago, we got married. It was the most perfect wedding in the lush garden of a Victorian-style home in Monterey, with all our friends and Jack's family. How could it be anything other than the perfect day after what we went through?

Sometimes, I can go for three days, maybe more, before real-izing with a start that I haven't thought of Bronwyn at all. The fact that she's dead helps. She died from her internal injuries three days after I pushed her down those stairs. I killed her. The prosecutor declined to file charges as a conviction would be unlikely. The whole world has seen that video by now.

Everyone says I was protecting my family. Some even called me a hero.

Apparently, had she been found sooner, she might have lived. If someone had stood at the top of those stairs and craned their neck, they might have seen a leg, a foot, they might have called for help. But nobody stood there and nobody looked, and I'd be lying if I said I wasn't deliriously happy about that.

I have wondered sometimes what she might have been thinking about, stuck on those stairs with a broken back for four-teen hours. Did she lie there and think, *I was on a good ticket with Jack. After I send Laura to jail with my made-up evidence, would Jack want to get back together with me? Of course he would. He's never stopped loving me. Anyone can see that. I could help him get his business back on track, which would simply entail not emailing potential clients pretending to be Jenny the babysitter. I could redecorate the house back to the way it was before Laura got her dirty hands on it: tasteful and elegant. We could renew our vows. I'll wear something spectacular; we'll go on a second honeymoon. To Paris, maybe? And I'll send Char-lotte to boarding school because that child is really demanding, and of course that would mean no babysitter in the house.*

But we'll never know what she thought because she's dead. Jack even joked once that when she was threatening to kill him, the best I could come up with was to go and get Harold next door. Sweet, old, slow, very slow Harold with his walking stick and his hearing aid and his poor eyesight. But when Bronwyn threatened to hurt Charlie, I turned into some raging beast, a cross between King Kong and the Incredible Hulk, picked her up like she was made of straw and threw her down the stairs.

"Thanks a lot," he quipped, rolling his eyes. I don't think it happened *quite* that way, but I know he's trying to help me stop the nightmares, reclaim the nights where I sit up screaming and claw at an invisible ghost.

Sometimes I dare myself to imagine what would have

happened if Jack and Charlie hadn't installed their wildlife cameras. The amount of evidence against me was staggering. Even the small bag of OxyContin had my fingerprints on it, and only mine. I wondered if that's what she was doing upstairs while I pretended to be asleep in the armchair: carefully retrieving the Ziploc bag from her underwear drawer and sticking it behind my bedside table. The gun, of course, had supposedly been purchased by me. And there was plenty of evidence of my irrational behavior, my paranoia, my jealousies about Bronwyn, about Summer, and let's face it, I can't even blame Bronwyn for that. Not for all of it, anyway.

But it doesn't matter. These days when I think of Bronwyn, I think of her as some warped version of the Evil Queen from Snow White. I can just see her gazing into her funhouse mirror. *Does everybody love me? Am I the best? The most admired?* And if she caught *anyone* not bestowing upon her the attention she felt she deserved, they had to die. *I don't make the rules.* She got it wrong, though. The three people she killed that we know of for sure – there are rumors there may be others – presented exactly zero threat to her.

Because something else happened: a month ago, my father died.

I hadn't seen him in years, decades even. Firstly, I didn't like him, so there was that, but even if I'd gone, he wouldn't have had a clue who I was.

I went to the nursing home where he lived to pack his few belongings, which consisted only of his clothes and a Bible. I donated it all to the facility for other residents who might find some use in those few things, but as I held the Bible, a letter fell out from its pages.

My hand was shaking when I bent to pick it up, because I'd recognized my mother's handwriting on the envelope, without even having to think about it. And yet if you'd asked me five minutes earlier what my mother's handwriting looked like, I would have said I had no idea. I just couldn't remember.

I went outside, sat on a bench overlooking the lake and opened the envelope.

Frank.

I told you a long time ago now that if you wouldn't get help I would have no choice but to leave. That time has come. I am not doing this for me, but for Laura. It's not right for her to grow up in a house filled with nothing but rage and anger, where she is afraid to speak her mind, afraid of being in the same room with you, afraid of you. I want her to have a normal and happy childhood, whatever is left of it, as happy and normal as I can give her. She needs to feel free to be herself, she needs to laugh, she needs love.

A friend has helped me find a house for Laura and me. Once we are settled, I will call you. If you accept my decision and promise not to argue for our return, I will give you our address if you wanted to visit her.

I wish you well, Frank. I really do. I hope you find peace in your heart one day.

God bless,

Margaret

I knew already my mother wasn't leaving me behind as I'd originally thought. Bronwyn, of all people, had told me this outside our house. *They were taking you with them, but not me.* But I didn't know I was the reason we were leaving. And I sure didn't know my father knew, all these years, because he never said a word.

"Was Mom planning to take a trip?"

"Your mother? Going on a trip? Where the hell would she go?"

I'll never know if my mother gave this letter to my father before she died, or if he found it later, or even why he kept it all these years. But the most shocking revelation, the one that is making my hand shake so much I can barely put the letter back in its envelope, is how devastatingly wrong Bronwyn had been about everything.

A friend has helped me find a house for Laura and me.

My mother wasn't running off with Bronwyn's father. He owned a real estate agency. He was helping her find a home for us, and he was doing it in secret so my father wouldn't find out. He was being a friend. But Bronwyn misunderstood those late-night calls and she killed my mother and, years later, her own father, too.

If Bronwyn had lived freely, would she have kept going? Knocking off every person who didn't worship her as she thought she deserved, until there was no one left but her and her stupid mirror? You bet she would.

I went to see Gavin once before we left for Carmel. I told him I had something for him, and I brought the paper bag with me. I think he thought I'd brought pastries or something. He smiled, then stared inside the bag for a long time. When he looked up again, he looked surprised. A little too much, even. Like he was putting it on.

"It's broken! What happened? Where did you find it?" he asked.

"I know it was you, Gavin. I saw the footage from the robbery. I saw the watch you wear on your right wrist."

He argued, but not very convincingly. In the end, he broke down.

"Okay, fine! I came back to the gallery, just as I said I would, and I saw you left the door unlocked."

I shook my head in disbelief. "And?"

"And..." He clicked his tongue, then told me petulantly, as if it was my fault, that he'd wanted to be the curator of Bruno's gallery, and that as his nephew, he thought he should have been. He told me that he took the job as my assistant, but he hated it. He hated the fact that his uncle treated him the way he did.

"When I saw the door was unlocked, I wanted to tell Bruno, you know? Show him that you weren't perfect, that you made mistakes too. That he should have given me the curator's job. I thought, heck, what if somebody came and took something!" He slapped his thighs. "So I did it. I went home, I got changed, came back in the middle of the night and I took one work, put it in the trunk of my car, and the next day you'd find it missing and you'd have to admit you'd left the door open. But then the gallery looked like it was broken into and I got really confused, and... well, you know, it just all snowballed. I had that thing in the trunk of my car and I didn't want it. You heard what the insurance guy said. I had to get rid of it. So when I brought the trestle tables to your house for your stepdaughter's party, I hid it in your garage. I didn't know what else to do. Are you going to tell Bruno?"

"No," I said. "You are."

———

Bruno didn't report him to the police in the end. He dropped the insurance claim and told the police the matter had been resolved. Then he told Claire Carter the work had been returned by an anonymous person.

It says everything about her talent that she fixed it up in no time and made it as enchanting and exquisite as the original. I went to her studio to pick it up, so I could deliver it to the couple who'd purchased it in the first place. I told her it was me who'd broken it. I didn't steal it, I said, but I broke it.

She shrugged, tapped my shoulder. "You were trapped with the devil," she said. As if that explained everything. And I thought, there you go. They say the greatest trick the devil ever pulled was to convince the world he didn't exist. Maybe the devil's greatest trick was to paint himself as dark and horned and grotesque, when in fact the devil is a beautiful woman with long raven hair and a face like a Renaissance painting. Or maybe he's a regular guy who works in a bar and has blue eyes and makes you laugh. The devil comes in many disguises, but one thing is for sure, when the devil comes knocking, you won't even look twice.

But Bronwyn did prove one thing about evil people. They die and take their evil deeds with them. Evil doesn't get passed on through generations. To think that someone as evil as Bronwyn could produce something as perfect and joyful and inspiring as Charlie proves that beyond a shadow of doubt.

Inside the package is a small, exquisite artwork from Claire, with a card, *For Charlie, congratulations.* The work is titled *The Magical Garden,* and it's exactly what it is. A colorful imaginary garden with shrubs and trees and fountains and hills, and a tiny figure of Charlie patting a dog, and when you look closely, you can see bees flying around Charlie's head.

She would have seen it on the news. We used to be on the news all the time after what happened. Not so much now, thank God, but then Charlie won the Young Scientist Research Award, the youngest recipient ever, for her work on monitoring beehives. She has a theory that when someone approaches a beehive, bees know whether that person is angry or sad, whether their intentions are good or not, and they'll adapt their buzzing accordingly.

If only that were true of people, I thought.

Everybody wanted to write about her when she won. It was a happy ending to a tragic story. They called her a genius, which is true, but she's also funny, and loving, and smart, and she has crinkly hair and a grin that makes you laugh. She's perfect. And incredibly, miraculously, in spite of everything, she's happy. She loves her new school, she loves her new friends, she *adores* her dog, Molly, a three-legged scraggly old thing we adopted from the pet rescue shelter. Since the moment Molly came home with us she has never left Charlie's side.

I'm admiring the gift when the door opens, and I look up to see Summer, her arms wide open in greeting, a big smile on her face and right behind her, Katie, who immediately squeals, "Oh my God! I love this space!"

I jump up to greet them. "You're here!" And for the next five minutes we embrace, we laugh, how was the flight? I ask. It was easy, Summer says, flapping a hand in front of her face. Katie tells me I have white paint in my hair.

"Where's Dexter?" I ask.

"Parking the rental car and buying cakes for dessert," Katie says.

We have become so close over the past two years. There's been so many tears, so many conversations, so much forgiveness, so much atonement. They have come to visit for Thanksgiving weekend and while they're here, they'll help me finish painting the gallery walls. My first show will be an exhibition of Summer's photographs. Not the black and white ones, she doesn't do those anymore. She's found her style. She does street photography now, focusing on small details like a crack in the sidewalk, the edge of a broken umbrella, an insect on a leaf, and her images are always surprising and always beautiful.

And now Dexter is here too and it's noisy again. Everyone admires the gift for Charlie and now it's time to leave, lock up and go to the house where we'll make dinner all of us together and sit at the big kitchen table and talk and laugh all night.

I don't think about Bronwyn often. I have my own little circle of love now, and it's bursting with joy and hope and it takes up all the space in my life. And one day, I just know, I won't think of Bronwyn at all.

A LETTER FROM NATALIE

Dear reader,

As always, a heartfelt thank-you from me for choosing to read *Unforgivable*. If you would like to keep up to date with my new releases, please sign up to my newsletter. Your email address will never be shared and you can unsubscribe at any time.

www.bookouture.com/natalie-barelli

I started writing *Unforgivable* with a completely different plot in mind, but as it often happens characters have different ideas. In *Unforgivable*, it's the relationship between Laura and her step-daughter Charlie that took over the story. I loved writing about their bond, and I thought a lot about what it must be like to raise step-children, and how uniquely special that bond must be.

So thank you, dear Reader, for getting this far, and I hope the characters in *Unforgivable* entertained you, and surprised you, as they did me.

You probably know this already, but reviews are the best way for readers to discover our books, and if you enjoyed *Unforgivable*, I would be hugely grateful if you would leave a review. It makes a massive difference, so thank you.

Until next time, Natalie

KEEP IN TOUCH WITH NATALIE BARELLI

nataliebarelli.com

facebook.com/NatalieBarelliBooks

ACKNOWLEDGMENTS

I am incredibly lucky to have many wonderful people looking over my shoulder, and this is where I thank them from the bottom of my heart.

Mark Freyberg, as always, thank you for your generosity in answering my legal questions.

Massive thanks to my editor Jessie Botterill, for being brilliant and for your support. Hugely appreciated! And my thanks to the team at Bookouture for their work and patience in bringing this book to life.

My writing buddy Debra Lynch for checking in and as always, making me laugh no matter what the heck is going on.

My wonderful friends and my extended family, thank you for your support and enthusiasm and in some cases for listening to me ramble on and on!

Thank you always to my husband for many things but especially for having the patience of a saint.

And always, thank you dear reader, for reading this book. It means the world.

82806423R00177